BLOOD RANSOM

Award-winning books from Sophie McKenzie

GIRL, MISSING
Winner Richard and Judy Best Kids' Books 2007, 12+
Winner of the Red House Children's Book Award 2007, 12+
Winner of the Manchester Children's Book Award 2008
Winner of the Bolton Children's Book Award 2007
Winner of the Grampian Children's Book Award 2008
Winner of the John Lewis Solihull Book Award 2008
Winner of the Lewisham Children's Book Award 2008-9
Winner of the 2008 Sakura Medal

BLOOD TIES
Overall winner of the Red House Children's
Book Award 2009
Winner of the North East Teenage Book Award 2010
Winner of the Leeds Book Award 2009, age 11–14 category
Winner of the Spellbinding Award 2009
Winner of the Lancashire Children's Book Award 2009
Winner of the Portsmouth Book Award 2009
(Longer Novel section)
Winner of the Staffordshire Children's Book Award 2009
Winner of the Southern Schools Book Award 2010
Winner of the RED Book Award 2010
Winner of the Warwickshire Book Award 2010
Winner of the Grampian Children's Book Award

SIX STEPS TO A GIRL
Winner of the Manchester Children's Book Award 2009

THE SET-UP
Winner of the North East Book Award (yrs 7 + 8)
Winner of the Portsmouth Book Award 2010 (Longer Novel section)

BLOOD RANSOM

SOPHIE McKENZIE

SIMON AND SCHUSTER

With thanks to Lou and Lily Kuenzler

First published in Great Britain in 2010 by
Simon and Schuster UK Ltd
A CBS COMPANY

Simon & Schuster UK Ltd
1st Floor
222 Gray's Inn Road
London WC1X 8HB

A CIP catalogue record for this book
is available from the British Library.

ISBN: 978-1-84738-763-9

1 3 5 7 9 10 8 6 4 2

Typeset by M Rules
Printed in the UK by CPI Cox & Wyman, Reading, Berkshire RG1 8EX

www.simonandschuster.co.uk
www.sophiemckenziebooks.com

For Ruth, Mark, Max, Freddie and Louisa Goodman

Nine months ago, Theo and Rachel discovered they were the world's first human clones. Captured by Elijah Lazio, the genius geneticist who cloned them, Theo learned not only that he was a clone of Elijah himself, but that the evil geneticist was planning to murder him to steal his heart, a perfect genetic match for his own failing organ.

Theo and Rachel managed to escape from Elijah, but were later separated and sent to new locations with their families. They are now in hiding from both Elijah and the Righteous Army against Genetic Engineering (RAGE) – an extremist group prepared to go to any lengths to destroy all the evidence of Elijah's cloning experiments, including the clones themselves . . .

Part One

The Hermes Project

1

Rachel

It was a Saturday afternoon in early July and I was looking forward to the highlight of my week – the hour or so
when Theo and I met online and everything else dropped
away.

I'd just been to a martial arts display at the old scout hall
past the docks. Not the sort of thing that happens often in
Roslinnon – or the sort of thing I go to on an average
Saturday – but I'd really enjoyed the moves in the show,
recognising quite a few of the basic techniques from the self-
defence lessons I'd been having.

Most of the audience was male and much older than me.
I'd caught a couple of guys staring at me during the interval
and, what with that and the way the hall stank like the boys'
changing room at school, it was a relief to be heading outside.

As I left the scout hall, I saw the two men who'd been staring at me earlier standing on the pavement. They were
watching everybody leave. For a second I wondered if they

were looking for me . . . waiting for me. Then I shook myself – told myself not to be paranoid.

It was drizzling with rain, so I pulled my hood up and headed for the internet café on the high street where I was going to message Theo. Rather than walk past the two men, I decided to take a slightly longer way round – nothing major, just a couple of extra streets, but it would bring me out at the top of the high street: a busy road where I knew I'd feel safe.

As I started walking, the rain got heavier. I sighed.

When the British government and the FBI had picked the port town of Roslinnon in Scotland as the location for my new life, they obviously hadn't known it was officially the rainiest place in the British Isles – not to mention a rubbish place to be young. Or at least I hoped they hadn't. Sometimes it felt like I was being punished for who I was.

Who I *am*. A clone of my dead sister.

Theo's a clone too. That's why we'd been hidden away and given new identities. Because there were people determined to find us – and kill us.

I checked the time. Four forty-five p.m. I had quarter of an hour before I was due online and, even going the long way round, it was only going to take a few minutes to reach the internet café. I decided to shelter from the rain.

Huddled in a doorway, I felt for the silver chain round my neck. The chain's special . . . my way of feeling closer to

Theo. I thought about what I was going to tell him this week. It was nine months since we'd seen each other, and yet our online conversations were more real to me now than my everyday life. Nobody knew that I was still in touch with Theo – I hadn't told a single person: not the agent who was our contact under the government protection programme; not Mum and Dad; not even the counsellor I'd been given to help me 'adjust' to my new life.

The government officials all thought we'd be safer if we didn't make contact with each other. There's this organisation called RAGE – the Righteous Army against Genetic Engineering. They don't think genetic copies of human beings – clones – should be allowed to exist. They think they're immoral. *We're* immoral. Then there's Elijah – the man who cloned us. He reckons he 'owns' us – that he's entitled to do what he likes with us.

The threat was real, so Theo and I didn't take unnecessary risks when we talked. I mean, I didn't even know exactly where Theo lived and I never asked

Across the street I caught sight of a girl from school and waved. Mhairi's sort of a friend, though we're not really close. I'm not that close to anyone at Roslinnon Academy, to be honest. It's better that way . . . you never know who you can trust.

Mhairi waved back at me, then pointed to the pale, anxious, plump woman beside her and made a face.

I nodded to show I understood. Mhairi's mum was a total nightmare . . . nearly as bad as mine. Still, at least Mhairi didn't have to put up with her mum berating her for not wanting to learn golf, or going on and on about how common everyone in Roslinnon was.

Emerging from my shelter, I walked on. I didn't know this area of town that well but from what people said it was kind of rough. The rain was pounding down now – and this was July. It was supposed to be summer! I tugged my hood further round my face and bent my head. The pavement was a dirty grey – shining in the rain.

I trudged into an alley, trying to avoid the puddles. Suddenly a large pair of Timberland boots appeared in front of me. I looked up. One of the men who'd been staring at me during the martial arts show – early twenties, with close-cropped red hair and a smashed-in nose – was blocking my way out of the alley.

'Hello, hen,' he said, a nasty smile creeping around his mouth.

'Hi.' I tried to step past him, but he put out his arm. My throat tightened.

'I saw you at the martial arts display just now,' he said. 'I was impressed. There's not many pretty girls go places like that, eh?'

Heart beating fast, I turned away.

The other man from the show, the one with dark, shaggy hair, was right behind me.

I was trapped in the alley.

'Hey, McRae,' the dark-haired guy sniggered. 'Shall we see if this wee girl is up for some action?'

'Get lost,' I said, but I could feel myself beginning to shake.

Both men moved closer. I clenched my fists and pressed my feet into the ground, breathing deep into my guts to calm myself, like Lewis had taught me when we were preparing to rescue Theo last year.

'Come on now, hen,' the dark-haired guy cooed in a silly voice. 'We just want you to show us what you've got.'

The first man – McRae – laughed. 'Aye.' He reached out for my arm, pulling me round to face him.

Something snapped inside me.

'Piss off.' I stared at McRae – right into his mean little eyes – then strode past him.

He grabbed me. Pulled me back.

I fisted my hand and punched, putting my whole weight behind the throw. The blow landed on McRae's shoulder, sending him reeling, doubled over with pain and shock.

I glared at the other man. His mouth fell open. I turned and sped away, out of the alley. I raced on, going over the route to the high street in my head. Left. Left. Then a long stretch before the right turn onto the high street. I'd come out further up from the internet café than I'd been planning – but who cared.

The sound of pounding feet echoed behind me. I glanced over my shoulder.

Damn. The two men were hot on my tail – vicious looks on their faces.

I ran faster. Took my two left turns. I was holding them off – but not getting away.

Almost at the high street now, I pushed myself on. The men were so close behind me I could hear them breathing as they ran. For a sick second I wondered if they were RAGE operatives, sent after me on purpose.

I darted down one final short road, then onto the high street. I raced into the first shop I came to – a charity clothes place. I ducked behind a large rail of overcoats. They smelled of dead men's sweat.

I glanced over the top of the rail. The two men had stopped outside the shop but they weren't looking inside. They were laughing, like hassling me had been the best game ever.

Pigs.

As I watched, they sauntered off, swaggering down the street like they owned it. I shook my head. Well, at least they were just stupid men, not people from RAGE.

It was a few minutes to five now . . . nearly time to speak to Theo. The internet café was just up the road. I moved away from the rail of overcoats, tugged my hood off my face and headed towards the door. Outside, a boy in a wheelchair propelled himself past the window.

I froze.

The boy was olive-skinned with short, dark hair and a square jaw. He looked older than I remembered him, but otherwise it was the same face I'd been remembering and seeing in my dreams for the last nine months.

No way.

It *couldn't* be him.

8

What was he doing here? What was he doing in a wheelchair?

I stared as the boy wheeled himself along the street. I knew that profile as well as I knew my own.

It was Theo.

2

Theo

Hot and humid, Philadelphia had been in the grip of a heat-wave for nearly a fortnight now and I was more fed up than I could remember. School had ended for the summer and I hadn't got good grades and Mum was annoyed at me.

She was worried too, I guess. She had made loads of friends, mostly through her new job. Why hadn't I?

Of course she wouldn't listen when I told her I didn't care. That I still hung out with the basketball mates I'd met in the first term – before I stopped playing basketball – and that that was enough.

I was fed up with much more than Mum, though. Some days, like today, my whole existence got on top of me. I hated the lie I was living. Pretending to be someone I wasn't in order to stay safe from Elijah and RAGE.

More than anything, I missed Rachel.

I was on my way to contact her now. I hated the fact that I had to find a random computer instead of being able to use my own PC at home, but it would have been too risky. I was certain the FBI, who'd rehoused Mum and me here, were monitoring all our phone calls and home computer use.

That annoyed me too.

This side of the street was in direct sunlight. Sweat trickled down the back of my neck.

Grumbling to myself, I went on.

At least I'd get to speak to Rachel soon.

That was something.

Actually, it was everything.

3

Rachel

I stood, too shocked to move for a few seconds, watching the boy in the wheelchair roll slowly along the pavement.

Now that I could only see the back of his head I immediately doubted it was Theo. I *must* have been wrong. I mean, for a start, what would Theo be *doing* here? We'd agreed it would be safer if we didn't reveal online exactly where we lived, but it's hard to write about your life without giving some information away. From various references he'd made, I'd guessed a while back that Theo was somewhere on the east coast of America.

I must have given away certain details myself. But I was sure I'd never told him I lived in Roslinnon.

And how could Theo *possibly* be in a wheelchair? It didn't make sense. I racked my brains, trying to remember if he'd dropped any kind of hint at all that he'd had some kind of accident.

I was probably mistaken, but I had to be sure. I darted out of the charity shop.

And ran – *wham* – straight into Mhairi's mum.

'Och, hello, hen,' she said, staggering backwards.

'Sorry.' I blinked, looking past her to where the boy in the wheelchair who *couldn't* be Theo was turning the corner into Rosmore Row – the busiest shopping street in Roslinnon.

Panic clutched at my throat. I *had* to catch up with him. Had to make sure.

'As you're here, Rachel, hen,' Mhairi's mum went on, 'maybe you'll help me talk some sense into my daughter now. I've left her trying on a pair of trousers at least two sizes too small for her. Will you come and—'

'I can't.' I stared at her pale, pasty face, barely able to focus. 'I'm sorry, I can't.' And I tore past her, darting across the road between honking cars, hardly registering the rain on my face.

I raced down the High Street and onto Rosmore Row.

It was *heaving*. I ran as hard as I could, dodging pedestrians laden with heavy shopping bags, glancing around me for any sign of the boy and his wheelchair.

There. He was up ahead, trundling slowly past the benches where most of my year hung out after school. No one there I recognised today, thank goodness.

He reached the end of Rosmore Row and turned into a much quieter side road. I ran on, only slowing when I'd reached the side road too and was just behind him.

I stared at the back of his head, remembering the moment when Theo had stepped in front of me, protecting me from Elijah.

13

And then I ran forward, jogging past him and stopping a few metres up at a lamppost.

The rain was still drizzling down my neck as I turned round, my heart thumping.

Oh God, it *was* him. And yet he looked different. With shorter hair and a hangdog expression, he looked like he'd aged about three years in the past nine months.

He caught me staring and looked up. He frowned, but there was no trace of recognition in his eyes.

For a second all my old insecurities flooded back. Had *I* changed too? My hair was a bit longer, maybe, but I didn't think I looked particularly different in any other way. Now I wished I'd checked my appearance before I'd left the martial arts show. Maybe my make-up had run in the rain, not that I was wearing much.

None of this made sense.

And then the boy smiled and mouthed the word 'hello'. I walked over, the bustle of Rosmore Row around us fading completely into the background.

The boy held my gaze. I was right next to him now.

'Theo?' I said, my voice trembling.

The boy frowned, looking confused. He shook his head. 'My name's Milo,' he said.

An American accent – and the tone of his voice was different from Theo's too. It was harsher, yet at the same time weaker.

'Er . . . do we know each other?' he said.

I stared at him. Close up I could see signs of stubble on his chin and a fullness to his face that Theo didn't – couldn't – have.

It wasn't Theo. Just someone who looked extraordinarily like him. The disappointment was crushing.

'I thought we knew each other,' I said, trying to keep my voice steady. 'I'm sorry.'

I took a step back.

'Wait.' Milo looked up at me. 'You just called me Theo, didn't you?'

'Er, yes, Theo's a friend of mine.' I blushed. 'You look a lot like him. An *awful* lot.'

A shocked smile crept over Milo's face. 'That wouldn't be the Theo who was kidnapped and taken to Washington D.C. last year?'

I could feel my eyes widening. *How on earth did he know about that?* I nodded, speechless.

There was a long pause.

'Well I guess I *do* look like him,' Milo said at last, 'seeing as we were cloned from the same person.'

4

Theo

My mood improved as soon as I walked inside the diner. Living in America does have *some* compensations, and the way every indoor space seems to be fully kitted out with aircon is one of them.

Cheri, one of the waitresses who knew me quite well, bustled over.

'Hi, hon.' She smiled. 'How're you doin'?'

I smiled back. 'Good, thanks. Can I use the computer?'

'Sure, when Jack's done.' Cheri nodded towards the counter, where the diner's only terminal stood between a stack of magazines and a shelf of salt and pepper pots. She let me use the internet for free when her boss wasn't around, which was most mornings.

The guy on the computer was middle-aged and huge. I'd seen him in the diner before, with his equally outsize wife and kids.

'Jack's having a bad time,' Cheri said, lowering her voice to a whisper. 'Wife's left him and taken the kids. Taken *everything*. Jack's emailing his attorney, trying to get a handle on it all.'

'Right.' I glanced at the clock. Five minutes before Rachel would be expecting me online. 'No worries,' I said.

'Strawberry Shake while you wait?' Cheri asked.

'Yeah, thanks.' I settled into the leatherette booth closest to the computer terminal and waited.

5

Rachel

The rain was coming down even harder now. Milo wheeled himself across the street to shelter under a deserted doorway. I followed him in a daze.

'Cloned from the same person?' I said, unsure I'd heard him correctly before. 'You and Theo?'

'Yes, we were both cloned from Elijah Lazio.' Milo nodded, his face serious. 'I'm guessing that if you know about Theo, then you know about Elijah too. Which means you must be Rachel, right?'

My legs felt like they might give way. 'How do you know about me?' I gasped. I stared at Milo. *Another* clone of Elijah, this one older than Theo. How was that even possible?

'Elijah's mentioned you,' Milo said.

'You've spoken to him?! Is he here . . .? Oh my God . . .' I stopped, panic filling me. Was Elijah nearby? Did he know *I* was here?

'Elijah cloned me three and a half years before he cloned Theo.' Milo explained, seemingly unaware of the effect his words had had on me. His face clouded over – an expression I knew well from Theo. In fact, the look he was giving me was such a powerful reminder of Theo that my heart actually skipped a beat.

Milo's eyes flickered to his wheelchair. 'As you can see, I didn't work out so well. I was born with a degenerative disease. My body's wearing out too fast. It's a genetic weakness caused by the cloning process. Elijah worked out how to stop it happening before he cloned Theo, but I can't walk and my heart and kidneys don't operate quite as well as they should.'

He looked up at me – an expression of defiance and humiliation on his face.

Again I was so strongly reminded of Theo that, for a second, I couldn't think straight.

'I'm . . . er, I'm sorry,' I stammered.

Milo shrugged. 'At least my heart was never strong enough for Elijah to want to steal it,' he said.

I huddled into the doorway. The rain had slowed to a drizzle and people were walking past again. No one gave us a second look.

'But where is Elijah?' I asked again, questions tumbling out now. 'When did you last see him? Does he know that you're here? That *I'm* here?'

'I live with him,' Milo said. 'And no, he doesn't know you're here.'

'But you weren't in Washington D.C.' I frowned, remembering how I'd gone to Elijah's underground headquarters,

19

hoping that while RAGE destroyed the building, Lewis and I would be able to find Theo and escape.

'Elijah sent me away to college,' Milo said bitterly. 'He sent me to school before that – and to camp in the holidays. He used to visit me occasionally but I don't think he could . . . that he can . . . stand the sight of me. It's like he feels he has a duty towards me, but underneath I remind him of his failures.'

'But you said you were with him now?' That meant Elijah must be nearby, surely?

'I *was*,' Milo said. 'He contacted me after the Washington compound was blown up. Said I'd have to leave college, that he was going on the run.' Milo sighed. 'I guess I could have gone off on my own, but I was pleased he wanted me with him . . . so I met him and came with him here . . . to Scotland.'

'*Here?*' I said, shocked. Elijah was in *Scotland?* 'Where exactly? *Why?*'

'Elijah's set up a private research base on a deserted island off the west coast,' Milo explained. 'It takes a few hours to reach it by boat. Roslinnon is the nearest port.'

A shiver snaked down my spine.

'And he really doesn't know I'm here in Roslinnon?' I said, hardly able to believe it.

Milo shook his head. 'To be honest he's stopped looking for you . . . for either of you . . . He's got other things on his mind.'

I looked round. The rain had stopped now, though the air

20

remained heavy with moisture. Rosmore Row was still buzzing with shoppers. A woman laden down with bags and a buggy marched past, scowling, a little boy trailing in her wake.

'What about Daniel?' I said. 'Is he OK? Does Elijah still have him?'

Daniel was the five-year-old clone of Elijah who Theo and I had met in Washington at Elijah's complex last year. When Elijah had escaped from the police and the FBI, he'd taken Daniel with him. No one knew what had happened to the little boy afterwards, but I could still picture his solemn little face and big brown eyes.

Milo looked away. 'Daniel's the reason why Elijah's stopped looking for Theo. He's the reason why I've run away too.'

I frowned. 'I don't understand.'

Milo sighed – a deep, heavy sigh. 'Elijah's worked out a way of adapting Daniel's heart so it will work inside him, even though it's not adult-sized – which means he doesn't need Theo's heart any more.'

I stared at him, unable to fully take in what he was saying. 'Are you sure?'

'Yes, Elijah's so arrogant he thinks killing Daniel is justi-fied because he's such a goddam genius.'

I nodded, feeling numb, remembering Elijah giving a sim-ilar reason to excuse his plan to take Theo's heart back in Washington D.C.

'Once I realised what Elijah was planning, I couldn't stand

21

to be around him any more,' Milo went on. 'I told Elijah I needed a break for the day. If I could have brought Daniel with me I would have, but there was no way I could get him out. Elijah sent me off in the boat with one of his guards. We moored a way along the coast – there's a car parked there that they use when they come to town to buy food and supplies for Elijah's research. I'm supposed to be hanging out here while the guard goes to the store, but I'm going to take a bus . . . get away . . .' Milo tailed off.

'Get away to where?' I said, my head reeling. I could still barely take in what Milo was saying. Elijah had Daniel – the sweet little boy that I'd thought about so often since our escape. And Daniel's life was now in terrible danger.

The urgency of the situation suddenly hit me. Never mind Milo's plans. We had to get help.

'Dunno where I'll go.' Milo shrugged. 'Edinburgh or Glasgow first, I guess . . . It's easier to get lost in the big cities . . . then a flight back to the States . . .'

'But what about Daniel?' I said. 'When's Elijah planning to do this transplant?'

'Tomorrow morning, first thing.'

'*What?*' I leaped up. 'We have to call the police. Get him stopped.'

'*No.*' Milo shook his head in another gesture that reminded me of Theo. 'Elijah's back working for the government. They know exactly what he's up to, though it's all under cover, of course. They're letting him use Daniel because Elijah's work is so valuable – they don't want to lose him.'

My mouth fell open. 'That's *terrible.*'

Milo grimaced. 'Yes, but there's nothing we can do.'

I stood silently for a second. Shoppers were still bustling around us, but I felt completely detached from my surroundings.

It was obscene that Elijah could consider taking Daniel's heart to replace his own. But somehow it was even worse that the governments which were supposed to be protecting me and Theo were turning a blind eye.

'We can't let this happen,' I said slowly.

Milo looked sadly up at me. 'How can we stop Elijah?' he said. 'He's too powerful.'

'I don't know exactly,' I said. 'But we have to try.'

6

Theo

The clock on the diner wall ticked slowly to midday and big, sad Jack was still hunched over the computer.

At one minute past noon, I went up to Cheri. 'I *have* to use the computer,' I said.

Cheri glanced over at Jack. 'I'm sure he won't be too much longer.'

At that moment Jack sighed. He shifted on his bar stool so that it creaked under his weight. Slowly he rolled the mouse over the shut-down button.

I was hovering beside him before he'd even clicked it, though it was another full minute before Jack managed to ease himself off the stool and shuffle to the door.

I glanced at the clock as I sat down. Three and a half minutes past twelve. Never mind. I was sure Rachel would wait. We'd both been a few minutes late before. Eager with anticipation, I logged on to the chat room we were using this month – we changed venues regularly – and searched for her user name.

She wasn't there. Oh well, maybe she was late too. I kept the screen up while I went to check my emails. A few minutes later I was back. Still no Rachel.

I started to feel a little irritated. All the effort I'd made to be here on time and she wasn't ready? It was probably her mum's fault. Rachel's mum was, basically, your worst nightmare. A hideous combo of martyr and snob. Rachel spent a lot of our time together online complaining about her. Recently Mrs Smith had been trying to force Rachel to play golf. Unbelievable.

I finished my shake and checked the chat room again. Rachel *still* wasn't there. It was now almost 12.15. I started to wonder if I'd got the place or the time wrong. But I knew I hadn't.

Cheri wandered over and I ordered another shake.

It arrived.

I drank it.

I checked the chat room again.

It was now 12.23 and Rachel wasn't there.

This was by far the latest either of us had ever been.

For the first time in nine months, I started to wonder if maybe she wasn't coming online at all.

7

Rachel

'You don't know what you're saying,' Milo said. 'Elijah's island is heavily guarded. Even if we could somehow reach Daniel, there's no way we'd be able to get away without being seen.'

'There has to be a way,' I insisted. 'We can't just let Daniel die.'

Milo shook his head.

My mind whirled with all the possible options as we made our way back down Rosmore Row towards the high street.

As we reached the corner, Milo looked up at me. It had stopped raining, but his hair was wet. The way the light fell across his face highlighted a deep crease in his forehead. Suddenly he looked much older than before – and a lot less like Theo.

'I don't want to go back there,' he said simply.

I bit my lip, realising for the first time how much courage it must have taken Milo to run away in the first place.

'It's only for a short time,' I said. 'And once Daniel's safe, I'll help you find somewhere to stay. My dad will help you.'

I was certain Dad wouldn't mind. Though, somehow, I'd have to talk to him without Mum finding out. I could just imagine her reaction. And I couldn't talk to Dad till it was all over. Even if he was prepared to help Milo, he'd still be furious that I was planning to put myself in danger after all I'd been through last year.

'I guess you could follow me back to Paul – he's the guard who drove me here,' Milo said, slowly. 'I'm due to meet him in the car park in a few minutes, but if I went on ahead, I could maybe distract him somehow so you could hide in the trunk of his car. Smuggling you onto the boat to the island won't be easy, but it's possible, I guess.'

I nodded. 'We can do this, Milo,' I said.

'Okay.' He smiled, his face lightening and looking more like Theo's again. 'I told Paul I'd meet him at five-thirty. It must be nearly that now.'

'Five-thirty? You're kidding.' I checked the time, a sense of dread filling me. Milo was right – it was just a couple of minutes off the half hour. Thirty minutes since I was supposed to be online with Theo. The shock of meeting Milo had pushed the time right out of my mind. 'Oh, no.'

'What?' Milo raised his eyebrows.

I sped up, turning along the high street towards the internet café. 'Theo and I are in touch,' I said. 'We meet up online every week. I've just missed our regular chat and I have to try him before we set off.'

Milo pushed his wheels faster. He was, I noted with the small part of my brain that wasn't consumed with worries about reaching Theo and what Milo and I were planning next, extremely dextrous at weaving his way through the throngs of shoppers still crowding the street.

'You'll have to be quick online, Rachel,' he said as we reached the café. 'If I'm late, Paul will worry about getting into trouble with Elijah and just want to get going. It'll be harder to distract him.'

I disappeared into the café, leaving Milo on the pavement taking out his mobile.

I hurried to a free terminal and logged on. My hands were shaking as I accessed the chat room. Would Theo still be there?

8

Theo

I sat, nursing my third strawberry milkshake and feeling sick. Cheri had kicked me off the computer so that another – paying – client could use it. I was waiting impatiently for her to finish so I could log on again.

Where *was* Rachel?

I tried to focus on the most likely possibilities.

1: She'd forgotten.

No. No way. I mean, she'd never forgotten before. Not one single time in nine months.

2: Something or someone had prevented her from coming.

More likely. Except Rachel had *always* had huge problems with her parents, especially her mum, and she'd never missed an online session with me before.

3: She was deliberately avoiding me.

I couldn't believe that was true. I mean, even if Rachel didn't want to call herself my girlfriend any more, we were still friends, weren't we? She wouldn't just break off all contact without saying something.

Unless she'd fallen for someone else, big time, and couldn't face either telling me or lying to me . . .

My stomach twisted into knots as I thought about this. The truth was, though I wouldn't have admitted it to anyone, Rachel was more than just a girlfriend to me. She was the only person I could truly be myself with. And the only person – apart from Mum, and a few government officials – who knew about us being clones. The idea of her not being in my life was too horrible to think about.

'You feeling all right, hon?' Cheri wandered over, a look of concern on her face.

'Sure.' I attempted a smile. 'But I need to get back on the internet as soon as possible.'

Cheri smiled back sympathetically. 'Problems at home?'

I nodded. Cheri knew all about my mum and her overprotective ways. Mum was better than she used to be, of course. Back before I tracked down Rachel and ran off to find Elijah, I'd had a bodyguard who never let me out of his sight. I understood later that Mum had been trying to protect me from RAGE, but even so it was a bit over the top. I guess Mum had no one to stop her from getting completely hysterical. There was never another man around and I'd been told my dad was dead. At least here in Philly she let me go out on my own – though I still had ridiculous curfews most nights.

A couple of minutes later the woman using the computer logged off and I raced over.

My hands shook as I accessed the chat room.

Please be there, Rachel. Please be there.

9

Rachel

I stayed in the chat room for a couple of minutes, but there was no sign of Theo. I could see he'd been there, though. I caught sight of one of his usernames on a couple of threads.

He'd obviously assumed I wasn't coming and logged off. I sat back in my chair, my heart sinking.

Wheels turned beside me. I looked up to see Milo's concerned face – *so* like Theo's – gazing at mine.

'He's gone,' I said. The words came out like a sob and I blushed at giving away how much my contact with Theo meant to me.

'Hey,' Milo said, awkwardly. 'You'll be able to try again later. Er, but if we're going we have to go now . . . I'm already late for Paul.'

I nodded, staring at the screen. I wanted to leave some kind of message for Theo but I couldn't think what to say.

Milo nudged my arm. 'Seriously, Rachel, we have to go.'

He wheeled himself to the door and looked over his shoulder expectantly.

Sighing, I switched off the terminal, paid at the counter and rushed outside to join him.

It took a few minutes to get to the car park. At least it wasn't raining.

I hung back as Milo approached Paul – a burly guy with blond hair wearing jeans and a rugby shirt. I watched them talking. Paul nodded, then the pair of them headed for the public toilets.

It suddenly occurred to me that if Milo couldn't walk, he probably had to be helped to get to the loo. I'd never really thought about that before – all the things I took for granted that he had to deal with because he was disabled.

I waited for Milo to pretend he needed something from the boot and come back to the car. Apparently the boot operated independently from the car's central locking system and the plan was that once Milo had opened it, he would only pre-tend to shut it properly, so I could sneak in.

The two men had almost reached the toilets before Milo turned in his chair and whizzed back to the car, his wheels spinning fast. He opened the boot and fumbled inside for a bit.

'Make sure you lock it!' Paul yelled from across the car park.

Milo nodded, then carefully lowered the boot and whizzed back to Paul. They disappeared inside the toilets.

Palms clammy with sweat, I rushed over to the car. The boot was open just a fraction. I looked round. The car park was vir-tually empty, just a young woman with a baby, emptying her shopping into her car. I waited, heart thumping, while she strapped in the baby and drove off. Now an elderly couple were strolling past, heading for their car.

I glanced over at the toilets. No sign of Milo and Paul. I had no idea how much time I'd have before they came back. I looked round. The elderly couple had reached their car. It was a couple of rows away so all I could see now were the tops of their heads. They both appeared to be bent over, looking at something inside the car.

This was my best chance. With a quick glance around to check the coast was clear, I flipped the boot fully open and clambered inside. It was spacious enough, though it smelled slightly musty. I reached my hand round and pulled the boot lid down hard, jerking my hand away just before it slammed shut.

It was done. I was trapped inside, my knees bunched up to my chest. My own breathing sounded loud in my ears. Suppose something went wrong – the car crashed or Milo forgot to let me out? I'd suffocate in here. How much air did I have, anyway?

I took a deep breath, trying to calm myself. Milo had assured me that Elijah's motorboat was tied up at a deserted beach just beyond the docks and that the journey would only take about ten minutes. I wasn't going to run out of air that fast.

I didn't want to think about Theo, and how I'd missed messaging with him earlier, so I focused on Lewis instead. Lewis was a former employee of Elijah's. He'd been sent to look after me, but had ended up working with me to defeat

Elijah. I missed him a lot. I mean, he was a good few years older than me and from a completely different background, but we'd got on really well from the start. I thought of him like an older brother. A very cool older brother. Lewis had shown me quite a few fighting moves – in fact it was him who'd sparked off my interest in self-defence – but he'd also taught me a lot about dealing with my fears.

When you feel anxious, press your feet into the ground and breathe in and out through the soles.

I couldn't use the ground, of course, but I pressed my feet against the side of the car and took a few calming breaths.

A minute later footsteps and the squeak of wheels signalled the return of Milo and Paul. I held my breath as two doors opened and – eventually – slammed shut. I knew, because Milo had told me, that the front passenger seat of this car had been adapted to contain the seat part of Milo's wheelchair and that, nine times out of ten, for short journeys Paul just folded the wheels and chucked them onto the back seat.

I just had time to pray that he didn't change his routine today and put them in the boot before another door opened and shut and the engine roared into life.

Paul reversed out of his parking space and we were off. It was hot, now, in the boot. I couldn't tell if Paul and Milo were talking or not. All I could hear was the car engine's low rumble and the whoosh of passing traffic.

Ten minutes later, the car stopped. I tensed, knowing that the next part of the plan was going to be the hardest to carry out successfully.

34

A thud outside. Paul muttering to himself. Then the crunch of wheels on gravel. Milo's voice sounded outside the boot.

'I need the can again, Paul.'

'*What?*' Paul's gruff American voice oozed irritation. 'You only went a moment ago.'

'Sorry, man.' Milo clicked the boot open and lowered his voice to a whisper. 'Rachel, you've got about two minutes.'

He wheeled himself off, whistling above the sound of the crushed gravel. I made myself count to twenty. That had to be enough time for the two men to get out of the way. Cautiously, I opened the boot and peered out.

Wind roared round me and the smell of rain – and the sea – hung heavy in the air. To one side of the car, about fifty metres away, was a line of trees. Milo, supported by Paul, was almost out of his wheelchair. He was going to have to pee in front of the man. *Ugh.*

I slipped out of the boot, ignoring the pins and needles that ran up my cramped right leg and taking care to disrupt the gravel at my feet as little as possible. The car was parked just metres from a small jetty that led down to a stony beach. There was no one else about.

I peered along the beach. A large motorboat was tied up at the end of the jetty.

Another glance at Milo and Paul. I could hear their voices, though not what they were saying, drifting towards me on the fierce wind. I lowered the car boot until it was almost shut and tiptoed across the gravel. As soon as I reached the jetty and felt the firm wooden boards beneath my feet I sped up. I ran as fast as I could, grateful that I was wearing trainers with rubber soles that made no sound.

As I reached the boat, I glanced round at Paul again. He was easing Milo back into his wheelchair. I had seconds left to get into the boat and hide.

I stepped down, into the back of the boat, and looked round for the red tarpaulin Milo had told me about. *There.* It was on the right-hand side of the boat, stretched over a collection of boxes and barrels. I raced over and crawled underneath, pushing a box out of the way, then pulling it back in front of me when I was properly in. It made a scraping noise, which sounded loud to my ears. I had to hope the sound wouldn't carry over the roaring wind.

I stretched out as far as I could. I was having to lie curled up again, with my right leg bent at an uncomfortable angle. Well, at least it was better than lying in the boot of that car.

In the distance I could hear the crunch of wheels and footsteps over the gravel – then thundering across the jetty.

Grunting, Paul leaped into the boat. I guessed he was lifting Milo down, then stowing the wheelchair. I held my breath as he stomped past my hiding place. The wind crept around me, chilling me through my top. I couldn't even move my arms to draw the hood around my face.

For a second I thought about crawling out from behind the boxes and jumping overboard. I didn't have to do this. In fact, surely what I was doing was *insane*, going right to the heart of Elijah's new operation.

And then I remembered Daniel's little face and huge

36

brown eyes and how I'd held him and comforted him when he'd cried.

And I knew that I didn't have a choice.

I was Daniel's only chance.

10

Theo

Where on earth was she? I'd gone back online several times and there was no sign of Rachel in *any* of the chat rooms we used. I threw all caution to the wind and started asking other users if anyone with any of Rachel's usernames had been online recently.

Every response was a 'no'.

By one p.m. the lunchtime crowd were starting to drift in and the diner was filling up. Several clients wanted access to the computer, and Cheri's boss turned up so I wasn't allowed to use the terminal any longer.

I went home, feeling seriously troubled. Having gone over all the options again, there seemed to be only one possibility.

Something had happened to Rachel.

Something bad.

I walked in the front door of our condo just after 1.30 p.m. It was a Saturday, so Mum was at home. Her new job involved her working from home quite a lot and her boss often came round 'to help'. He was in our living room right

38

now, on the couch next to Mum. They were looking at a magazine together, but there was an odd atmosphere about them too – like maybe I'd walked in and interrupted them and the magazine was just a cover for what they'd *actually* been doing.

I *really* didn't want to think about that, so I just grunted a hello and went to my room. It's not bad, as bedrooms go. In fact, our condo here in Philadelphia is much nicer than the flat we had in London. My room's twice the size of my old one, with a huge, light window and loads of space to hang out in. The bed's big and so's the couch – not that I have friends round here very often.

I hurried over to the desk in the corner and opened my laptop. Another bonus of our new life was the money we'd been given to start us off. Mum used most of it to buy furniture and stuff, but there had been enough left to get me an okay phone and a laptop.

Normally I wouldn't have dreamed of trying to contact Rachel from home. I was fully aware of how easy it is to trace computer use back to physical locations – and of how dangerous Elijah and RAGE really were.

But this was an emergency.

First off, I went back to all the chat rooms. There was still no sign of Rachel.

Okay, I was going to have to track her down some other way. I thought for a while, trying to remember everything Rachel had said about where she lived. We deliberately hadn't revealed any details online but I'd picked up enough bits of information to be pretty sure she was somewhere in Scotland, near the coast.

She was always complaining about the rain too – not that that was going to help me narrow my search down much.

I wasn't sure what I hoped to find out, but I had to do something. I'd start with local newspapers, then move on to schools. Maybe something on a website somewhere would give me a clue about what had happened to Rachel.

It wasn't a lot, but it was all I could think of.

11

Rachel

It felt like hours had passed, but when I switched on my phone and checked the time, it was only 7.30 p.m. and still very light.

Milo and Paul had left the boat ages ago. I couldn't tell where it was moored because I didn't dare emerge from under the tarpaulin yet.

Milo had said that though the docking area wasn't visible from any of the buildings on the island, there was a security camera which did a regular sweep of the bay and that I should wait till he gave me the signal to emerge – which wouldn't be until after it was properly dark.

I reckoned I had another two to three hours to wait until then.

At least I'd been able to shift the boxes and barrels a little so I could stretch my legs out fully. I flexed my feet and pointed my frozen toes, trying to get some feeling back into them. I tried to breathe steadily too, mindful of Lewis's advice about keeping calm.

I'd never wished he were with me more than I did now. I missed him almost as much as I missed Theo.

I felt for the chain round my neck once more, feeling my way down to the tiny letter 't' at the end and remembering the last time I'd seen them both – in that hotel in Washington D.C. . . . Lewis, hugging me goodbye with tears in his eyes . . . and Theo holding me and kissing me . . .

It was tough remembering being that close to Theo.

The floor of the boat was hard and cold and, even though I'd pulled my hood up and covered myself with a bit of spare tarp that I found crushed up behind one of the boxes, I was freezing. And hungry. I'd gone through the small bag I had with me and chewed my way through an entire pack of chewing gum.

I couldn't find my purse and school identity card, for some reason. I guessed I must have left them somewhere, probably the internet café. I knew I'd taken out my purse then, because I used it to pay for my time on the terminal. Or maybe the purse and the card had fallen out of my bag when I got into the car.

At least Paul didn't seem to have found it. If he had he would surely be searching the boat. Wouldn't he?

12

Theo

I searched online for hours, stopping only when Mum insisted I come into the kitchen to say goodbye to her boss and get some food. The guy tried to talk to me, asking me questions about the exams I'd just taken, but I made my excuses – and a sandwich – and got away as fast as I could.

Even though I'd been starving, the sandwich tasted like dust in my mouth. I was certain now that something terrible had happened to Rachel. Even if there'd been some kind of delay, there was no way she wouldn't have gone online as soon as she could and left some message for me. She would know, after everything we went through last year, that I would worry. Even if she never wanted to speak to me again, I was absolutely certain she wouldn't want to put me through that.

But I could find nothing from her. By five p.m., I was ready to hit something.

And then I saw the news story. It was on a Scottish local

news website and had obviously only been added to the site in the past hour or so.

Roslinnon girl in suspected suicide

Another teen suicide brings to five the number of teenagers who have taken their lives in the Renfrewshire area this year.

The girl, 15, is not being named at present, but is believed to have left her purse and school ID card on a beach near Roslinnon this afternoon before apparently walking into the sea. An eyewitness called the emergency services immediately but no body has yet been found. Strong currents may mean it is not retrieved for days, perhaps weeks.

The girl's parents have requested that their daughter's identity not be released until all friends and family members have been informed.

My stomach gave a sick lurch as I read the piece. Was this Rachel? I couldn't believe it, and yet something kept me searching for more versions of the story. Within an hour I'd found three. Though Rachel wasn't named in any of them – and I wouldn't have recognised her cover ID even if she had been – one of the stories did publish a blurry picture of her parents getting into a car. Even though the photo was small and grainy, it was enough.

I'd met Mr and Mrs Smith last year when I was trying to

find out information about Elijah. It was definitely them.

I stared, blinking, at the picture, letting what it meant sink in.

Rachel was dead.

Rachel had killed herself.

No. Every cell in my body revolted at the idea of it. It was unthinkable. Impossible.

I switched off my computer and paced up and down in my room. Outside, the sun was still bright and children's voices rose up from the playground nearby, laughing and arguing.

Somehow my world had exploded and yet everything else was still exactly the same. Rachel was gone.

Except she *couldn't* be. I *knew* her. And, sure, she was annoyed at her Mum and fed up with the dull, rainy town where she lived, but there was *no way* she would ever contemplate killing herself.

Even as I thought this, a tiny sliver of doubt curled itself around my brain.

How do you know what she really thought or felt?

How do you know what she was going through?

How do you know that she told you the truth about anything?

I sank onto my bed, my head in my hands.

No. I wouldn't accept it. Apart from anything else, Rachel would *never* have gone away deliberately without saying goodbye to me.

I stood up. This was something to do with RAGE or Elijah. It *had* to be. There was no body . . . no proof at all that Rachel was dead, other than her things being found on the shore and this eyewitness, whoever they were, telling the police what they'd seen. Anyone could have faked such a suicide.

Yes, if somebody wanted Rachel dead, why not just kill her outright? More than ever, I was sure Rachel was alive, but in some kind of danger.

I paced the room, trying to formulate a plan.

I was going to have to get to Scotland without the US authorities knowing, which meant I needed a fresh passport and money for a plane ticket.

But how the hell was I going to get hold of either?

13

Rachel

I'd never been so cold in my life. It was only the thought of poor little Daniel – and what Elijah would do to him if we couldn't save him – that kept me going.

Outside, the tiny patch of sky I could see was dark grey. Rain pattered on my tarpaulin.

Come on, Milo, I kept muttering under my breath. *Come on*.

I checked my phone again. There was no signal and the battery was nearly out but I couldn't bear to turn it off. Out here – in what felt like the middle of a wilderness – it seemed like the only thing left connecting me to the outside world. I knew Lewis, in that kindly big-brotherly way of his, would have told me not to be so silly and to conserve its power for when I did have a signal, but I couldn't help it.

The minutes crawled by.

Where the hell was Milo? Had something gone wrong? I was half tempted to go outside and attempt the break-in alone – but I didn't know the layout of the island or where Daniel was. It would have been crazy.

I closed my eyes, exhausted, and let an image of Theo swim in front of me . . . his smile crinkling his face . . . I wondered if he was out with his friends right now, if he was thinking about me.

Then I wondered whether Mum and Dad were worrying. Hopefully they'd assumed I was out with friends and had forgotten to charge my phone.

A soft shower of earth, heavier than the rain, fell on to my cover.

I jumped, my heart pounding.

Was that Milo?

I crawled out from under the tarpaulin and peered over the side of the boat. It was moored to a short jetty above a sandy beach. I couldn't see far in any direction – the coastline curved sharply round on both sides, with trees blocking the view and the island ahead rising up towards a hill.

At the end of the jetty was a wooden shelter. Milo was in his wheelchair, huddled underneath.

'Over here!' His voice was a soft hiss, almost lost in the wind and rain. 'Hurry!' He pointed to a camera positioned above him. Its lens was swivelling slowly in my direction.

I didn't need to be told twice. Forcing my stiff, cold legs to move, I stumbled across the boat and onto the jetty. I raced over to the shelter and threw myself, panting, at Milo's feet, just as the camera passed overhead.

'Well done,' Milo whispered. 'No one suspects a thing.'

14

Theo

First things first.

Money.

I only had a few dollars, but Mum was bound to have more.

I could use her credit card to buy a plane ticket to Scotland, and her cash to go to the guy in my year at school who specialised in creating fake ID. If anyone could fix me a new passport, it was him – and there was no way I could travel on the passport that had brought me to the States. The authorities would be able to trace me far too quickly and easily.

I still couldn't work out what could have happened to Rachel. If RAGE had taken her, they would surely have killed her straight away. No games. No 'suicide' cover story. RAGE didn't believe clones like us had a right to life.

And if Elijah had taken her . . . well, that seemed even more unlikely. What would Elijah want with her? It was my heart he'd been after last year. Rachel couldn't provide him with useful body parts. *She* wasn't his clone. So why else would he risk exposure to kidnap her – if he had?

My guts twisted into knots. Thinking about what might or might not have happened was just making me feel sick. I had to act.

I opened my bedroom door and crept down the corridor. Mum was on the phone, laughing at something the person on the other end had just said. Her bag was hanging on the coat peg by the front door. As I passed by, I reached for it . . . took it down.

My palms were sweating as I opened the flap on the bag and peered inside. Mum's usual jumble of pens and pills and receipts and lists written on scraps of paper met my eyes. I took out the paperback she was reading, lifted a Hershey bar – she'd become totally addicted to those since we'd moved here – and saw her purse. It was bulging with coins, notes, and cards. Holding my breath and listening out for any sound of move-ment from the living room, I carefully unzipped the purse.

And then my phone rang. It was in my trouser pocket and the ring tone sounded so loud that I jumped.

'Is that you in the hall, Theo?' Mum called.

'Er, yeah,' I said, struggling to zip her purse back up and retrieve my phone at the same time.

I heard Mum say goodbye to whoever was on the landline, then her footsteps sounded on the living-room floor.

I shoved her purse back and quickly hung the bag back on the wall. Hands trembling, I checked the caller display on my mobile. Name and number withheld.

'Theo?' Mum appeared in the doorway.

'Just a minute, Mum.' I put the phone to my ear and retreated to my room.

'Hello?' I said.

'Theo?'

There was something familiar about the male voice on the other end. The accent was American, but he sounded older than any of my friends at school.

'Who is this?' I said.

'We can't talk on this line,' the man said. 'I need you to go outside . . . there's a diner a few blocks away. The Chili Popper. D'you know it?'

'Yes,' I said, shutting my bedroom door. 'But what's this about?'

'Just get to the diner. Order something. I'm going to call the number there. We can speak properly then.'

He rang off and I suddenly realised who it was.

Lewis Michael. He'd helped Rachel rescue me from Elijah's Washington compound . . . and nearly died trying to protect us.

Man, Lewis must have heard the news about Rachel too. I was sure he wouldn't believe she'd killed herself either.

Maybe he knew something about what had happened to her.

Completely forgetting that Mum wanted to speak to me, I raced out of the house, letting the front door slam shut behind me.

51

15

Rachel

The rain fell steadily. I stood under the shelter at the end of the jetty as Milo went over the plan.

'The place where Daniel is being kept is just up ahead,' he explained.

I nodded. 'Will it be guarded?' I said.

'Not right now,' Milo said. 'The guy on duty is out patrolling the island. I know his route. We can avoid him.'

I nodded, feeling the rain dripping off my hair and running down the back of my neck. 'What research is Elijah doing?'

'I don't know, I'm not allowed into the lab he's set up here.' Milo shuffled uneasily in his wheelchair. 'Hey, I brought you some food . . . figured you'd be hungry by now.'

He took a plastic bag from beside him in his wheelchair and handed it to me.

Inside was a pack of roughly-made cheese sandwiches, a bag of crisps and a carton of milk.

I fell on the food. Milo watched me eat, an expression I couldn't read on his face. 'Rachel?' he said.

'What is it?'

'I'm . . . er, I'm sorry . . .'

'What for?' I suddenly felt uneasy.

'Nothing . . . just that this is so dangerous.' Milo hesitated. 'Are you ready?'

My whole body was stiff and sore but, already, I could feel the adrenalin pumping through me.

'I'm ready,' I said.

'Come on, then. Let's go.'

16

Theo

I ran hard all the way to the Chili Popper. I'd never been inside it before. It wasn't as nice as Cheri's diner – a bit run-down with rips in the cushions on the booths and stains on the tables. I looked round for a phone but couldn't see one. I took a seat near the main counter. A middle-aged woman with dark roots and bleached blonde hair glanced over at me with a scowl.

'What d'you want?' she said. 'You have to order food.'

I raised my eyebrows, then glanced at the menu scrawled on the plastic board beside the waitress's head.

'A Coke, please,' I said, 'and some chilli fries.'

The waitress grunted in acknowledgement and disappeared into the kitchen. I glanced round. The diner was pretty deserted – just a couple in the corner and a group of girls in the largest booth.

A few minutes later my food and drink arrived. The chilli fries weren't bad and I was hungry. I'd nearly finished wolfing them down when I heard a phone ring in the kitchen.

'Who?' The scowling waitress didn't exactly sound thrilled to be taking the call.

I looked up. She came into the restaurant area, holding a phone.

'Some guy wants to talk to you, says he's your brother,' the waitress said. 'Something about meetin' up.'

'Thanks.' I took the handset. 'Hello?'

'Theo, you're here. Good. Sorry I couldn't talk before. Listen, it's Lewis. I've got some bad news about Rachel . . .' He spoke in a rush, his voice strained, then stopped abruptly.

'She didn't kill herself.' I spoke more loudly than I meant to and the waitress, who was hanging around by the counter, clearly worried I was going to steal the stupid phone, pursed her lips.

Lewis sucked in his breath. 'You know? But it only happened a few hours ago!' He sounded shocked.

'Rachel and I, we are . . . were . . . in touch,' I said shortly. 'We were supposed to be online earlier, but Rachel didn't show.'

'Right, er, okay.' Lewis sounded confused, as if that was the last thing he'd expected to hear.

'How did you find me?' I said. 'I thought all our locations were top secret.'

'There are ways. I always knew you were in Philly and Rachel was on the west coast of Scotland – finding the exact addresses and numbers wasn't hard after that. Look, I need to speak to you about Rachel.'

'Like I said, she didn't kill herself,' I said again, more quietly than before. 'There's no way she would have.'

'I agree with you. But nobody else seems to. She's gone and her parents think she's dead . . . but . . . I'm certain it's Elijah. I'm sure he's taken her . . .'

'Or RAGE . . .'

'Possibly,' Lewis said. 'It could be RAGE, but I don't see why they'd fake a suicide.'

'Well, why would Elijah?'

'I don't know,' Lewis said. 'I just wanted to warn you that Rachel had gone. And to find out if you'd seen or heard anything suspicious.'

'No, nothing,' I said. 'But I've been trying to work out how I can get over to Scotland to help find her . . .'

'No way.' Lewis's voice was sharp and insistent. 'There's no point you putting yourself in danger too, Theo. I can find Rachel. I'm here in Scotland already.'

'I'm going whether you like it or not,' I said angrily. What right did Lewis have to stick his nose in? Or assume I couldn't look after myself?

'Come on, Theo, you'll be stopped at the airport. The US government won't let you leave the country. You're too valuable to them.'

'I can sort that,' I snapped. 'I'll get a fake passport.'

'How?' Lewis said. 'How will you pay for it?'

'I'll manage somehow. And I'll get the money for a ticket too.'

'You mean you'll *steal* the money?' Lewis said.

'That's none of your business.'

There was a pause, then Lewis sighed. 'I understand you wanting to get involved, but it's dangerous for you.'

'It'll be dangerous for you too,' I said.

'Sure, but I'm trained and anyway . . .' Lewis hesitated and when he spoke his voice broke over the words. 'I owe it to Mel to take the risk.'

That shut me up for a moment. I'd met Mel last year. She was young and beautiful – and she'd looked after me in Elijah's Washington compound. She was supposed to be Elijah's girlfriend but she was really in love with Lewis and worked with him to help me escape. Elijah had killed her when he found out she and Lewis had betrayed him.

'It's *not* your decision whether I go to find Rachel,' I went on. 'If you won't help me, I'll sort it myself.'

'Yeah, by robbing a convenience store and hoping some student friend of yours can create a passport that'll get you past airport security?' Lewis gave a sarcastic laugh. 'I don't think so, Theo.'

I hesitated, thrown by Lewis's apparent mindreading of aspects of my plan *and* his ability to pinpoint the flaws in it.

'I'd have thought you'd *want* me with you,' I said. 'Whether it's RAGE or Elijah who's got Rachel, they must be after me too. I'm like . . . bait, which makes me an asset. And I'm not a child any more. Not even legally – I'll be sixteen next month. I'll find Rachel on my own if I have to.'

'Man, you're stubborn.' Lewis let out a low hissing sound. 'Okay, you're right. It will help – and I don't want you here in Scotland without back-up, so listen. There's a guy I know who lives near you. He owes me a favour. I'll get him to sort out a passport. Just wait for my text. Deal?'

'I can sort this myself,' I said stubbornly.

'I'm only helping you because it might just help Rachel,' Lewis said. 'Maybe *you* should start putting her first too.'

There was a bitter note to his voice I didn't remember ever hearing before, but I knew he was right. Accepting Lewis's help was the fastest way to get to Rachel.

'Do we have a deal, Theo?'

'Yes,' I said. 'Er, thanks.'

'Good,' Lewis said. 'I'll be in touch within the hour.'

17

Rachel

Milo led me along the stony path for about two hundred metres. He had a hard time steering his chair around the larger pebbles.

I looked round, my heart thudding. I could see more of the island now. It wasn't big. From the higher ground, most of the coastline was visible. The sea beyond stretched for miles. I shivered at how isolated it was. Suppose we couldn't get back to the boat with Daniel? Or suppose Milo couldn't start the engine and get us away from here?

'Don't worry,' Milo said. 'The guard is down by the trees on the west of the island. He won't see us from there.' He pointed towards the single building up ahead. It was still some way off, but from here it looked like a traditional farmhouse – made of stone with a tiled roof.

'Aren't you worried about Elijah seeing us?' I asked, wondering why we weren't taking more trouble to keep ourselves out of view.

'Everyone's in the basement getting ready for the operation,'

Milo said. 'There's a camera over the front door of the house, but I'll be able to disable that. Daniel's still in his room. Once we're inside, we'll grab him, then get straight back to the jetty. I've already stolen the boat keys. If you can help me on deck I can steer us out of here and back to the mainland.'

It sounded suspiciously easy. I nodded, my mouth dry.

We reached the house. It was fairly bleak-looking, built on two storeys and ringed by a high wire-mesh fence. I took a deep breath as we walked through the gate in the fence and headed for the door. The camera on the wall above was pointing directly at the entrance. It was too high for me to reach. I couldn't see how on earth Milo was planning to disable it.

And then a twig snapped somewhere behind me.

I froze, then looked round, my skin prickling. I still couldn't see anyone, but they were there, I was sure. And we were trapped between the fence and the door.

'Someone's following us,' I whispered.

18

Theo

I'd waited for what felt like ages for Lewis to contact me again. Maybe I should have felt guilty insisting on going to Scotland, but I didn't. I was determined to save Rachel. And being with Lewis, actively trying to find her, seemed like the best way to do that.

Eventually Lewis texted me, and told me to send a picture of myself to some dodgy-looking email address. I did what he asked, then waited again. It was a while before I heard from him, but when I did he told me to go to Rittenhouse Square in the centre of Philadelphia, and wait for someone to bring me my fake passport.

I took a small bag with me. It wasn't that I particularly cared about having a change of clothes, but it occurred to me that I'd look highly suspicious if I turned up at an airport with no luggage at all.

Mum asked me what I was doing, of course. She was well annoyed at me for not waiting to speak to her earlier. She'd wanted to ask if I minded her and Jeff (her boss) popping out to dinner.

I told her it was fine, and that I was planning to go out myself, to see some friends. Before Mum could even mention my curfew, I promised I'd be back by 10.15. Hours away.

She bought the whole thing, which should have made me feel bad but didn't.

Anyway, I got to Rittenhouse Square and sat on a bench. A couple of minutes later a man in a baseball cap walked past me and dropped an envelope in my lap.

I opened it eagerly, to find a US passport with a fake name and two years added to my age, plus an e-ticket in the same fake name for a flight to Edinburgh. At the bottom of the envelope was a cellphone – fully charged and loaded with Lewis's phone number – plus two thick wedges of cash, one in ten-dollar bills, the other in ten-pound notes.

This was it. At the back of my mind I realised I had no idea what Lewis and I were going to do when I got to Scotland, but it didn't matter. We could work it out when I arrived. I was on my way to find Rachel.

That was all that counted.

Shoving everything back in the envelope, I stood up and walked out of the square in search of a taxi to take me to the airport.

19

Rachel

I heard another twig snap. Where was the noise coming from? Milo and I were close to the house, inside the wire-mesh fence. Trapped. My heart thudded as I scanned the patch of dense woodland just outside the fence.

A figure emerged from behind one of the trees. It was the blond guard who'd brought us to the island. He strode towards us, his hard eyes fixed on me.

In his hand was a gun.

For a second I was so frightened I thought I might wet myself, and then Milo spoke.

'I'm sorry, Rachel,' he said.

I turned to him, bewildered, then looked back at the guard. The expression in the man's eyes said it all. He knew I was here. He wasn't surprised.

Oh God.

I took a step back, towards the house.

The guard raised his gun. 'Don't move,' he ordered.

'Do what Paul says.' Milo's voice shook.

'What's going on?' But as I turned to look at Milo, I already knew. I didn't need to see the shame on his face or the way he wouldn't meet my eyes.

This had been Milo's plan from the beginning.

20

Theo

I found a taxi and set off for the airport. I spent most of the journey agonising over what text to send Mum. In the end I opted for short and sweet:

GNG AWAY 4 BIT. DNT B MAD. DNT WRRY. I LL B FINE. LOOK
AFTR YRSELF. TX

I added the last sentence as an afterthought. I meant it, though. Mum and I might not be close, but I've grown up since last year and I now recognised how hard being a single mum had been for her.

I sent the text on my old mobile and, having sent it, decided to get rid of the phone itself. I could be traced on it – Lewis had found it, after all, and the FBI were certainly aware of my calls.

I hesitated just a second, then switched it off and chucked it out of the taxi window.

Weird. Without my phone I felt disconnected from my old

life – as if I were doing more than just getting on a plane tonight . . . as if I were leaving everything I knew behind.

Which was also strangely liberating.

I checked in easily enough at the airport – the fake passport didn't raise any eyebrows – then had ages before my flight took off. I looked round the shops, then bought a burger and headed for the gate. I'd flown before, of course, but never on my own. Though I wouldn't have admitted it to anyone, I was terrified.

At first I was just scared of what I was doing – running away and using fake ID to get on a plane, possibly to walk right into the hands of the very people who most wanted Rachel and me dead.

And then, as I bit into my burger, I suddenly felt scared for Rachel, like something terrible had happened.

I hoped it was all in my head.

21

Rachel

I blinked, unable to breath, unable to move. My mind seemed to slow right down. I registered Paul, the guard, walking towards me . . . the frayed edge of his rugby shirt collar . . . the crunch of the stones under his feet.

'Get inside,' he snapped.

I backed towards the house as Milo wheeled past me. Behind me I could hear him opening the front door.

'Inside, Rachel,' Paul barked.

I stared at him, my legs threatening to give way.

'What are you doing?' I said. 'Milo, where's Daniel?'

Milo said nothing, just wheeled himself inside.

'Where's Daniel?' I repeated, more forcefully.

'He's not here,' Milo muttered.

Not here? 'You mean Elijah doesn't have him . . .? He's not on the island . . . not about to be operated on?'

'No. Now come inside.'

I stumbled into the house after him. It was cold and dimly lit, with whitewashed walls, but I barely noticed.

'Why did you trick me into coming here?' My voice sounded hoarse as a terrifying stream of possibilities rushed through my head. 'What are you going to do with me?'

Paul came inside after us and shut the door. He grabbed my arm. 'This way.'

'I was just following orders,' Milo muttered. He wheeled himself past me.

I felt sick.

'*Whose* orders?' I called after him. 'For God's sake, Milo, you can't do this. People will come looking for me . . . My parents . . . The police . . .'

'Actually, they won't,' Milo said. 'I took your purse and card from your bag before you got into the boot of the car. We left them on the jetty, so that it looked as if you'd drowned . . . deliberately . . .'

'*Killed* myself?' I couldn't believe it. 'No one's going to accept that.'

'They will,' Milo went on. 'There was an eyewitness . . .'

'*What?*' I thought back to the desolate patch of coastline where I'd smuggled myself onto the boat. 'Who? *How?*'

'I need to get her into her room,' Paul said, his hand still gripping my arm.

Milo nodded. 'You'll find out more in the morning, Rachel.'

'No, wait!'

But Paul was already pushing me along the corridor. We reached a door on the left and Paul opened it and shoved me inside.

The door shut – then locked.

I stood stock-still, trying to make sense of what had happened.

I looked round the room. It was empty and painted a dirty off-white. There was no furniture apart from a narrow camp bed which was pushed against the far wall. No windows.

I went over to the bed. The mattress was stained but a thick wool blanket had been laid on top of it.

Milo had tricked me . . . had faked my death.

Anger rose from deep inside me. How *dare* anyone do that? And *why*? It didn't make sense.

I wrapped the blanket around myself, my anger shot through with confusion. What was Milo playing at? Was Daniel *really* not here? And what about Elijah? Was he on the island?

My heart seemed to shrink inside me as I thought it through. Faking my suicide meant that no one would know I'd been taken. Everyone would think I was dead. I imagined the shock for my parents . . . the pain that they and Theo and Lewis would feel when they heard the news. *Surely* they wouldn't believe it? Would they?

I closed my eyes as sheer terror gripped me. My hand closed on the tiny silver 't' on the chain round my neck but, tonight, even that didn't comfort me.

I'd been betrayed and was locked up on an island for reasons I didn't understand.

No one knew I was here. No one even knew I was still alive.

I was totally alone.

22

Theo

My flight touched down just after noon – though it felt much earlier to me, still on US time.

As I made my way through passport control at Edinburgh Airport, anxiety surged through me. What if the UK authorities realised I was using a fake passport? What if there was a picture of me on their files that would flash up next to my false identity? What if Lewis didn't make contact?

In the end, none of those things happened. I sailed through security in Edinburgh and there was a text from Lewis waiting when I switched on my phone.

GET A TAXI TO THE HUDSON HOTEL. I'LL MEET YOU
OUTSIDE.

I found the taxi rank and set off.

After sunny Philadelphia, cloudy Edinburgh was a bit of a shock. The air was mild enough, but the sky seemed to press down on me, reminding me – now I was actually here – of the enormous task that lay ahead.

I saw Lewis before he saw me – he was leaning against the wall of the hotel, in jeans, sunglasses and a leather jacket. He looked exactly the same as before, his hair cut in a short dark crop and that slight air of danger about him. Except, I realised, we were now the same height. Six foot exactly. Just a couple of inches shorter than Elijah though, as Elijah's clone, I was presumably going to end up the same height as him.

Lewis came over as I got out of the cab. 'You've grown,' he said.

I shrugged. 'Not any smarter,' I said.

Lewis grinned. 'Good to see you, man. Was everything okay with the passport?'

'Yeah, no problem.'

Lewis nodded. 'That guy's brilliant – the best.'

There was a slight pause.

'You hungry?'

'Starving – the breakfast on the plane was, like, a roll and some jam with two teaspoons of egg and bacon.'

'Forget breakfast.' Lewis laughed. 'It's lunchtime here.'

We headed for a café across the road. Once we'd ordered our food, and I'd thanked Lewis for all his help getting me here, I asked him the all-important question:

'So, what leads do you have on where Rachel might be?'

'I don't have any.' He sighed, taking off his sunglasses and laying them on the table between us. 'The police have totally bought this suicide thing. There's even an eyewitness account of Rachel walking into the sea.'

'I told you before, she wouldn't have done that. Not in a million years.'

Lewis looked up. His eyes were a bright blue against his tanned skin. 'I know,' he said.

'Which means that eyewitness is lying and we need to find out why – and who for,' I said.

'I agree. The only trouble is that the inquest into Rachel's death won't be held until next week, which is the first time we'll get to see the eyewitness.'

'We can't wait that long . . . anything could have happened to her by then!'

'I agree,' Lewis said with a groan, 'but I've already been to the place where she was supposed to have killed herself. There are no clues – nothing for us to follow up at all. A few people apparently remember seeing her on the high street, but that's it.'

I shook my head. 'Then we have to speak to her parents, find out what they know.'

'After yesterday, that's what I was thinking too, but we have to be careful. They won't want to talk to us, especially me,' Lewis cautioned. 'We're a reminder of the past – a threat to their safety.'

'Tough.' I gritted my teeth. 'They're the only option right now.'

*

Two hours later, we reached the place where Rachel had been living in Roslinnon – a neat semi-detached house at the end of a long terrace.

'I've been keeping an eye on her for months,' Lewis explained as he parked his car. 'After Mel . . .' he hesitated, his voice growing bitter, 'well, I requested relocation to Edinburgh, so I could be near Rachel.'

I nodded, trying not to feel jealous. I knew Rachel saw Lewis as a big brother, but it was still hard to think he'd been looking out for her all this time while I'd been stuck on the other side of the Atlantic.

'How've you been getting money?' I said, thinking about the cost of my false passport and ticket.

'Security guard job,' Lewis said. 'The pay's okay and I get plenty of time off.'

He had to ring the doorbell of Mr and Mrs Smith's house twice before anyone answered. In the end Mr Smith came to the door. He looked terrible – ashen-faced and dead-eyed.

His mouth fell open when he saw us. '*You*. What the hell are you two doing here . . .?'

'Rachel,' I said.

Mr Smith's eyes widened. 'How did you even find us?'

'I've always known,' Lewis explained quickly. 'It was part of my deal with the FBI.'

'Your *deal*!' Mr Smith's voice rose. 'What the hell are you *thinking*, coming here?'

'We're certain she didn't kill herself, Richard,' Lewis said quickly. 'Somebody's covering up what really happened.'

Mr Smith hesitated for a second. 'You'd better come in.' He stepped back to allow us to pass, then ushered us into the living room. With its rose-patterned wallpaper and polished wooden furniture, it looked like a cheaper, smaller version of the house I remembered visiting last year in South London, that first day I met Rachel.

Mr Smith didn't bother to sit down – or invite us to. He simply shut the living-room door and folded his arms.

'Now, listen,' he said, his voice terse. 'I appreciate Rachel may have meant something to both of you, but there are still risks involved in us all being together. I also understand why you don't want to believe she's gone . . . especially *that* way, but there was an eyewitness and . . .'

'Whoever he is, he's lying,' I said.

Mr Smith shook his head helplessly. 'My wife and I . . . we've been over it and over it . . . the government are certain that neither Elijah nor RAGE had any idea where Rachel was. Her . . . what she did, it's the only logical explanation, no matter how much it hurts . . .'

There was a pause as we all stood in awkward silence.

'What makes you so sure Rachel would do something . . . like that,' Lewis said gently.

'She wasn't getting on with her mother,' Mr Smith said, heavily.

Well, that was true. I thought back to the many times Rachel had complained online about how controlling her mum was.

'Plus, she didn't seem to have any appropriate interests –

just this ridiculous obsession with self-defence . . . she'd been to a martial arts show just before she . . .' He tailed off.

Lewis and I exchanged glances. I knew he'd taught her some martial arts fight moves while the two of them had been preparing to rescue me from Elijah's compound in Washington D.C. I didn't much like the idea that Lewis had sparked off such a big interest. On the other hand, maybe having an in-depth knowledge of self-defence techniques might help keep Rachel safe.

'She didn't even seem to have any friends . . .' Mr Smith went on, his forehead creased with a deep frown. 'I mean, maybe a couple of girls at school . . . She saw one the day it happened, in the high street. The girl's mother stopped to speak to her and apparently Rachel just ran past, saying "I can't . . . I can't . . ." Terribly agitated, the woman said.' Mr Smith sighed. 'That sums it up really – the last few years Rachel turned into such a loner. Things were bad back in London, then, after the . . . episode in Washington, she seemed stronger for a while – but recently she's been more walled up in herself than ever. She's stopped confiding in us . . . God, she must have felt she didn't have *anyone* she could talk to.'

'She had *me*.' The words just blurted out.

'*You?*' Mr Smith looked at me, his eyes worn and strained behind his glasses.

I could feel Lewis looking at me too. My face grew red as I explained.

'Rachel and I met online every week. Don't worry, we

were careful. We used different internet cafés . . . different chat rooms . . . She told me stuff – about friends, home, school . . .' I hesitated. 'She told me lots of things and, yes, she was bored and annoyed with some of her life but she was happy too – and . . .' I tailed off, not knowing how to express my certain feeling that Rachel would never have gone away without saying goodbye to me.

Mr Smith was still staring at me, his mouth gaping open. Lewis went over and touched him on the shoulder.

'We just want to look around for a minute or two, Richard. To see if we can spot anything that would give us a clue . . . just in case . . .'

Mr Smith nodded slowly, his expression dazed. 'The police already went through her things, but . . . well, all right. Just don't make a noise. My wife . . . Rachel's mother . . . she's taken some tranquillisers – it's the only way she's getting any rest at all and . . .' He tailed off.

'We understand.' Lewis lowered his sharp blue eyes. 'This is the second time.'

With a jolt, I registered what he was saying. I knew that Rachel had been cloned from her dead older sister, Rebecca. I'd never thought about it before, but that must mean that Mr and Mrs Smith had already gone through the death of one daughter.

No wonder this apparent loss of Rachel was so unbearable.

Mr Smith said nothing more, just led us up some stairs and towards Rachel's bedroom. He stopped at the door. 'I can't go in there,' he whispered, sagging slightly against the wall. 'We haven't touched anything. You go ahead.'

I pushed open the door, eager to see Rachel's room. It was blue. Very blue. Blue blinds, blue duvet cover, blue walls. There was a wardrobe and a bookshelf and a desk. Two pictures of ballerinas hung from the wall above the bed.

I looked round, disappointed. I'd hoped being here would give me a sense of Rachel, but this room was just like the rest of the house. This was Rachel's mother's version of a girl's room. It didn't tell me anything about Rachel herself.

Lewis was examining the bookshelves. I went over – a few novels and textbooks and a whole shelf of martial arts books and pamphlets. Lewis picked one up and flicked through it.

I turned my attention to the desk. It was as neat and tidy as everywhere else. A few tubes of cream and a couple of bits of make-up were stacked in the corner. It was all so middle-aged and formal – rather like the ballerina pictures on the opposite wall – and not at all like Rachel.

At least, not the Rachel I knew . . .

I fingered the two huge necklaces that lay across the desk. One was made of large brown and blue beads . . . the other of thick golden leaf shapes. They looked like the sort of thing Rachel's mother would wear. I couldn't imagine Rachel herself in either of them.

What was that?

A tiny hairgrip with a diamante arrow at the tip was nestling under one of the large golden leaves on the second necklace. It was much simpler and prettier than anything else on the desk.

I picked it up. Rachel had worn this before . . . At her school disco and, later, in the cottage in Scotland.

I glanced round. Lewis was opening the big drawers under Rachel's bed, his back turned. I slipped the hairgrip into my pocket and turned back to the desk.

It wasn't much, but it was all that was here that truly reminded me of her.

A few minutes later and Mr Smith came in. He kept his eyes fixed on me as he spoke, clearly not wanting to look at the reminders of Rachel in the room.

'You'll have to go now,' he said. 'My wife's waking up.'

Lewis nodded.

'But we haven't found anything yet,' I said.

'We can come back.' Lewis turned to Mr Smith. 'What can you tell us about the eyewitness who said he saw Rachel on the beach?'

Mr Smith shrugged. 'Local police took a statement. It was a man in his early twenties. He only spoke to us for a moment – said how awful it had been not to be able to get to her in time . . . how sorry he was for us . . .'

I exchanged looks with Lewis. 'What was his name? What does he look like?'

'Dean McRae,' Mr Smith said. 'Cropped red hair, squashed nose. A student, nothing special. He doesn't live round here, he said he was just in the area for the weekend. Apparently he noticed Rachel at the martial arts show then, later, saw her again while he was driving along the coast, looking for a pub. She was in the distance, on the beach . . . then . . .' Mr Smith's mouth trembled.

'Where does this guy live?'

78

Mr Smith shrugged. 'Glasgow somewhere.'

'How many McRaes d'you think there are in the Glasgow phone book?' I asked Lewis.

But before he could answer, the bedroom door was flung open.

Rachel's mother appeared in the doorway, dressed in a floor-length satin dressing gown. Her hair was a mess, with grey roots showing, and her eyes were wild with fury.

'What the hell is going on?' she yelled, taking in first me, then Lewis. She turned to her husband. 'What are *they* doing here?'

Mr Smith started stammering out an answer, but Rachel's mother was clearly beyond listening. I stared, transfixed by her mean, tight face with the skin stretched weirdly round her eyes.

'Get out . . . get them out!' she shrieked.

Lewis grabbed my arm. 'Come on.'

We nodded goodbye to poor Mr Smith, then raced down the stairs and out of the house. We didn't speak again for a while. Lewis drove fast and hard, hissing softly under his breath . . . lost in his own thoughts.

I looked out of the window as we drove, watching the passing houses and trees and fields. Even though it was the height of summer here, everything seemed grey and life-less.

'At least we know who we're looking for,' Lewis said at last. 'Even if finding him is going to take forever and max out our cash.'

Max out.

Max.

Of course. 'I've just thought of someone who could help us do it faster,' I said with a grin.

23

Rachel

I woke with a start. For a second I was completely disoriented. Then everything that had happened flooded back.

Trying to save Daniel. Milo's betrayal. The suicide he'd faked . . . *my* suicide.

A chill raced through me, as the horror of my situation fully registered.

I looked around the room. No window. And my phone was totally out of power – I couldn't even check to see what time it was.

Across the room, the door handle turned. I sat up as it opened and a tall man with dark hair and a designer suit walked in.

'Hello, Rachel,' he said smoothly. 'What a great pleasure it is to see you again.'

A small part of the answer to the million questions in my head slid into place, as I registered who I was looking at – Elijah Lazio.

24

Theo

My amazing hacker friend Max was gobsmacked to hear from me. I found her mum's number through the online directory, then called her that evening – Sunday. After she'd stopped demanding to know where I'd been for the past nine months, she agreed to do a search on Dean McRae, though I refused to tell her why.

'It's for your own protection,' I said.

'Jesus, Theo.' Max laughed. 'You sound just like your mum back when she wouldn't tell you why you had a bodyguard.'

The reminder of Mum made me feel guilty. I quickly changed the subject, asking Max about her own life. We'd known each other since we were babies – our mothers were friends. As she spoke I found myself lost in thoughts of my old life at school in London, when Max and I were kids and this other guy, Jake, was my best friend.

'D'you still see Jake?' I said.

'Yeah, he comes round all the time.' Max laughed. 'Mostly just to annoy me.'

'Sounds like Jake,' I said.

For a second I wished I was back in the safety and ignorance of the past, a place where I'd never even heard of RAGE or Elijah Lazio.

Then I pushed the thought away. There was no point in wishing anything different. Everything was as it was.

Anyway, without all those other things I would never have met Rachel.

True to her ace hacker reputation, Max found six Dean McRaes in the Glasgow area within half an hour. A couple of them had some kind of police record. Lewis discounted those two straight away.

'RAGE wouldn't use anyone like that. Neither would Elijah. They'd want their witness to be completely credible.'

I nodded, checking through the details Max had sent through for the other four men.

'It's him,' I said, pointing to the second on the list.

Lewis looked over my shoulder and read out loud:

'Dean McRae, 22, engineering student . . . interests include war memorabilia and martial arts.'

Lewis raised his eyebrows. 'Why him?'

'It's the martial arts,' I said. 'Remember all those books in Rachel's room? Her dad said she'd been to some sort of martial arts show just before she disappeared.'

'It's definitely a connection,' Lewis said. 'The witness who saw her on the beach said he recognised her from that same show.' Lewis clicked through to the attached pic of

83

Dean McRae. It was from a student ID card and fairly blurry, but his hair was close-cropped and his nose looked squashed and broken, just as Mr Smith had described.

'I reckon he works for RAGE.' I looked at Lewis. 'You worked undercover there for a year, didn't you? What d'you think? Does he look like he'd fit in there?'

Lewis shrugged. 'RAGE takes in all sorts – from idealistic hippies against genetic modification to thugs who are just looking for an excuse to beat up on people. This guy might just as well work for Elijah as for RAGE.'

There was something particularly bitter about the way he said Elijah's name. I'd only heard him sound that bitter once before . . . about Mel.

I stared at him, suddenly realising what Lewis was really focused on. 'You *hope* McRae works for Elijah, don't you? You hope all this will lead you to Elijah.'

'Don't be stupid,' Lewis muttered.

'I'm not,' I said. 'You might care about Rachel and want to save her, but you're also hoping that you'll find Elijah. *That's* why you're spending all this time and money. It's to lead you to Elijah so you can take revenge for Mel!'

Lewis glared at me. 'He killed her in front of me . . . in front of you and Rachel . . . totally unprovoked . . . just because she'd been with me . . .'

I nodded. 'I know.' I felt uncomfortable now. Lewis looked so angry and upset. 'I'm just saying our priority has to be Rachel, that's all.'

'Of course.' Lewis looked away.

There was an awkward silence for a moment or two.

'Let's check in with Max,' I said eventually. 'See how she's getting on.'

It turned out that Max hadn't managed to find an address for McRae, but the college where he was studying engineering was listed. Lewis and I set off for it straight away, hoping that McRae would turn up for school first thing on Monday morning.

We found a B&B near the college and, while Lewis took a shower, I went outside and used the call box I'd noticed to phone Mum.

It was now almost twenty-four hours since I'd sent her the text from my old mobile. I took a deep breath as I punched in our home number. I knew I had to let her know I was okay – Lewis had already nagged me about it several times – but I wasn't looking forward to the bollocking I was likely to receive.

In the end, I just got the answerphone. I left a short message, repeating my lie about having gone off for a few days with a friend. I knew Mum wouldn't buy it, just like I knew she would be beyond furious when we finally saw each other again. But, right then, I didn't care.

I rang off, wondering vaguely if I should try Mum's mobile. After all, if she wasn't at home that probably meant she was out looking for me somewhere.

Another twinge of guilt.

I got into bed and tried to focus on what we had to do tomorrow: find McRae and make him tell us what really happened to Rachel.

I hoped it was going to be as easy as it sounded.

85

25

Rachel

Elijah Lazio folded his arms, clearly enjoying the shocked look on my face.

'Surprised to see me, Rachel?' He stared at me appraisingly. A mean smile twisted across his lips. 'Milo did well to trick you – I can see you've lost that innocent, trusting manner you had last year.'

'What are you going to do with me?' I said. 'And where's Daniel? What've you done with him?'

'All in good time, Rachel,' Elijah said, brushing a speck of dust off his expensively-cut suit.

'I see Milo was lying about you needing a heart transplant,' I said.

'I had one.' Elijah flicked his little finger impatiently.

'Is that . . .?' I couldn't bear to think what that might mean. 'How . . .?'

Elijah sighed. 'I worked out a way of adapting Daniel's heart so that the transplant I needed could take place. It was performed nearly seven months ago and it worked. Obviously.'

I stared at him, unable to take in what he was saying. 'So . . . Daniel's dead?'

Elijah shrugged. 'A necessary sacrifice, I'm afraid.' He paused. 'I had to take Daniel's heart, but the procedure was not unproductive. As you can see, I'm fitter than ever.'

I looked at him. It was true, his face was less lined and grey than I remembered. My whole being filled with hatred and revulsion. I clenched my fists, feeling the bile rise in my throat. How *could* Elijah do such a thing – and to a little boy?

'I'm sorry you were lied to, Rachel, but it was necessary to bring you here.'

'H-how did you find me?'

'One of the agents assigned to you under the government protection programme sold you out.' Elijah smiled at my shocked face. 'In case you were wondering, I have limited security on the island, which is why I had Milo bring you straight to the house. Plus I wanted to give Milo a chance to prove himself. He may be crippled, but he has his uses.' He paused. 'His code name is Hephaestus, you know . . . the lame God . . . another son of Zeus. You remember my code name, Zeus?'

I nodded. *God*, it was all flooding back, the detached, dispassionate way that Elijah always spoke about his cloning work. A sob rose inside me.

He had killed Daniel. I couldn't believe it. Except it made sense. Elijah had been prepared to sacrifice Theo in exactly the same way, for exactly the same reason . . .

I closed my eyes, feeling the grief swell inside me.

'Rachel?'

'You're . . . *evil* . . .' My voice broke as I looked up at him.

Elijah sighed. 'I'll leave you alone . . . talk to you later . . .' He took a step to the door.

'No.' I wiped at my eyes; I needed answers. 'Tell me why I'm here.'

Elijah leaned against the wall. His dark eyes – so like Theo's – studied me carefully. 'I need you,' he said.

'*Need* me?' I said suspiciously. 'What for?'

'Did Theo ever mention the Hermes Project to you?'

I tried to remember. The name was familiar and Hermes, I knew, was another of the Greek gods.

'Isn't . . . wasn't Hermes . . . er, *Daniel*'s code name?' I said. As I said his name, another wave of misery threatened to overwhelm me. Daniel had looked just like Theo when he was younger. It was like . . . like learning Theo's little brother had been killed.

I couldn't imagine how awful Theo was going to feel when he found out.

Elijah was still leaning against the wall, his cold, dark eyes intent on my face. 'I called my project after Daniel – Hermes – because he was the first healthy clone that I kept with me. Which meant he was the first clone I was able to experiment on.'

Ugh. 'What sort of experiments?'

'Lots of things . . .' Elijah said with a vague wave of his hand. 'The Hermes Project is a research programme designed to compare clones with non-clones, to find out what strengths and weaknesses belong to each. Part of the programme examines IQ and physical abilities. The other looks at genetic codes and DNA programming.'

'And the government let you stay on this island, working on *that*? Not . . . not caring that you've *killed* people?'

'No, the government does not allow this, Rachel.' Elijah sighed and ran his hand through his hair – a gesture I'd often seen Theo make. 'If Milo told you that, it was another lie. I'm still a wanted man you'll be pleased to hear, although I do have a backer who believes in my research. And he has powerful connections which offer me some degree of protection. But we're not talking about me, we're talking about the Hermes Project – and that's where you come in.'

'Me?'

'As you know, I cloned you from your older sister, after she died. I don't know whether your sister carried this . . . genetic quirk, or whether it's only in you, but there's something . . . special . . . in your DNA which I need to examine. I've been working off a single strand of your hair – that's all I had with me – but now my tests can be more extensive. It's just some blood I need, nothing too invasive.'

I stared at him. 'You brought me all the way to this island just to do some blood tests on me?'

I didn't believe it, but Elijah stared back at me, his dark eyes steady.

'Yes.'

26

Theo

Monday morning. Nine a.m. Lewis and I were standing outside McRae's college, waiting for him to arrive.

We'd already checked and there was a lecture on his subject that morning at 10.30. We kept our eyes peeled as a steady stream of male students wandered past us.

At about 9.45, it started raining. There was still no sign of McRae. If he didn't show up we were going to have to ask around, find out where he lived . . . track him down some other way. We were closing in, I knew, but I couldn't help but feel impatient. Rachel had last been seen on Saturday afternoon – over thirty-six hours ago. Anything could have happened to her since then . . . *be* happening to her.

The rain drizzled down. Rachel hadn't exaggerated how wet it was here. I pulled my hood up and huddled back against the wall. More time passed. Ten a.m. . . . 10.15 . . . 10.25 . . . Most students had arrived. The rain stopped, though the sky stayed iron grey.

And then I saw him. Dean McRae – complete with close-cropped red hair and squashed-in nose. He was sauntering across the pavement, a bag of books slung over his back, chatting to the guy next to him. I caught Lewis's eye across the doorway. He nodded, then set off towards McRae.

I hung back for a second, watching.

Lewis reached McRae. He flipped open a wallet, showing what I knew was a fake press ID card.

'I'm a reporter from the *Gazette*,' he said, in an English accent. 'I'd like to ask you some questions about the suicide you witnessed at the weekend.'

McRae frowned. 'I'm not supposed to talk to any—'

'It's all off the record.'

McRae hesitated. He whispered something to the guy he'd been walking with, who chuckled and hurried on inside.

'Off the record?' McRae said. 'That means you won't quote my name or say I'm the eyewitness?'

'Absolutely.' Lewis held up his wallet again: this time a line of twenty-pound notes poked out of the top. 'I can make it worth your while.'

Another pause. McRae glanced at his watch, clearly wondering if the conversation Lewis wanted to have was worth ditching his lecture for.

'Okay,' he said. 'But not inside the college.'

'Sure,' Lewis said. 'It won't take long. Why don't we just go round the corner, out of the rain?'

They set off. I followed at a short distance.

Round the corner, out of sight, Lewis darted forward. He shoved McRae against the wall. The man's eyes widened.

'What the . . .?' McRae raised his hand, turning sideways to aim a kick. But Lewis was too fast. He skipped past McRae's leg, grabbed his arm and twisted it behind his back. With his other hand he made a fist and pushed it against McRae's throat. McRae gasped, straining to breathe.

For a second I thought he was going to crush McRae's windpipe. That same furious-bitter look was in his eyes from earlier, when he'd talked about Elijah.

'Hey!' I shouted.

Lewis released his grip on McRae's throat slightly. McRae turned his head away and Lewis pressed his cheek against the brick. McRae's squashed nose went white at the tip.

'What do you want?' he said, his voice shaking.

I was suddenly sure this was no trained RAGE operative. McRae might look tough, but underneath he was just an ordinary student – a guy with no criminal record, who'd been paid to lie to the police.

'You lied about that girl's suicide,' I said walking over. 'What really happened?'

'Happened?' McRae was trying to twist his face round, to look at me, but Lewis kept his cheek pressed against the wall. 'It was like I told the cops. She put her purse down on the beach, then walked into the water.'

'That's not true.' Lewis twisted McRae's arm.

McRae winced with pain.

'Tell us what really happened,' I repeated. 'Were you even *at* the beach?'

'I don't know what you're—'

Lewis twisted McRae's arm higher.

'Okay, okay . . .' McRae paused, his breath coming out in shallow little gasps. 'I didn't see anyone walk into the water.'

'Why did you lie?'

McRae was silent, his body trembling.

'*Talk.*' Lewis pressed McRae harder against the wall.

'They told me to pretend I'd seen her . . .' McRae was really shaking now.

'Who?' I said.

'It was this young guy in a wheelchair . . . he turned up here one day . . . just told me to follow her after the Roslinnon martial arts show, make her run towards the high street where he'd be waiting. That's all I know, I swear.'

Anger rose up inside me. If Rachel had been followed, then she must have been scared. 'Why did this wheelchair guy tell you to say you saw her drowning?' I said, trying to control the rage that was boiling inside me.

'I told you, I don't know. He just said I had to tell the police I saw her walk into the sea just up the coast. He told me where to find her purse and ID card . . . said I had to pretend I found them on the beach after I'd seen her kill herself.'

'What was his name?' Lewis asked.

'I don't know, I only met him once. He didn't give me a name or a number or anything.'

'How did he pay you?'

'Cash. I'll get the rest after the inquest.'

I frowned, trying to make sense of what McRae was saying. Who was this guy in a wheelchair? What on earth was his connection to RAGE or Elijah? And why would he go to such lengths to fake Rachel's death?

'Did you hear or see *anything* else?' Lewis demanded.

'No,' McRae insisted. 'Except . . . the only time I met him he took a phone call which was obviously connected. He said something about taking the girl to see someone called Calla . . . Yes, that was it: Calla . . .'

Lewis and I exchanged glances. I was still mystified, but at least we had a couple of leads now – a young guy in a wheelchair and a woman called Calla. Not that we knew where to find either of them.

Lewis took his hands off McRae, who slowly turned round.

'So what did this wheelchair guy look like?' I asked.

McRae stared at me, his eyes widening.

'Actually,' he said, 'he looked a lot like you . . .'

27

Rachel

I slept badly, waking several times in a panic.

I had no idea what time it was. After Elijah's visit I hadn't seen anyone for hours, then the guard, Paul, brought me some food on a tray, and took me along the corridor to use the bathroom. As I went in to wash, he handed me a change of clothes – combats and a sweatshirt and some boxer shorts.

'These are *men's*,' I said, staring at them.

Paul shrugged. 'They're all we have.'

Paul had left me with instructions to get some sleep, but my body was too wound up to rest. On top of which I felt completely disoriented. There was no natural light in the room and I only had the vaguest sense of how much time had passed.

There was a light tap on the door, then the sound of the lock turning. I sat up as Milo entered in his wheelchair. He was wearing a leather jacket that looked a little too big for him. There were dark shadows under his eyes.

'Elijah says I can take you out today,' he said.

I had barely noticed it yesterday, but today the harsh American edge to his accent grated on my nerves.

'What time is it?' I asked.

'Just gone eleven a.m.'

I leaned against the wall – it was cold against my back.

I glared at Milo. 'I don't want to go anywhere with you,' I said.

Milo looked at me, his face reddening. 'I understand you're mad right now, Rach—'

'Well, that's big of you,' I snapped.

There was an awkward silence.

Then Milo took a deep breath. 'Look, I'm real sorry I had to lie to you to get you to come here. Believe me, once I'd met you and seen just how . . . how . . . what a great person you are, I hated myself for what I had to do, but it was *Elijah*, so . . .' He tailed off.

I shook my head. Nothing could excuse what Milo had done. Nothing.

'Okay.' Milo wheeled himself backwards, towards the door. 'I just thought you'd like some fresh air. If it were down to Elijah he'd leave you in here for days on end.' He paused. 'You know Elijah. He acts like he owns us because his science created us. I mean all those experiments he did to make the cloning work in the first place.' Milo shuddered.

What experiments?

I bit my lip, my thoughts fighting with each other. I couldn't bear the thought of spending time with Milo. It was humiliating to think how easily he'd tricked me. On the other

96

hand, I was desperate to get out of this room. Most importantly, I was never going to find a way off the island if I didn't know more about it. And Milo was, clearly, a good source of information.

Milo opened the door.

'Hold on,' I said. 'I'll go with you.'

Milo nodded. He waited while I put my shoes on, then led me out into the corridor. Glancing up and down I could see no windows.

'What's this building used for?' I said.

'It's where Elijah, me and the two guards eat and sleep.' Milo glanced at me. 'There's a kitchen along the corridor – I prepare the food, it's all really basic. I think the building used to be some kind of farmhouse. Goodness knows what they farmed here, though.' We reached the main door. Milo pushed it open and light flooded in. I shielded my eyes as we stepped outside.

Blinking against the glare, I followed Milo along the path. Paul was on duty at the gate, dressed in jeans and another rugby shirt.

He nodded at Milo, who nodded back.

I looked round as we passed the gate. We were surrounded by moorland – wild and green. The land rose up into hills on either side and up ahead, meeting a bright blue sky. Milo led me through the trees that surrounded the fence round the house. As we emerged on the other side, my mouth fell open. The rest of the island was bleak and scrubby but here the land dropped sharply, leading down to a long, smooth sandy beach. The sea sparkled beyond. It was beautiful.

As soon as I saw the water I started planning how I could slip away from Milo and swim out to sea. Surely another island – hopefully an inhabited one – couldn't be far away?

'Awesome, isn't it?' Milo said with a grin.

We went down onto the beach. Milo couldn't take his wheelchair onto the sand, so he stayed on the path, but I walked onto the sand and peered out to sea.

'The nearest island is fifteen miles in that direction,' Milo said, pointing to our right. 'Also deserted.'

I sighed. So much for my idea of swimming for it.

'And there's a cave over there.' Milo indicated a line of rocks that separated the beach from the trees beyond. He smiled, clearly enjoying his role as tour guide. 'The cave's cool, but wait till you see the view from the hill in the middle of the island.'

I nodded. Getting the full lie of the land would definitely be useful. I followed Milo back along the path. Beyond the house the land rose steeply. My heart beat faster. The little jetty where we'd docked before was just over this hill. Maybe there were other jetties and other boats. If I could work out how to start the motor I'd surely be able to steer a small boat until I reached land.

'I'm going to go down to the sea over there.' I pointed to the coastline. It was partially hidden from view by trees. Milo wouldn't be able to see me.

'That's fine, but just so you know, you won't find a way off the island, Rachel,' Milo said, shielding his eyes from the sun. 'John – the other guard – he's taken the boat to the mainland

98

for supplies and even if it wasn't miles to the nearest island there are rocks everywhere. The jetty we tied up at is the only place on the island where you can get close enough to shore to moor a boat – and even that's dangerous.'

'Right.' I didn't want Milo to see that he'd read my mind so well. Without looking back I jogged over the moorland and towards the sea. It really was the most beautiful day – not a cloud in the sky and just a gentle breeze drifting in off the water.

I reached the beach and walked along it, looking out at the endless sea beyond. The rocks Milo had mentioned were clearly visible close to shore. My heart sank as I realised he was right. You couldn't land a boat here, much less swim – those rocks would cut your legs to ribbons in seconds.

I trudged back towards Milo, a heavy weight in the pit of my stomach. There was, clearly, no way off the island unless I could somehow manage to get hold of the keys to the one boat when it returned, reach the jetty where it was tied up and work out how to drive it without running myself aground on the rocks just below the surface of the water.

Milo had trundled himself further along the path while I'd been gone and was now at the foot of the hill he'd mentioned earlier.

He watched me as I walked towards him, his dark eyes anxious and intent.

I couldn't work him out. He looked so like Theo and yet there was something about him that was completely different –

an awkwardness, a defensiveness . . . and the way he was acting about tricking me before . . . like it wasn't really his fault . . .

I was seized with a sudden thought. 'How many more clones of Elijah are there?' I asked.

'None after me and Theo and Daniel.' Milo's face took on a pained expression. 'At least, I don't think so.'

There was a moment's silence, the only sound the wind whistling off the sea.

'How could you just stand by while Elijah killed a totally innocent little boy?' I said.

'I didn't know that's what he was going to do,' Milo insisted. 'He doesn't really talk to me – like I told you, I think I remind him of his failures.'

'But you knew he wanted to kidnap *me*,' I said. 'Maybe he's planning on killing me too.' My throat tightened as I said the words.

'I honestly don't believe that,' Milo said, his face screwing up into an anxious frown.

'No?' I said. 'Are you sure? He told me that he was researching the difference between clones and non-clones and that he needed to do some tests on my blood . . . that there's something in me – a genetic quirk, he called it – that his other clones don't have. D'you know what that's all about?'

'No,' Milo confessed. 'Like I told you before, Elijah does all his research in an old barn at the other end of the island. Some guy pays for it – a private backer. Elijah built a kind of lab there when we came to the island four months ago. I've never been inside.'

'Then you don't know anything about Elijah's intentions, do you?' I said. 'For all you know, he might be planning to murder me tomorrow.'

Milo fell silent.

I glanced up the hill beside us. Even if there was no way off the island, it would be worth climbing it just to get my bearings.

Milo followed my gaze. 'Go on,' he said. 'I'll wait for you here.'

The wind whipped up as I climbed the hill. I had to hold my hair back to stop it flying into my eyes. I reached the top and looked around. Now, at last, I had a sense of the island as a whole. Straight ahead of me was the farm building where I'd spent the night – with the pretty beach and the cave beyond. At the opposite end of the island was a crumbling, stone barn – that must be the place where Elijah had set up his lab.

There were no other buildings. In fact, the only other man-made structure at all was the jetty with its little shelter. There were no boats in sight.

I strained my eyes, looking for other islands. It was a really clear day, I realised, so I must be able to see for miles and yet there was nothing but water all around.

I stomped back down to Milo.

We stood staring at each other for a moment.

'Your hair looks really pretty in the sunlight,' he stammered.

I rolled my eyes. 'I'd like to wash it,' I said, feeling irritated. What on earth did Milo think he'd achieve by paying me compliments?

'I'm sure I can arrange that,' Milo said eagerly. 'There's a proper bathroom at the end of your corridor next to that restroom you've already used and—'

'Don't do me any favours,' I snapped.

Milo looked crestfallen. 'Rachel, I'm real, real sorry everything's turned out like this . . .'

I opened my mouth to snap at him again. It was beyond irritating that he should act so polite around me when it was entirely thanks to him that I was a prisoner here in the first place.

But I stopped myself. Whatever the reason Milo was trying to be so friendly, it was surely worth my while taking advantage of it. If I couldn't get myself off the island then I was going to have to find some way of communicating with someone who could rescue me.

'How do you stay in contact with the outside world here?' I asked. 'I mean, I know from when we came here that there's no signal for a mobile.'

'That's right,' Milo said. 'There's no landline or mains electricity or anything. We bring everything in and there's a generator for the lights and heating.'

'What about the internet?' I said.

'Nope, nothing,' Milo went on. 'Elijah has some sort of radio, but it's kept in his office which has about three locks on the door.'

102

At last, something I could maybe use. It wasn't much, but some hope was better than nothing. If I could reach the radio, then I had a chance of contacting the police and my parents.

Milo glanced at his watch. 'I've got to make some sandwiches for lunch. You're supposed to come with me, but I don't want to force you. You can go back to your room if you'd rather.' He looked up at me hopefully.

Wow, thanks.

Again, I resisted the impulse to bite his head off. I hesitated, holding my hair off my face again. The wind was definitely getting stronger, though the sun was still burning down.

'Sure.' I attempted a smile. 'Would you like me to push your chair?'

28

Theo

'What do you mean, he looked like me?' I said. 'You said he was in a wheelchair.'

'Yeah.' Dean McRae stared at me, anxiously. 'He *was*. I didn't mean that . . . his face was a bit like yours, just older, late teens maybe.'

Lewis and I glanced at each other. We pushed McRae for more details but it was soon obvious he didn't have any. The only person he'd dealt with was this mysterious guy in a wheelchair who looked like me and the only name he'd picked up was that of the woman Rachel was being taken to see: 'Calla'.

We left McRae with dire warnings not to tell the wheelchair guy we'd been asking questions. We found a café out of the rain, and sat down over egg and chips to discuss what to do next.

Lewis was stumped.

'I just don't get it,' he said. 'In all the time I was with Elijah I didn't *ever* see or hear about anyone in a wheelchair *or* anyone called Calla.'

'What about when you worked undercover at RAGE?'

Lewis shook his head.

'Maybe it's a code name?' I said.

Or maybe Rachel's disappearance doesn't have anything to do with Elijah or RAGE.

The thought sat between us, unvoiced. Lewis stared at his plate of food, his eyes hard. I rested my head in my hands. The idea that Rachel might be in some sort of random trouble that Lewis and I couldn't know anything about was more than I could bear.

The egg on the plate in front of me was congealing around one of the chips. I pushed it away.

'Let's go back to where McRae told the police he saw Rachel kill herself, the place where Wheelchair Guy told him to say he'd found her purse and ID card . . .'

Lewis nodded. He paid and we left the café. We drove back towards the West coast. Once we'd arrived in Roslinnan, it only took ten minutes to get to the beach where Rachel was supposed to have drowned. We walked up and down the shore, but saw nothing that could possibly be connected.

I don't really know what I'd been expecting, anyway. Lewis and the police had already been here – not to mention several days' worth of tides ebbing in and out, clearing away everything left on the sand.

It was late afternoon by now and had turned into a beautiful day. I stared out over the sparkling water. Somehow the glittering waves just reinforced how helpless I felt.

'It's certainly deserted round here,' Lewis mused. 'A good place to fake a suicide.'

I looked up and down the beach. Not a single person in sight and rocks blocking the view on either side.

'We don't even know if Rachel was ever really here,' I said with a sigh.

We trudged back to Roslinnon. Lewis found a B&B and insisted I set up a new email account and email my mum from the local internet café while he called Rachel's dad to tell him what we'd found out from McRae. I sent my email, reassuring Mum once again that I was fine.

I couldn't stop thinking about Rachel the whole time. Was she okay? Was she trying to find a way out of wherever she was? Was she thinking of me?

In the end I couldn't bear my own thoughts. I went for a walk, arriving back at the B&B just before I was due to meet up with Lewis – who we'd claimed was my older brother – for dinner.

I sat in the little dining area next to the pub part of the B&B – staring blankly at the map of Scotland on the wall above the fire. It was one of those ancient maps, drawn centuries back, with the land divided up into the clans that, I assumed, had once owned them.

The woman who ran the B&B bustled over several times. I think she felt sorry for me having to wait for my 'older brother' to come down from his room.

I tried to smile and be polite, but to be honest everything felt like it was spinning out of control. I'd come all this way and Mum would be mad and Lewis and I had, surely, done everything we could to find Rachel. But nothing had worked.

'So where are you and your brother going on your trip?' the B&B lady was asking.

'Dunno,' I said, staring at the map and hoping she would go away.

The B&B lady followed my gaze. 'Are you planning to visit any of the islands while you're here?'

'I'm not sure yet,' I said carefully. 'I suppose they're all really built up now, aren't they?'

'Not at all.' The lady paused. 'That is, there's a fair amount going on, on some of the bigger islands like Eigg and Muck . . .'

'There's an island called *Muck*?' I said.

'Aye, but when you come to the Outer Hebrides there's some isles that are still completely deserted.'

Deserted. I stared at her. What would make a better hiding place for an outlaw like Elijah, or a terrorist organisation like RAGE, than an empty island?

At that moment Lewis arrived, his hair wet from the shower, and the B&B lady bustled away.

I leaned forward in my chair. 'Let's do a search on the islands off the coast here,' I said in a low voice. 'See if there's anywhere Elijah or RAGE could be hiding out.'

Lewis shrugged, clearly not as sold on the idea as I was, but he took out his phone and we both bent over our mobiles.

Intent on my search, I found a list of Outer Hebrides islands straightaway. There were loads of them, most of them absolutely tiny.

One name immediately jumped out at me.

'*Calla*,' I said, looking up at Lewis. 'That's *it*. The Isle of Calla – it's a *place*, not a person.'

Lewis nodded, staring intently at the map of the islands showing his own phone.

I jumped to my feet. 'Lewis, that island *has* to be where Rachel is,' I said, my voice trembling with excitement. 'We have to go there now!'

29

Rachel

After we came inside, Milo took me to the kitchen and cooked lunch. The food was better than I expected – tender lamb stew with crisp green beans and creamy mashed potatoes. I made sure I praised Milo's cooking, noting the way he blushed when I did so.

After an hour or so, Elijah came in. He looked tired and preoccupied and his presence changed the atmosphere, as if a storm cloud was hovering in the room.

Milo fingered his shirt buttons nervously. 'Is everything okay?' he said.

Elijah threw him a contemptuous glance. 'Enjoying playing nursemaid to Rachel . . .?' he sneered. 'Fetch me some food.'

Milo's face burned red with humiliation.

I wasn't going to be intimidated by his rudeness.

'Why am I here, Elijah?' I asked. 'What are these blood tests you want to do?'

Elijah waved my questions away with a weary flick of his

fingers, as Milo trundled towards him with a plate of stew in his hand.

'Please, Rachel, I've been up since the night before last. I can't answer your questions now.'

Milo set the plate down in front of Elijah. His hand was trembling.

Elijah ate a couple of mouthfuls of stew, then another man walked in.

'I got the things you asked for, sir,' he said, glancing briefly in my direction.

This must be the other guard, John – he was as broad and beefy as Paul, only with longer, darker hair. Milo had said he'd taken the boat to the mainland to fetch supplies. My mind raced with fresh possibilities. If John was back, then so was Elijah's motorboat – but where had John put the keys? And what supplies had he bought? Would these give me any clue as to what Elijah was planning to do with me?

'Good, John,' Elijah said. 'Leave everything in the radio room.'

'That's where I've just come from, sir.' John glanced from me to Milo, a cold, hard look in his eye, clearly gauging how much it was okay for him to say in front of us.

Elijah looked up. 'What is it?'

'He's on the radio, sir. He wants to speak to you,' John said.

'*Already?*' Elijah gazed longingly at his stew, but pushed himself up from the table and strode off. John followed.

I looked round. If I went too, I might learn something

useful. At the very least I'd get to see where the radio was kept.

Milo had picked up Elijah's plate and was heading for the oven, presumably to put the food inside to keep it warm. His back was turned.

I jumped up and raced down the corridor after John and Elijah. They disappeared round the corner into another, shorter corridor. Two doors, one on either side of the passageway, with a huge, locked fire door at the end. John and Elijah went into the room on the left.

Heart thumping, I crept after them and peered in round the doorway.

It was a fair-sized room, lit by an overhead bulb. The windows were shuttered and padlocked. A radio stood on the table at one end. Two black-and-white, grainy-screened TV monitors hung above it. One showed moving pictures of the beach and jetty where our boat had landed three days ago. The other showed the entrance to the barn I'd seen earlier . . . the place where Elijah had set up his lab.

Elijah was bent over the radio, some sort of head set clamped to his ear. John stood beside him. Two large plastic bags – presumably containing the supplies John had brought from the mainland – were at his feet. Neither man noticed me.

'Yes,' Elijah was saying into the radio mic. 'Yes, we lost another.'

I held my breath. What was he talking about?

'I don't know.' Elijah sounded impatient. 'But the

Aphrodite Experiment is . . . it just *happens* . . . I *don't know*.'

A tug on my arm. I turned. Milo had wheeled up behind me. He reached past me and pushed the open door shut.

'They'll be real mad if they see you,' he whispered. 'Probably lock you up again.' He turned and wheeled himself back to the kitchen.

I followed, my head spinning with what I'd heard. What had Elijah lost? What was the Aphrodite Experiment? Elijah used Greek names as codes for people. I was Artemis. Theo was Apollo. Elijah himself was Zeus. How did Aphrodite fit in?

Milo and I reached the kitchen. 'You can't let them see you snooping around like that, Rachel,' he said quietly.

'I thought you said I was free to move about here,' I snapped. 'It's not as if there's any way off this bloody island.'

'It *is* okay . . . I mean, within reason . . . so long as I can see you.'

Like a stalker.

I took a deep breath, biting back the impulse to say the words. I wanted to storm off . . . give myself time alone to think . . . but it was not in my interests to upset Milo.

'Can we go back outside?' I said. 'I'd like some air.'

'Sure.' Milo wheeled his way to the front door.

We went down to the beach and sat on the path, staring out to sea. After a while I left Milo and wandered across the sand, my thoughts caught up in Theo, wondering what he was doing right now . . . and how he would feel if he knew about Daniel.

112

I came back along the opposite path, stopping off at the cave Milo had mentioned earlier. It was smaller than I'd expected – a dark, low-ceilinged shell cut into the stone. Empty, apart from a pile of rubble at the back.

I peered into the dim recesses of the cave and shivered.

I needed a plan . . . some way of getting off the island. But how? I still didn't know how to drive the boat . . . or where the keys were kept. And I still had no idea what Elijah was doing here other than that it was something to do with me and this *Aphrodite Experiment* he'd mentioned.

Sighing, I wandered back to Milo.

He looked up at me, his hand shielding his eyes from the glare of the sun.

'So, what's Theo like?' he said.

He was trying to sound casual, but I could hear the hunger for information in his voice. I bit my lip, working out what to say. It wasn't surprising Milo was interested. After all, Theo was a clone of Elijah just like him, though Theo's body worked better. It was almost like they were brothers.

'We-ll,' I said slowly. 'He's nice.'

'*Nice?*' Milo sounded scornful. For a second he looked just like Elijah had earlier – that same expression of contempt.

'He's lovely,' I said. My heart beat fast. I didn't want to give away how much Theo meant to me. That was private. 'A lovely guy. Kind. Loyal. Brave.'

Milo shook his head. 'Sounds a bit all-American action-hero.'

113

'He's not American,' I said. 'He's British, like his mum. And . . . and—'

'Is he smart?' Milo asked.

I frowned. 'Smart enough,' I said. 'I don't think he's a scientific genius like Elijah.'

'Who is?' Milo said, bitterly. He paused. 'Actually, I don't think Elijah *is* such a genius, you know. The main reason he's achieved so much scientifically is that he doesn't know when to stop. I mean, the work he did before I was created . . .' He shook his head. 'Some of that was real horrific.'

'What work?' I asked, my curiosity piqued.

'I'm not supposed to talk about it.' Milo looked uncomfortable. 'I'm not even supposed to *know* about it. Er . . .' He paused, like he was plucking up courage to ask me something.

'What is it?' I said.

'Tell me more about Theo.' Milo looked out to sea, carefully avoiding my gaze. 'Are you in love with him?'

Yes.

I looked away, knowing my face was blushing furiously. 'Don't be stupid.'

'Sorry,' Milo said gruffly.

A few minutes later we went back to the house. I used the bathroom, then Milo said I could either stay with him in the kitchen or be locked into my room. I chose my room and lay, curled up on the bed, my fingers wrapped round the little 't' at the end of my silver chain.

Everything was so surreal. Being here . . . with Milo

114

acting like I was his *guest* almost . . . with thoughts of Mum and Dad always at the back of my mind.

And Theo . . . what was he going to do when I didn't get in touch again this week? Part of me wanted to believe he would try and find me – though I couldn't bear to think of him being captured and put in danger.

Then I remembered the fake suicide. If Theo tried to trace me, that's what he'd discover. How would he feel then? Would he believe it? If he did, how long would it be before he forgot all about me?

I swallowed down the sob that rose inside me. I couldn't give into this. I had to make a plan. At least I'd found out where the radio was kept.

Yeah, right. That's a big help, Rachel.

I sighed. Knowing the location of the radio was all very well, but how I was going to get past a locked door, work out how to use it and contact someone on the mainland was still way beyond me.

30

Theo

'We can't just drop everything and set off for this island!' Lewis didn't look up from his phone. 'We don't even have a boat yet.'

'Then let's hurry up and hire one,' I said. 'Come *on*, Rachel *has* to be on Calla. That's the same name Dean McRae heard.'

Lewis glanced up at last, irritation all over his face. It was late and we hadn't eaten. But I'd lost my appetite. Why couldn't Lewis see that every minute we waited put Rachel in more danger?

'Your impatience will get us killed, Theo,' he said. 'This stuff I'm reading says that it's virtually impossible to land on Calla because of the rocks. I'll need to study the area . . . find the best way in . . .' He turned back to his phone.

Frustration surged through me. 'Can't we just get going and work out about the rocks on the way?'

'No,' Lewis snapped. 'We're only going to have one chance to get to Rachel and we need to make the most of it.

That means being as prepared as possible. Whoever's got her will almost certainly be armed.'

'We don't know anything about them!' I protested. 'How can we prepare for something we don't know about?'

'That's exactly *why* we have to prepare.'

'But—'

'I want this as much as you, Theo, believe me.' Lewis's eyes filled with bitterness and I knew he was thinking about Mel again. 'But we have to do it properly. Understand?'

I turned away.

Sleep came in fits and starts that night. At last it was morning – as grey as yesterday had been sunny. Lewis was already up.

'I've worked out how to get to Calla,' he said. 'Now I just have to hire us a boat.'

'So we'll be able to leave in an hour or so?' I said, leaping out of bed.

'No.' Lewis glared at me. 'Obviously we can't just pitch up in the middle of the day. We'll go tonight.'

My eyes widened. 'But anything could be happening to Rachel,' I said.

'I know, but there's no sense risking arriving while it's light.' Lewis rubbed his chin. He hadn't shaved for several days and the stubble was dark against his skin. 'Why don't you get down to Rachel's school, see if you can pick up any clues.'

I stared at him. What was the point in that? *Man*, he was clearly just trying to get rid of me.

On the other hand, it was certainly better than hanging around here.

I set off for Roslinnon Academy. It was easy enough to slip in through the gates when a teacher came out at break-time. I wandered about the grounds, searching for people likely to be in Rachel's year. Eventually I found a girl called Mhairi – the one whose mother had spoken to Rachel the day she disappeared.

I was expecting more suspicion about who I was from Rachel's friends, but Mhairi was eager to talk, especially when I told her that Rachel and I went way back.

'*Really?*' she said. 'How do you know her? Rachel never talked about before she moved here. I wondered if something had happened to her before she came.'

I fended off her questions as best I could and asked my own. I didn't learn much. Just enough to know that Rachel had never mentioned my existence – not even as some kind of cover story.

I knew this was probably a sensible move on her part, but I didn't much like hearing it.

'Did she ever mention other friends or people she saw apart from her family?' I asked. 'Anyone at all outside of school?'

Mhairi gazed at me quizzically. 'No . . . well, not to me. She was kind of secretive. Quite a few boys liked her, but she never showed any interest.'

Well, that was something.

Not that it mattered if we didn't find her soon.

I went back to the B&B, still deeply frustrated.

Once in the room, I stared out of the window. It was a grim view, especially when the sky was so overcast: a small car park, some rubbish bins and the backs of a row of squat, brick houses.

'I've found a boat,' Lewis said. 'Though the owner's asking for more money than I want to spend. My savings are running low.'

I stared at him. I hadn't really thought about it much before, but Lewis must be spending a fortune on our efforts to find Rachel. There was the cost of all the travelling we'd done . . . plus my fake documents . . . petrol for the car . . . the B&Bs . . .

'You're spending your savings?' I said. 'I thought you had a job?'

'It doesn't pay *that* well,' Lewis said. 'I'm a security guard, not a professional soccer player.'

'Sorry,' I said, feeling irritated again.

There was a pause, then Lewis sighed. 'No, I'm sorry. It's just since Mel, looking out for Rachel's been all that mattered.'

I looked away, remembering Lewis's smart, beautiful girl-friend again . . . and how Elijah had shot her dead in front of us both.

'Most days I just go to work and come home again,' Lewis went on in a low voice. 'And when I get home I tend to stay there, though I have been keeping an eye on Rachel's dad's work friends . . . making sure no one was in a position to harm her . . .'

I felt another stab of jealousy. It should have been *me* looking out for Rachel, not him. 'Did anyone ever see you checking up on her?'

'No.' Lewis ran his hands over his head. 'I was careful.'

'Are you sure? I mean, maybe whoever has got Rachel found her through you.' The words were out of my mouth before I could stop them.

I felt mean inside for saying them . . . for thinking them . . . and yet . . .

Lewis stared at me, horrified. 'I hope not,' he said. 'Man, I hope not.'

'It doesn't matter now anyway,' I said awkwardly. 'All that matters is getting her out.'

The time until we left passed slowly. Lewis went over the plan several times.

'Apparently there's only one place we can land on Calla, so whoever's on the island will probably be guarding, or at least monitoring, what happens there. Once we've arrived we're going to have to move as quietly as possible.'

'I know,' I said. 'I get it.'

'Do you?' Lewis fixed me with a stare. 'If Rachel's on this island there'll be people there with guns. I don't have one. D'you get that? All I have is a knife. We have to be quiet and we have to be quick. Get in. Get Rachel. Get out.'

I swallowed. 'I'm not afraid.'

Lewis muttered something I didn't quite catch.

I didn't ask him to repeat it.

*

At last it was time. We drove well out of Roslinnon to a bat-tered old marina, where Lewis took charge of the boat he'd hired.

As Lewis went over the controls, I tugged my wool hat down round my ears. Lewis and I were both dressed in dark trousers and black jumpers, with dark jackets. We had to hope this would help keep us unseen when we reached Calla.

I sat, as directed, in the bow of the boat as the motor revved. It was a small motorboat – just room for me at the front and Lewis at the back. I looked into the darkness. There were lights on one of the large islands nearby, but I knew Calla was much further away.

I took deep breaths of the cold salty air as we set off.

This was it.

It felt like hours later when Lewis turned off the light in the boat and slowed the engine to a chug. The sea spray that had been spattering my face fell away and the moon came out from behind a dark cloud.

I could just make out the coastline ahead – a dark beach under a jetty lit with a single lamp. Another boat – larger than ours – was already moored against the jetty.

'Only one boat to disable,' Lewis muttered.

I peered at the lamp. It was fastened to the shelter at the end of the jetty. Beneath it, a small security camera was swivelling away from us.

'That camera is sweeping the jetty,' I whispered. 'We'll have to moor up behind the big boat so it doesn't see us.'

Lewis followed my gaze. 'Good thinking,' he said.

He cut the engine and paddled us up to the hull of the other boat. As the camera on the jetty shelter turned away from us, Lewis hauled himself up, clambering silently into the other boat. There was the swift ripping sound of a knife tearing through plastic. I watched the camera. It was still focused on the other end of the jetty. Lewis's head appeared over the hull. He beckoned me towards him and I crawled into the other boat too.

My heart was hammering away, the adrenalin coursing through me.

'Okay, I've killed the engine,' Lewis whispered. 'Their boat's out of action.'

I nodded, pointing towards the camera, which was now moving slowly back in our direction. We lay face down, prostrate against the deck, as we waited for the camera to swing all the way towards us and begin its journey back again.

Several long seconds passed. There was no sound from the shore, just the slap of the waves against the boats and the whistle of the wind above our heads.

At last I risked a glance. The camera was pointing away from us again. I raised myself, ready to move.

Damn.

A tall, thick-set man was walking along the path towards the jetty. I dropped back down, my breath ragged and shallow. Had he seen us?

31

Rachel

I lay awake for hours on Tuesday night. Another long day had passed. Elijah had appeared at lunchtime – looking exhausted again – and taken blood from me. He hadn't explained any more about why I was here. I'd spent most of my time talking to Milo and walking on the beach when it wasn't raining.

I was still no closer to finding a way into the radio room, but at least I had a better sense of how life here at the house worked.

Elijah's word was law. Both bodyguards and Milo were clearly terrified of him – and he, in turn, expected absolute and immediate obedience from them.

Elijah kept odd hours, spending most of his time in the mysterious lab he'd set up in the barn. However, whenever he did appear, he expected Milo to be on hand providing him with food at a moment's notice.

One guard was on duty at all times. John and Paul took shifts outside the barn that contained Elijah's lab while Elijah was inside – and through the night. I was pretty sure that, most of the time, the house where we all ate and slept was unguarded, but there was still no way for me to get outside. Though I was allowed to roam about under Milo's supervision during the day, I was locked in my room after supper and left there till morning.

I pumped Milo for more information while we ate the shepherd's pie he'd made.

'Once or twice a week one of the guards goes to the mainland for fresh provisions. I've only been off the island that one time – to fetch you.' He blushed.

I smiled, determined to make him think I was interested. 'It was clever, the way you tricked me,' I said. 'I mean, I hate to admit it, but you really fooled me.'

Milo blushed even more deeply. 'I know, I'm so sorry I had to lie to you Rachel, but I promise everything else I've told you is the truth.'

'I understand,' I said, forcing another smile. 'It's hard to say "no" to Elijah.'

Milo nodded.

'There is one thing . . .' I hesitated, trying to assume a look of slight embarrassment. 'I hate being locked in that room overnight,' I said softly. 'It's humiliating not being able to go to the bathroom. I was wondering . . . please? I mean, maybe you could leave it unlocked? It's not as if I can get anywhere – the front door and all the windows are barred overnight.' I gazed at Milo with what I hoped was a helpless, beseeching look on my face. '*Please*, Milo?'

He bit his lip. 'I can't,' he said, 'but if I'm up in the night, I'll definitely come to see if your light's on. If it is, then I'll let you out to go to the bathroom. Okay?'

'Thank you.' I smiled again.

It wasn't much, but maybe I'd be able to use it to my advantage.

32

Theo

We lay rigid-still on the deck of the large boat. Lewis was right beside me, his eyes intent. A soft, hissing sound escaped from under his breath.

The man I'd seen jumped onto the jetty. His weight sent a vibration through the boards and across to where we were lying. His footsteps sounded as he paced up the jetty.

I held my breath.

The footsteps stopped, then receded. Another jump, this time off the jetty. There was a dull thud as he landed on the beach.

I risked a look. The man was disappearing into the trees on our right. The camera had almost reached the end of its journey away from us.

'Give it a moment,' Lewis whispered.

We waited until the camera had swung back towards us, and then turned away again.

'Come on.' Lewis prodded my arm. 'To the trees on the left.'

We wriggled, commando-style, along the deck and up onto the jetty, then crawled across the wooden boards until we reached the shelter containing the light and the camera.

We scrambled to our feet, well out of sight of the camera now, then jumped down and raced into the woodland to the left of the beach.

I stood under cover of the trees. The sand was compacted – damp under my feet. I had no idea what the area further inland looked like. A few feet past the light at the jetty and the whole island faded to gloom, lit only by faint moonlight.

A stony path led into the darkness.

'Our best bet is to follow that path, keeping close to the trees,' Lewis whispered. 'We should see any buildings in the moonlight as we get closer.'

I glanced up as the wind dropped. The moon was misty behind clouds. The air was crisp and clear and cold.

We set off in the darkness, keeping the path just in view.

It was spooky; the only sounds the rustling of the trees above our heads and the swish of the waves beyond. The woodland thinned out as we rounded a curve, making it harder for us to find cover.

I kept my eyes open for any sign of the guard from before – or other men like him – but there was no one about.

And then I saw it . . . a single electric light burning in the distance, outlining a small building. From here I couldn't make out exactly how big the building was, or what it was made from, but the light – which I quickly realised was positioned above a door – suggested it was inhabited.

'Look.' I pointed the light out to Lewis. 'Let's go.'

'We'll approach from the rear of the building,' Lewis said, grabbing my arm to stop me rushing ahead. 'There may be more cameras. And guards.'

I nodded and we set off across the grass.

33

Rachel

The lights outside flashed on, brightness seeping under my door, waking me.

Was that Milo? I switched on the overhead light by the door – so that he could see I was up if he passed.

Two minutes went by. I heard nothing . . . then the sound of wheels trundling along the corridor.

'Milo?' I hissed, rattling at the door knob. 'Milo, open the door.'

The wheelchair stopped outside. I could hear a metal clink as Milo fiddled with the key.

The door opened. Milo wheeled backwards to let me out.

'Elijah and Paul are in the radio room,' he whispered. 'They think they saw something moving along the jetty. It's probably just a seal or something, but they've sent John to the lab to check everything's okay. You can go to the bathroom if you want, but be quick.'

'Thanks.' I headed away from him, down to the bathroom. The stone floor was cold on my bare feet.

As I reached the door, Elijah called out for Milo. I turned. Milo was beckoning me to come back, but I shook my head. *Two minutes*, I mouthed, then disappeared into the bathroom.

A few seconds later I heard Elijah shout out for Milo again, then the wheelchair moving away down the corridor.

I waited a moment then followed after Milo, back past my room and round the corner, towards the radio room.

Elijah was barking out orders.

'That's definitely an intruder,' he was saying. 'Get going, Paul. Milo, get my gun. Now.'

I flattened myself against the wall beside the radio room as Paul dashed out. He didn't notice me. Neither did Milo, who followed right after him, zooming down the corridor at high speed.

I crept to the doorway and peered inside, my pulse drumming against my throat. Elijah was leaning over the desk, fists clenched, all his focus on the monitor in front of him. It showed the entrance to the barn where the lab was situated. John was standing outside its door, looking round, a gun in his hand.

And then the light above the door went out.

Elijah let out a stream of swear words. He leaned into the radio mic on the desk. 'What's going on, John . . . report . . .'

I stared at the screen. John's silhouette was still visible in the moonlight. He was backed against the barn door.

'Someone threw a stone, sir.' John's voice crackled through the radio. 'Knocked out the light. I can't see—'

'Stand firm.' Elijah spoke into the radio mic on the desk. 'Paul's on his way.'

'Yes, sir.' John nodded, his face lit now by the moon.

Elijah covered the mic and swore again. He still hadn't noticed me standing behind him. I looked around. If only I had some weapon, something I could use to attack him, I could get to the radio right now – both the guards were gone and Milo was still away, fetching Elijah's gun.

I was on the verge of going back to my room to find something when new movement on the screen caught my eye.

Elijah thumped the desk. I froze, trying to make out what was happening. A man . . . no, two men . . . were now silhouetted beside John. One punched, the other chopped his hand against John's neck.

John fell. One of the attackers turned towards the camera.

My hand flew to my mouth, my eyes piercing the screen. I stared – the moment lasting an eternity – as Theo's unmistakable face flashed for a second in the moonlight, then vanished, as he disappeared into the barn.

34

Theo

The guard fell against Lewis, who eased him to the ground.

I turned to the door. Rachel was inside. She *had* to be.

The door seemed to take an ordinary key. No sign of anything flashier. I pushed on the handle.

It was locked.

'Find the key,' I urged.

Lewis was already fumbling in the guard's pockets. 'There's nothing on him,' he said, glancing at the door. 'That lock doesn't look very sophisticated, though. If I had a pin I could pick it.'

A pin . . . My eyes widened. 'You mean, like a hairpin?'

I fished Rachel's diamante arrow-shaped hairgrip out of my pocket and handed it to Lewis.

He stood up and fitted it to the lock. 'Where the hell did you get this?'

I didn't want to tell him where I'd taken it from . . . or why.

'Thought it might suit me,' I muttered.

Lewis grunted as he fiddled with the pin. 'Keep a lookout, Theo.'

It was impossible to see more than a few metres in the darkness but I strained my ears. Was that faint sound just the wind in the trees? Or distant footsteps?

Behind me, Lewis eased open the door. Inside it was pitch black. Disorientated, I felt on the wall for a light switch. *There.* I turned it on. We were in a small stone hallway. No furniture. No floorboards, even. The overhead light cast a dim glow across the empty room.

I frowned. 'There's nothing here,' I said.

'What about through there?' Lewis pointed to a door I hadn't noticed on the other side of the dingy hallway. It was made from metal – completely different from the rest of the building. Beside the door a small screen was set into the wall. A faint red light glowed from inside it.

'That's a retinal scanner.' I raced over. Elijah had used these back in his Washington compound. 'Who'd put a door that secure into an old barn unless they wanted to hide what was on the other side?'

'How do we get through it?' Lewis held up the hairgrip. 'I don't see this working.'

I pocketed the hairgrip. 'If it's Elijah's door, then we're okay.' I strode over to the screen and positioned myself so that the red light could 'read' the imprint of my eye. As a clone of Elijah, I was a genetic match for his retina.

The metal door gave a soft click as the lock sprang back.

'Typical Elijah.' I could hear the bitter satisfaction in

Lewis's whisper. 'Let's hope there isn't anyone waiting for us on the other side.'

I took a deep breath and pushed the door open. The room beyond was dimly lit, bathed in a warm pinky glow. I crept inside. I could just make out the rounded shapes of a short row of plastic cases. A low, mechanical humming noise was coming from somewhere, but there was no other sound. No people.

I took a closer look at the cases.

My mouth fell open.

'Oh my God.' Lewis stood beside me. 'What the hell *is* this place?'

35

Rachel

He was here. He was here.

A tornado of feelings swept through me, paralysing me for a second. Elijah appeared similarly shocked. He stood, rigid, in front of the screen for a moment, then picked up the radio mic again.

He was so intent on the image before him, he still hadn't realised I was standing by the door.

'Breach!' Elijah shouted into the mic. 'There's been a breach at the lab. John is down. Paul . . . *Paul*, do you read me?'

'Yes, sir!' Paul sounded breathless.

His distant footsteps pounded along the path. He was going to reach the barn in less than a minute.

I stared at the screen. John was still in a heap on the ground. I wondered for a second who the person with Theo was, then focused all my thoughts into a single aim . . . I had to warn Theo that Paul was coming. Even if I couldn't reach him before Paul did, surely he'd hear me yell if I could just get outside the house?

I turned and tore off down the corridor.

36

Theo

I shook my head, trying to make sense of what I was seeing: row after row of clear oval pods. Each one contained some sort of tiny, semi-transparent blob, suspended in liquid and attached to long tubes that led out of the pods to a large central tank. A low hum emanated from the tank. I stared at the blob inside the nearest pod.

Man, was it *moving*?

The skin on the back of my neck prickled.

What on earth was Elijah up to?

Outside the room a radio crackled. The muffled voice giving orders was just audible. 'Do not shoot inside the laboratory. Repeat. Do *not* shoot.' It was Elijah.

His voice sent a bolt of fear shooting through me.

'Hide,' Lewis hissed, ducking behind the large tank.

I darted behind the row of pods just as a man charged into the room.

37

Rachel

I reached the front door of the farmhouse, running hard, just as Milo wheeled himself round the corner. He was coming in my direction – fast. The small black gun Elijah had sent him to fetch rested on his lap.

'Rachel, stop!'

No. I raced out of the front door. Down the path. The stones were hard and cold on my feet and the air freezing against my skin, but I barely noticed.

I *had* to warn Theo.

38

Theo

I crouched behind the row of pods. The man by the door was tall and bulky – another of Elijah's security guards, I guessed. The low lighting in the room glinted off his blond hair as he looked around, his gun at the ready in front of him.

The guard's eyes widened as he took in the sinister-looking pods. Had he not seen them before?

I crouched lower, but it was impossible to hide.

'Stand up,' the guard ordered. 'Hands in the air.'

I stood, my stomach constricting into a tight knot. The guard turned towards me. I kept my gaze averted from the large tank behind him, not wanting to give away Lewis's hiding place.

The man's dark blue eyes widened, his mouth falling open in shock.

'*Milo?*' he said. He stared at my legs, lowering his gun.

Who the hell was Milo?

'No, you're not him.' The guard raised his gun again.

Lewis flew out from behind the tank. His hand chopped at

the guard's neck and he fell to the ground. Lewis stood over him, panting.

I watched him, breathless. I would *never* get used to how fast Lewis could move.

Lewis grabbed the man's gun and glanced up at me, his eyes fierce.

'Go!' he yelled.

We pelted out of the door, past the unconscious guard outside and down the path.

'Into the trees,' Lewis ordered. 'We'll follow the path up the island – but keep under cover. There must be another building further on.'

'Right.' It wasn't good news. For all we knew there could be loads of buildings – with Rachel hidden in any one of them.

We reached the trees. I darted into the pitch black and turned to look back the way we'd come. A distant shout echoed towards us.

Lewis put his finger to his lips. I listened hard.

'THEO!' The yell came closer. 'THEO!'

It was her . . . I was *sure* it was her. I stared into the darkness.

And then she ran into view, past the hill in the moonlight, flying over the rough stones.

Rachel.

39

Rachel

'Theo!' I yelled again.

He walked out from the trees beyond the lab. It was too dark to see him properly, but I knew it was him. Then he stepped into the moonlight. My breath burned in my throat as I made out his face . . . the slope of his nose . . . the silky brown of his hair . . .

I raced on. A second later I was there, right in front of him. I stood, panting, my eyes soaking up Theo's face. Even in the moonlight I could see how different he was from Milo. Something stronger and sweeter in his eyes. *So* beautiful. And taller than I remembered too.

'Rachel.' A second figure emerged from the trees.

'Lewis,' I breathed.

He grabbed my arm, unsmiling. 'Come on. Our boat's by the jetty.'

He was different somehow, but my head was too full of Theo to think about the how or why of anything to do with

Lewis. I could feel his eyes on me as we stumbled in the darkness. Distracted, I tripped over the thick root of a tree, landing heavily on the ground.

'Quiet!' Lewis hissed.

We were nearly at the jetty. Elijah's roar rang out.

'Theo! You won't get away with this!'

Lewis froze. Then he turned to me. 'How many guards are there?'

'Just two,' I said. 'Two men and Elijah. That's all.'

'What about the guy in the wheelchair?' Theo said.

'Yes, but he's not like the others.' I hesitated. 'I don't even think he has a gun of his own.'

'Both the guards are unconscious,' Lewis said. There was a hard look in his eyes I didn't remember seeing before. A terrible bitterness. He stood a step away from us. 'I'm going after Elijah,' he said. 'This ends tonight.'

'*What?*' I said.

Theo stared at him. 'That wasn't the plan . . . you said "get in, get Rachel, get out", not—'

'I know what I said, but I have to do this. It's the only way we'll all be safe.' Lewis took another step away. 'Get back to the beach. Wait in the trees near the boat until you hear me. I'll be there in ten minutes . . . max.'

'But—' Before I could say any more, Lewis sped off.

Theo and I looked at each other.

'Is Lewis going to kill Elijah?' I whispered, shocked.

Theo nodded. 'It's because of Mel. Lewis is obsessed with getting revenge on Elijah for killing her. It's all he talks about.'

141

I nodded, letting this latest bit of information settle as Theo took my hand and led me on, through the trees towards the jetty. My feet were numb with cold now, but my hand was warm under Theo's touch. After a minute we reached the edge of the wooded area. An expanse of beach lay ahead. Above the beach, the jetty stretched into the sea. I could make out the vague outline of Elijah's boat bobbing in the water at the end.

'Our boat is hidden behind that one,' Theo explained.

I glanced up at the camera, which was still scanning the beach.

'Should we make a run for it?' I said.

Theo shook his head. 'Lewis said to wait by the trees. There's more cover.'

'Okay.' I shivered.

Theo tugged off his jacket. 'Put this on.'

I took the jacket gratefully. It was too big, but I wrapped it round me, instantly feeling the protection it gave against the wind.

There was no sight or sound of either Elijah or Lewis.

Theo looked at me. He took my hand again. 'Are you okay?'

I nodded.

'Did Elijah hurt you?' Theo's eyes were dark and intense.

'No.' The word came out as a whisper. Immediately I thought of Daniel. How did I tell Theo about him?

We stared at each other.

You risked everything to find me. The thought was overwhelming. Impossible to put into words.

'You're here,' I stammered.

'For you,' Theo said.

I gazed into his deep brown eyes. He moved closer. The silence between us grew as we looked at each other. In the background the trees rustled and the wind whistled and the sea lapped against the shore. And then those sounds faded away and all I could hear was Theo's breathing, as rapid and shallow as my own.

'They made out you were dead,' Theo said. 'But I knew it wasn't true.'

I looked into his eyes, my heart racing again.

'Elijah wants me for some tests he's doing . . .' I stammered.

'Are they anything to do with those weird pods in that lab of his?'

I frowned. 'Was that what you saw?' I said, wondering what he meant. '*Pods?*'

Theo nodded.

'I don't know anything about Elijah's research,' I admitted. 'He doesn't let anyone into his lab, but I think his tests on me have got something to do with the Hermes Project . . .'

'I remember that from Elijah's compound in America.' Theo's eyes rounded. 'It's connected to Daniel . . . Wait . . . is *he* here?'

I stared at him, a hundred thoughts fizzing round my head. Theo had felt terrible last year in Washington that he hadn't saved Daniel. How was he going to feel now, knowing that the little boy had paid for that with his life?

'No, Daniel's not here.' I took a breath, unsure how to tell him that Daniel was dead.

Theo didn't wait for me to say any more. He dropped my hand and cupped my face in his palms. 'It's good to see you,' he said softly. 'I missed you.'

'Me too,' I whispered.

Theo stroked his thumb down my face. My cheek burned where he'd touched it. He drew closer still, until our lips were almost touching.

'Rachel,' he whispered.

I closed my eyes as his kiss ricocheted through my body.

And then a series of shouts ripped through the air.

We broke away from each other, turning towards the shore.

More shouts. Elijah. Getting nearer.

'Theo!' That was Lewis. A warning yell.

'Come on, we should get to the boat now.' Theo grabbed my hand and we raced off across the beach. In a few strides we were at the jetty. It was just above our heads. Theo reached up, gripped hold of the edge and hauled himself up. More yells. They were definitely getting closer. I turned to see if I could catch sight of either Lewis or Elijah and stepped on a jagged stone. It sliced into my foot.

'*Ow!*'

Theo was half on the jetty, scrabbling to get a purchase with his legs. 'What's the matter?'

'Nothing.' I lifted my foot off the ground. I could feel blood seeping out of it.

Theo was on the jetty now. He reached down for me.

Wham. A shape lunged at me out of nowhere. Strong arms pushed me. Caught off balance, I toppled over. The sand rushed up to meet me. *Thud.* Sharp grains flew into my eyes and nose and mouth.

'Stay down.' Elijah was pressing hard on the back of my neck.

I gasped for breath, spluttering mouthfuls of sand, the panic rising . . . choking me . . .

Above me, Theo was yelling, 'Let her go!'

And then a shot fired.

40

Theo

The bullet whistled past my head. It only missed me by a few centimetres or so, but at that range Elijah could easily have killed me.

I froze, staring down at him. It was all flooding back – the events of the year before . . . Elijah and the way he had manipulated me, imprisoned me, been prepared to murder me . . .

My hands started shaking. Elijah gave me an icy smile.

'Hello, Theo,' he said.

'What have you done with Lewis?'

'Get down from the jetty,' Elijah said, ignoring my question. 'No sudden moves, please, or I shoot you for real.'

'I thought you needed me?' I glanced at Rachel. She was lying quite still in the sand, her head turned sideways. Elijah's foot was still on her neck, but her eyes showed no pain. Only fear. 'Don't you need my heart, Elijah?'

'I have a perfectly healthy heart now, Theo,' Elijah said briskly. 'My experiments have moved on. It's Rachel I need. Not you.'

I stared at him. Was that true?

'Now, get down onto the beach,' Elijah went on. '*Slowly*. Sit before you jump, please.'

I looked round, trying to work out what to do. Our boat was only a metre away, just past Elijah's. From up here on the jetty I could make out the outline of the hull.

With a jolt I realised Lewis was inside, carefully unwinding the rope that bound our boat to Elijah's. He must have swum there from the beach and got on board without me or Elijah hearing him.

As I stared at him he looked up. Our eyes met. Seawater was dripping silently down his face. He put his finger to his lips. *Sssh.*

'*Now*, Theo.' Elijah cocked his gun.

I turned back to him and slowly lowered myself so that I was squatting on the jetty.

'Where is your boat moored?' Elijah said. *Man*, if he walked a few more metres down the beach he'd be able to see it – and Lewis inside.

'What are you going to do with Rachel?' I said, trying to keep his focus on me. 'What are those creepy things in your lab?'

'I suggest you stop asking questions and start answering mine, Theo. Now get down here!'

I couldn't stop myself glancing over at Lewis again. Except he wasn't there. Neither was the boat.

Had he taken it somewhere? How, without using the motor?

'Theo?' Elijah had followed my gaze. He bent down, keeping his gun tightly gripped in his hand, and pulled Rachel to her feet.

Damn, he'd realised I was looking for the boat.

Holding the gun pressed against Rachel's side, Elijah walked along the beach. He was frowning, peering into the darkness, trying to see past his own, bigger boat.

I raised myself up a little, my muscles tensing. There must be some way I could jump him . . . get that gun off him . . .

A faint creak sounded behind me. As Elijah looked out to sea, I glanced over my shoulder. Lewis was easing our boat round the jetty. I could just see the tips of his fingers, and the boat, a dark shadow moving through the water. I turned to face Elijah again. He was still staring out at the ocean, frowning.

'How far off shore are you moored, Theo?'

'Miles,' I lied.

And then several things happened at once. The boat bumped against the jetty behind me. Lewis – who had manoeuvred it into position – reached out and grabbed my legs, pulling me backwards off the jetty. I fell on my side, into the boat, all the wind knocked out of me.

Across the jetty, Elijah's gun fired.

I froze in the bottom of the boat, then yelled out, 'Rachel!'

Lewis was swearing, tugging at something. The motor roared into life. And, with a huge surge that brought a deluge of spray in on top of me, the boat stormed away out to sea.

41

Rachel

Theo's cry rang in my ears as Elijah dragged me, cursing, up the beach and onto the path. He held my arms behind my back. I struggled to free myself, desperate to get back to Lewis and Theo, but his grip on my arms just tightened.

'They're gone. Calm down,' he spat, then broke into an angry torrent of swear words.

'You shot at them!' I shouted. Fear and fury swirled in my head.

'Of course I shot at them,' Elijah roared. 'They were trying to steal you.'

'I'm not a 'thing' you can steal.'

'Quiet!' Elijah shoved me forwards again. I stumbled on the unlit path. We were heading for the barn and Elijah's sinister laboratory.

'Where are you taking me?' I said, suddenly terrified. 'What're you going to do?'

Elijah said nothing. A minute later, we reached the barn. John was leaning against the door, his head in his hands.

As we approached, Paul staggered out through the door.

Both guards straightened up when they saw Elijah.

'Go to the jetty,' he ordered Paul, still keeping tight hold of my wrist. 'See what they've done to the boat. Lewis will have disabled it. Assess the damage, then report back.' Elijah turned to John. 'You. Get Jamieson on the radio. Immediately.'

'Yes, sir.' The guards set off.

Muttering angrily to himself, Elijah shoved me inside the barn, then through another, metal door. The door slammed shut and Elijah let go of my arm at last. I rubbed my sore eyes, trying to work out where the door handle was.

There wasn't one. Just a small, infra-red screen on the wall beside the door. I'd seen one like it in Elijah's Washington compound. It was a scanner, programmed to respond only to Elijah's eyes.

I was trapped.

Slowly I turned, taking in the rest of the room.

It was lit with a soft pink glow – and appeared as high-tech on the inside as it was old and crumbling on the outside. A bank of computers ran down one side of the room. A massive metal tank stood in the middle. Clear tubes came out from the tank and then narrowed as they passed into each one of a row of clear oval pods.

Inside these were the weird beings that Theo had talked about.

I peered into the nearest pod. It contained something vaguely oval, and alien-looking, with a rounded head and tiny flippers budding out of its sides. It was semi-transparent and definitely alive, moving slowly from side to side and vibrating internally with a fluttering motion. It was suspended in a thick, syrupy liquid that was obviously being pumped into the pod via the clear tubes that led from the central tank.

The pods themselves were made of some sort of thick plastic – solid, but not entirely rigid. I'd never seen anything remotely like any of this . . . and the overall effect made me shiver.

Elijah charged around the room, checking on various cases. He seemed to have forgotten I was there. I hugged Theo's jacket tighter around me. Whatever Elijah was working on here must be directly connected to why he'd gone to such lengths to kidnap me. I shivered again. Theo and Lewis had gone – at least for now – but maybe in here I could find some answers.

'What *are* these things?' I said.

Elijah's head shot up. He was bending over a pod in the far corner of the room, partly hidden by the huge tank. He had taken off his jacket. The small black gun Milo had brought him earlier was strapped to his belt.

'Ah, Rachel.' His voice was icy. 'Come here. We don't have much time.'

He beckoned me over.

I stood my ground. 'Tell me what these things in the pods are first,' I said.

Elijah rubbed his hand through his hair. 'Can't you tell, Rachel?' His tone was lightly mocking . . . challenging.

151

'Come on, we have to move fast. I can't give you long to work it out.'

I looked round the room. Each pod contained an identical, alien-looking creature. Except ... I stared more closely. Some of the creatures were slightly bigger than the rest. Maybe two to three centimetres longer.

One of the creatures kicked out its flipper and I realised, with a jolt, that the flipper was actually a tiny foot ... attached to a leg.

I met Elijah's gaze. *Oh. My. God.*

'Babies,' I gasped. 'You're growing babies.'

42

Theo

The boat roared off into the darkness. Spray splashed on my face with every wave we bounced over.

'No!' I yelled.

'It's okay,' Lewis shouted over the noise of the motor, leaning down to where I was still lying in the bottom of the boat. 'You're safe, I damaged the engine on their boat, remember? They can't follow us.'

'It's not *me*!' I reared up, full of indignation. 'It's *Rachel*. We left her behind!' Furious tears streaked through the spray on my face.

Lewis met my eyes. 'There was no choice. We had to retreat. Elijah would have killed both of us before we reached her. This way we get a second chance.'

'We still should have stayed . . . tried to help her.' My guts twisted over and over. All I could see in my mind's eye was Rachel . . . her frightened face.

'Rachel will be okay,' Lewis sat down beside me. 'Elijah went to a lot of trouble to take her and to fake that suicide.

He's not going to hurt her now. Anyway, we're not going far. We're just going to anchor off shore for a bit, then go back later, give the rescue another go.'

'If you hadn't gone after Elijah then all three of us would have got away,' I yelled at him.

'It's done now.' Lewis's mouth tightened into a thin line. 'And we will go back. I promise you, Theo, you can't want this any more than I do.'

'Oh yeah? *This?* What I want is to save Rachel. What *you* want is to get even with Elijah.'

'We can do both,' Lewis said.

'Not on our own. Those two guards will be coming round soon.'

Lewis shook his head. I suddenly realised he was shivering, soaked to the skin from his swim to the boat. 'We can take them,' he said. 'We can do it.'

'There's no way,' I protested. 'Come *on*, we *know* Rachel is on that island now. We can make her parents believe it. We can get the police out here. And we *should*.'

'No. We can handle Elijah on our own,' Lewis said stubbornly. 'If we call the police then someone, somewhere, will protect Elijah. You saw that weird lab of his – he's working again, which means he's got funds and backing . . . which means the government's behind him.'

I shook my head. 'You don't know that for sure. And Elijah and both those guards have *guns*. All we have is a cheap knife.'

Lewis opened his mouth to argue back, but the chugging

154

engine of a distant boat made us turn our heads towards the sound.

The outline of the boat appeared on the horizon, lit by moonlight.

What was another boat doing out here?

And then a bright light shone suddenly, right into our eyes.

Lewis reached for the engine, but before he could touch it a shot fired. He slumped down. I stared at his shoulder. A dart was sticking out of it.

No. I ducked down, shielding my eyes from the light now glaring closer and closer. And then I felt a sharp prick in my own shoulder. A second of sickness. And the light faded to black.

43

Rachel

I stared at Elijah in horror.

'Well done, Rachel,' he said, running his hand through his hair. 'These are indeed babies – or, to be exact, a foetus and several embryos.'

'But . . . but . . .' I gazed around the room. 'But they're growing . . . developing . . . in . . . in . . . *pods*! There's no *mother*.'

Elijah pointed to the huge metal tank and its tubular tentacles. 'This contains a blend of proteins and amino acids that gives the babies all the nutrients they need.'

I shook my head, unable to take it in.

'The new embryos are doing well. It seems I've managed to overcome most of the previous problems that undermined the earlier experiments.'

'Experiments?' I echoed faintly.

'Yes.' He nodded, his eyes glittering with excitement. 'Gestating the embryos in these artificial wombs has proved a huge challenge but once I got the right balance for the

156

feeding tubes and the right matrix for the pods it became easier.'

'What are the pods made of?' I stared at the plastic cases.

'A blend of materials, including collagen and chondroitin. Sort of like an artificial skin.' Elijah said. 'Even with that in place, most of the early experiments failed by the end of the first trimester, but now all the problems have been ironed out.' He paused. 'I'm explaining this, Rachel, so that you can see what's at stake here.'

I shook my head, gazing at the tiny creatures inside the pods. 'But what's this got to do with me?' I said. 'Are these embryos part of your Hermes Project?'

'Not exactly.' Elijah frowned. 'I told you already. The Hermes Project is my study of the differences between cloned and non-cloned humans. This is a much more ambitious programme which arose *out* of the Hermes Project.'

My head spun. 'Ambitious how?'

Elijah looked pityingly at me. 'Don't you see it, Rachel?' he said, a touch of acid in his voice. 'Don't you see what I've created here?'

'*Created?*' I said. As I spoke the truth crashed down on me.

Of course.

'Oh my God, all these babies are clones, aren't they?'

'More than that, Rachel,' Elijah said, walking over to me. 'All these babies are clones of *you*.'

44

Theo

I woke, sore all over. As I came to, I realised there were bindings on my feet and wrists and a blindfold over my eyes. Low voices were speaking above my head. Beyond them was the steady chug of an engine.

I was lying on something hard that smelled of wood, but I was warm for the first time in hours. Really warm.

I listened hard, trying to make out what the voices were saying. A man and a woman were speaking.

'We go in one hour,' the woman was saying. A soft Scottish accent.

'Yes, ma'am.'

Footsteps coming closer. I stiffened.

'Are you awake, Theo?' The woman's voice was surprisingly gentle.

Well, there was nothing to be gained by pretending to be asleep. Not trussed up like this, anyway.

'Yes.' The word came out as a croak. I suddenly realised my throat was parched. I was desperate for a drink.

Someone tugged at the knot of my blindfold. It fell away and I found myself looking at a red-haired woman with a long, oval face and startling green eyes.

For a second she stared back at me. Then she smiled – a soft smile, but it didn't reach her eyes.

'Where am I?' I said. 'Where's Lewis?'

'Lewis is fine,' the woman said, drawing back a little. She took a glass of water from a ledge beside her and held the straw inside it to my lips. 'And you're on *our* boat now. Quite safe.'

I sipped at the water, looking around. I was clearly in some kind of engine room. Pipes and metal machinery were all around. A man stood by the door. He was staring at me, an expression of curiosity on his face. A rifle swung from his hand.

The woman took the drink away and placed it back on the shelf.

'Who are you?' I said. 'What . . . why have you taken me and Lewis?'

The woman tilted her head to one side, studying me. She had long eyelashes that perfectly framed her green eyes. Not beautiful exactly, but striking.

'We've been following you for a while,' she said. 'Once Lewis hired that boat it was easy to place a tracking device on the hull. We hoped you'd lead us to Elijah Lazio. You have. Now we just need all the information you can give us on the layout of the island and Lazio's resources.'

I frowned, still unable to make sense of what she was saying.

'Who are you?' I said again.

'I'm Amanda Lennox,' the woman replied.

'Never heard of you,' I said, sitting up.

'Good.' Another smile curled across Amanda Lennox's mouth. 'But you'll have heard of the organisation I work for. I'm the new chief.'

'The new chief of what?'

'The Righteous Army against Genetic Engineering, of course,' she said. 'Also known as RAGE.'

45

Rachel

'Clones of *me*?' I gazed around the dimly-lit room. There had to be nearly twenty embryos in here. '*All* of them?'

Elijah nodded. 'I tried to clone other people – male and female – but your blastocysts are the only ones that have survived in the artificial womb.'

'Why?' I said. 'Why do you want so many babies? Why are you trying to make an artificial womb?'

Elijah frowned. 'Because I can,' he said, as if it were too obvious an answer to be necessary. 'It is great science.'

'Why were my clones the only ones that worked?' I asked.

'I don't know,' Elijah admitted, 'but I think it's connected to this special property in your blood . . . in your DNA. That's why I brought you here, to Calla, Rachel, to find out what it is in your genetic make-up that makes this possible.' He waved his arm to indicate the room. 'And it's also why I've brought you here now . . . to ask for your help.'

'My help?'

'Over here.' Elijah pointed to a pod I hadn't noticed before, right in the corner of the room.

I gasped. The pod held a fully-grown baby, or so it looked to me. Ten fingers. Ten toes. Her little legs were kicking at the syrupy liquid. I put my hand on the glass case and the baby must have felt the vibration because her head turned towards me.

I stared into her open blue eyes, totally shocked. 'This is a clone of *me*?' I said.

'Yes,' Elijah replied. 'A full genetic replica.' He paused. 'I call her Aphrodite. It's just over eight months since I created her. She's stronger than the others, the only one to have survived more than a few weeks, until this new batch.'

I stared at the baby, my horror mounting. A baby growing in a pod. Worse, a clone of *me*. It was a freak show. Disgusting.

Elijah's radio crackled. He held the handset to his ear. Paul's voice came through.

'The boat engine is damaged beyond our ability to repair it here, sir,' he said.

Elijah swore. 'Get back to the house,' he snarled. 'Find out why John is taking so long to get Jamieson on the line.'

My ears pricked up. *Who was Jamieson?*

Elijah switched off the radio and ran his hand through his hair. 'Okay, Rachel,' he said. 'This is the situation. Lewis and Theo have escaped.' Elijah spoke calmly. 'But they will be back. And they will bring the police. This work I'm doing is illegal and whoever comes and whatever they do, there is a

162

strong chance we will be overcome and all these babies . . . all these little Rachels . . . will die.'

I stared around the room. Most of the tiny shapes in the pods didn't even look human.

And yet they *were*.

I couldn't get my head around it. All I knew for sure was that creating babies without proper mothers was grotesque.

'I thought you were working for the government?' I said. 'I thought they knew all about this . . . your . . . research . . . Surely the police won't destroy it?'

'I've told you already, I am not working for the government, Rachel, though my backer has powerful government contacts. Milo lied to convince you that you were Daniel's only hope. But it is not true. When the police come, they will destroy this work. Unwittingly or on purpose, they will destroy it.'

'Can't you move the . . . the embryos?'

'Not without moving all of them *and* the central tank at the same time – or organising an individual tank for each case.'

'Why?'

'Without the nutrients – especially the liquid oxygen – from the tank, they won't survive more than a few minutes.'

Elijah put his hand on the case containing the fully-grown baby. He tapped his finger and she moved her head in his direction. 'There is a chance for Aphrodite,' he said softly. 'She may be ready . . . may be able to survive outside her artificial womb.' He looked at me. 'It's a risk, especially without proper neonatal care, but many ordinary babies live far earlier than her thirty-six weeks.'

I met his eyes. 'Why are you telling me this?'

'Because I want you to help me give birth to her . . . to release her from the case . . . I can't do it alone.'

'*Me?*'

'I was going to use Milo – he is, right now, back at the house waiting for me to call him – but it strikes me *you* would be better,' Elijah said. 'I think you will care for her more. And she will need a lot of care. Once she is in the world, you will have to take her back to the house and look after her. Keep her safe until whatever happens is over. I must stay here, do what I can for my younger experiments, but if we can extract Aphrodite from her artificial womb, we have a good chance of keeping her safe.'

My eyes widened. 'No *way*,' I said. 'I can't look after a *baby.*'

'I can't force you to do this, Rachel, but I can't do it myself. I must prepare for the police attack. Apart from Milo we are just three men, with three guns and no way off the island. I hope that Don Jamieson will get here in time to save us, but there is no guarantee.'

'Who is Don Jamieson?'

'My backer. The man who is paying for all this – our research, our food . . .' He hesitated. 'So, will you help me with Aphrodite?'

I shook my head. 'Suppose . . . suppose she dies?' I said.

'Then the Aphrodite Experiment will have failed and I have to hope that we can protect the clinic and the other embryos.' Elijah turned his keen brown eyes onto me again.

'Rachel, I need her to live. There are many tests to do on her once she is alive.'

'What tests?' I didn't like the sound of that.

Elijah waved his little finger dismissively. 'Nothing harmful. We can discuss that later. Now, are you ready? We must start.'

'*Now?*'

'Yes.' Elijah walked round the other side of the glass pod and pulled on a pair of rubber gloves. 'Fetch a blanket from that pile under the computer table over there, and clear some space – it's not nearly warm enough in this room for a baby.'

I walked over to the table he had indicated and took a soft blanket from the pile underneath it. Then I shunted one of the terminals along the table and laid out the blanket in the space. I worked silently, in a total daze. I was about to attend a birth. The weirdest birth of all time, without a mother . . . or . . .

'Focus, Rachel.' Elijah snapped the end of his latex glove against his skin. 'I need you over here, now.'

As I walked back to him, his radio beeped again. He cursed and ripped off the gloves.

'Yes?' he barked into the handset.

John's voice answered: 'Patching Don Jamieson through to terminal two, sir.'

Elijah turned to the computer at the end of the table and tapped a couple of keys. The screen fizzled, then a balding, middle-aged man appeared, scowling, in the centre of the screen.

'What the hell is going on, Elijah?' His voice was deep, with a strong Scottish accent.

165

'Our cover is blown.'

'How?' Jamieson spat.

'Doesn't matter. I anticipate an attack within hours,' Elijah said. 'The Aphrodite Experiment is under threat. We need to leave as soon as possible.'

'Then leave.' Don Jamieson swore. 'Why do you need my help?'

Elijah rolled his eyes. 'Don, we are three men and a disabled boy with a handful of small guns and no working boat. We can't do this alone.'

A pause, then Jamieson spoke. 'I'll send a copter. It should be with you in an hour.'

'Thank you. Over.' Elijah flicked off the radio and pulled on another pair of gloves.

'Where will you . . . we . . . go?' I said.

'Later.' Elijah flicked his hand again. 'Now, put on some gloves and get ready to hold her while I dismantle the tubing. We're going to have to move fast.'

He cursed again, then reached for a lever I hadn't noticed at the end of the case. He gave it a twist and the syrupy liquid that held the baby in suspension started draining slowly into the compartment beneath the pod.

I backed further away from the pod. 'If your research is all about Aphrodite and these other babies, why do you need me?' I said.

'Please, Rachel. I cannot explain it all now.'

I shook my head. The liquid cleared from around the baby as I pulled on a pair of latex gloves. As soon as Aphrodite's toe touched the bottom of the case, Elijah grasped the sides of the pod.

'Get ready to hold her, Rachel. One hand under her neck, the other on her lower back. Come *on*. She's just a baby. She won't bite you.'

Bloody hell.

'Okay,' I agreed, holding out my gloved hands. Elijah fiddled with the catches for a second, then opened up the pod. The remaining liquid poured out, splashing, lukewarm, over my bare feet and onto the floor around us. I reached for Aphrodite. She was unbelievably light and fragile. Scarily floppy, in fact.

'Ease her down onto the table,' Elijah ordered, placing the sides of the pod on the floor. 'Cup her head and neck in your palm.'

I did what he told me. My heart was totally in my mouth. This was a *real* baby. A million thoughts crowded into my head as Elijah bent over her, his deft fingers gently stroking her arm.

'There.' He stood back. 'Now she must breathe alone.'

I waited, holding my own breath, my hand still under Aphrodite's head. The liquid had drained fully away now and my sore, bare feet were soaked, but I barely noticed.

Aphrodite was still limp in my hands. Her eyes were shut, her face an alarming shade of blue.

I looked up at Elijah. 'What's wrong?' I said. 'Why isn't she breathing?'

Elijah shook his head. 'Bring her over here.'

I picked her up and followed Elijah to the dry table where

I'd laid out the blanket. I set the baby down as gently as I could, then stood back, my heart thumping.

'Come on, come on,' Elijah muttered under his breath. He started talking to himself in Spanish which, I remembered, was the language he'd been brought up speaking. It sounded as if he were giving himself instructions. After a moment he inserted his little finger into the baby's mouth, gently turning her head sideways. A trickle of thick fluid dribbled out, then her face scrunched up.

'*Waaa!*' It was a thinner wail than I thought babies made; more like the sound of a kitten meowing.

Elijah prodded at the baby with his finger.

'What are you doing?'

'Testing her reflexes,' he said. A minute later he stood back, a satisfied expression on his face. 'An Apgar of nine. She's fine. Take off your gloves, wrap her and pick her up. Be real careful around her neck, remember.'

I hesitated. The idea of picking up such a tiny, floppy scrap of life again was terrifying.

'Rachel, *please.*'

Reluctantly, I took off my gloves and wrapped the blanket over the baby, tucking it under and round her tiny body. God, she was *so* fragile. The babies I'd seen in the past had all been chubbier and more robust-looking than this. Aphrodite felt like she might break in my hands.

I bound the blanket round her a third time, tucking it carefully under her head. The baby stopped crying and looked up at me. Her eyes were blue. My heart missed a beat. This was a clone of me . . . this was how I'd looked as a baby.

'Is she really all right?' I said, looking anxiously at Elijah. 'She's just so . . . so . . . delicate.'

Elijah was studying me, an amused expression on his face. 'She's perfectly normal. No vernix, even . . . I don't know why,' he said.

I nodded, though I hadn't understood the last part of what he'd said.

'Hold her closer, she needs to be kept warm.' Elijah took off his rubber gloves.

I held the baby close. I could feel her tiny heart racing away and the warmth of her body. I took one trembling finger and touched her little cheek. The skin was soft and smooth.

With a jolt I felt the pull of the blood tie. This was my sister. I glanced over my shoulder at the less developed embryos. These were *all* my sisters. But this one was properly *alive*. As I stared back at her tiny, perfectly-formed face, her mouth curved into what could have been a smile.

'Why did you call her Aphrodite?' I said.

'Aphrodite is the goddess of beauty, famous for being born from the sea,' Elijah said. 'I thought it was appropriate, but she should have an everyday name too. Just as Apollo is also Theo and you are Rachel *and* Artemis.' He paused. 'Why don't *you* choose her name.'

I flashed him a glance. I knew he was manipulating me, trying to make me care about the baby. Part of me wanted to tell him to shove his name-choosing. On the other hand, I had to admit, it was pretty cool being able to pick any name I wanted.

'Grace,' I said, gazing down at the baby. 'I'd like to call her Grace.'

'Fine, Grace it is.' Elijah nodded approvingly. 'Now make sure she's sheltered from the wind under that big jacket you're wearing and take her back to the house. I want you to keep her and yourself safe until the helicopter arrives.'

'You're still planning to do tests on us?' I asked, remembering what he'd said earlier.

'Of course.' Elijah nodded, flicking his little finger at me impatiently. 'Now go.'

'But what about feeding and . . . and nappies . . .?' I stammered, feeling the panic rise. 'I don't know that—'

'Girls younger than you have looked after babies before,' Elijah said dismissively. 'You'll find some formula milk and bottles and sterilising equipment in the storeroom. Nappies too, I think. Get Milo to help you find what you need.'

We left the clinic as Elijah's radio mic beeped again. I could hear Paul on the other end, this time asking what they needed to pack for the escape off the island. Elijah stopped walking to talk to him, but waved me on to the house.

Rain was falling, but only a drizzle. I kept Theo's jacket completely over Grace as I walked carefully, making sure I didn't trip. She was getting heavier as I went on, a warm pulse against my chest.

I made it back to the house, past Paul who was still talking on the radio with Elijah. He didn't even look at me properly, but Milo's jaw dropped as I walked into the kitchen where he was busy making sandwiches.

'Jesus, Rachel, what happened? Paul said you were with Elijah but . . .'

I uncovered my jacket, revealing Grace.

Milo's eyes widened. 'What the hell is that?'

'A baby,' I said. 'And I need milk and nappies and stuff. Elijah said they'd be in the storeroom. That you'd show me.'

Milo was still staring at Grace. 'Where did she come from?'

'The barn,' I said. 'Well . . . the lab inside the barn . . .'

Milo's face was ashen. 'Where's the mom?'

'There wasn't one,' I said. 'Elijah basically grew her in a pod. Anyway she's a clone . . . a clone of me . . .'

Milo's mouth fell open.

'Milo,' I snapped. 'I know it's weird, but you need to show me where the storeroom is. *Now.*'

'Sure. This way.' Roused by my irritation, Milo wheeled himself out of the room. I followed him down the corridor.

As I walked, it struck me that the attack Elijah was so sure was coming would be a great chance for me to get away from him. If I could just reach the police, I'd be able to tell them everything.

The storeroom turned out to be opposite the radio room. Milo unlocked it and let me in. 'Sit there.' He switched on the light and pointed to a chair by the door. 'I'll look for the stuff you need.'

I sank into the chair, little Grace still in my arms.

171

As I peered down at her, she opened her eyes and looked up, right into mine.

'Hello, Grace,' I murmured under my breath. 'I'm Rachel. I'm your big sister.'

Grace stared back at me. I couldn't tell if she was really seeing me or not. It suddenly struck me that she had no mother to look after her. That her biological mother was the same as mine. Which made her my sister twice over.

I smiled down at her, unable to tear my eyes away, and reached inside the blanket for her little hand.

The fingers were unbelievably tiny and perfect. I stroked my own finger over her palm and she grasped it so tightly I gasped.

'You're strong, Grace,' I murmured, still staring into her eyes. 'Strong and beautiful. Don't ever let anyone tell you otherwise.'

She carried on gripping my finger . . . hard. And in that moment something shifted in my heart and I knew that what I was feeling was love.

Pure and unconditional love.

46

Theo

I'd drawn Amanda Lennox the map she'd asked for, showing the location of the barn building containing Elijah's weird experiments – and how to reach it from the jetty.

I didn't like giving away the information, but Elijah's sinister lab was completely expendable as far as I was concerned. More importantly, if RAGE were focused on destroying the lab, then there was a greater chance that I could somehow get off the boat, find Rachel and rescue us both.

Not that I had any idea how on earth I was going to do any of those things.

Amanda Lennox had explained, rather boastfully, how RAGE had picked up my trail since I started looking for information on Rachel's supposed suicide. I asked for more details, but she refused to give any.

A little later, the man with the rifle brought Lewis in. He'd obviously been badly beaten: his face was bruised on both cheeks, his lip was split and one eye was so swollen it was nearly closed.

'What have you done to him?' I demanded.

'Nothing he didn't deserve,' the RAGE operative said. 'He shouldn't have crossed us.'

His words didn't make sense for a moment. Then I remembered how Lewis had worked undercover at RAGE last year, keeping tabs on their activities for Elijah.

No wonder they were mad at him.

The RAGE man pushed Lewis to the floor and chained his wrist to a pipe sticking out of the wall opposite. He left without speaking again.

I stared at Lewis's crumpled body. He opened his eyes with a groan.

'You look like crap,' I said.

'Thanks,' Lewis mumbled.

'D'you know what the time is?' I asked.

Lewis twisted round so he could see his watch. 'Almost 2.30 a.m.'

'What d'you think they'll do with us?' I said.

'That woman . . . Amanda Lennox . . . has ordered that you're kept safe until after the attack. I think she thinks you could be a useful bargaining chip with Elijah,' Lewis said.

'What about you?'

Lewis shook his head.

At that moment, the man who'd chained him reappeared at the door with a bunch of other guys. How many RAGE operatives were there on board?

'Take the kid to a cabin,' he ordered.

I was quickly untied and led out of the room. As I walked

along the corridor, I heard the thud of a boot kick, followed by Lewis's groan.

Suddenly I was terrified. RAGE was ruthless – and Lewis was of no value to the organisation. How far were they prepared to go to punish him for double-crossing them last year?

A few doors down, and I was locked inside a proper cabin, tied by a padlocked chain to the bed. I had enough slack on the chain to walk to the toilet and back, but not to reach the door. There was a single porthole but it was covered with a locked shutter. If I'd had a crowbar I might have been able to force it open, but I didn't. Apart from the bed and an empty fitted cupboard, the cabin contained just a single shelf stacked with a pile of RAGE leaflets.

I sank down onto the bed. Along the corridor, Lewis yelled out in pain.

I shut my eyes, not wanting to imagine what might be happening to him. After another thirty seconds, footsteps pounded past. They stopped outside the room Lewis was in.

'What's going on?' It was Amanda Lennox, her soft Scottish accent suddenly sharp.

One of the men growled a response.

'He's unconscious,' Lennox said angrily. 'This could have waited. Now, come up on deck.'

Footsteps trudged past me and faded away.

I closed my eyes. If Lewis was unconscious that meant I was on my own in the rescue attempt.

And I still had no plan.

I sat on the bed feeling seasick as the waves grew choppier.

47

Rachel

It took a while, but eventually Milo found the nappies, milk, bottles and sterilising equipment in the storeroom. Keeping Grace carefully swaddled in her blanket, I followed him back to the kitchen.

'I'll work out the milk while you put a nappy on her, yeah?' Milo said.

'Okay.' I laid Grace carefully on the table. She was still fast asleep.

Keeping one hand over her stomach, I tried to get my head round the nappy instructions.

'Why is Elijah cloning babies?' Milo asked from the sink.

'I don't know,' I admitted. 'He said something about tests – on Grace, not just me – but I don't know what he's looking for. He calls it the Aphrodite Experiment. Apparently there's something I've got in my blood that's different from every other clone. Something that makes me special. He's looking for the same thing in Grace, I guess.'

'Well, she'll certainly be easier to do tests on,' Milo said. 'No one's going to be coming after her . . .'

'What d'you mean?' I said.

'Just that Grace is in Elijah's power. He can test anything he likes on her. No one even knows she exists.'

I shook my head, not wanting to think about what Elijah's tests might mean for Grace.

We worked on in silence. In the end, the nappy was quite simple, though it was a bit big for Grace. Milo struggled with the sterilising equipment but eventually produced two small bottles of milk.

Grace stayed asleep through the whole thing. Nappy on, I wrapped her in the blanket again and picked her up. 'God, that was exhausting,' I said.

Milo nodded. 'Hey, your foot looks really bad. Can I check it out?'

I'd completely forgotten about the deep cut on my sole, not to mention all the bruises, but now Milo mentioned them my feet seemed to throb painfully. Milo took a tube of anti-septic and a pack of bandages out from under the sink. He held them out to me.

'Please, Rachel, let me help you.'

Part of me wanted to tell him where he could shove his bandages and yet he had been so helpful with Grace – and it would be easier to get away from him if he trusted me . . . and if my feet were less sore.

I let him wash and bandage the cut.

'Thanks,' I said. 'Er, what's going to happen now?'

'Dunno,' he said. 'Paul told me to get some food ready in case we had to move fast. They're expecting the police in about two hours, but hopefully we'll be gone in the helicopter before that. Last I heard it should be here in the next twenty minutes, maybe less.'

My mouth felt dry. This was going to be my chance. I had to get away from Milo, take Grace and hide somewhere for a few hours . . . then Elijah would be forced to leave us both behind and I'd be alone when the police arrived.

'Rachel?' Milo was staring at me. 'Did you hear what I just said?'

'No, sorry. What?'

'Elijah's got one thing right,' he said softly. 'You *are* different. Special.' He hesitated. 'I think you're beautiful.'

I looked quickly down at Grace, blushing. I didn't know what to say . . . What was Milo doing, talking like that?

'Milo . . .' I started.

'Anyway,' he said, his tone suddenly brisk and cheery. 'Do you want a sandwich, I'm making—'

Boom. An explosion echoed across the island. I froze, clinging to Grace as another went off, then another.

'What was that?' I said.

Milo careered to the door, almost colliding with John.

'It's RAGE,' John gasped. 'They're here – and the helicopter's still ten minutes away!'

No. What was *RAGE* doing here? Like everyone else, I'd been expecting the police. But RAGE was *far* worse. The people at RAGE would have no qualms about blowing up Elijah's lab – or, indeed, killing Grace and me.

'Get out of the house,' John shouted. 'Elijah says you have to go to the cave on the beach and hide till the helicopter gets here. I'll come and find you then.'

Milo and I both stared at him. He thumped the door with his hand.

'Come on!' he yelled. 'Hurry!'

48

Theo

One look at the RAGE leaflets and I was reminded of how extreme the organisation really was.

We'd moored just over five minutes ago. I was pretty certain everyone apart from Lewis had left the boat, leaving me chained up in the cabin.

Since his yell of pain a while back, I hadn't heard Lewis make a sound. And he hadn't responded to my shouts either.

I didn't want to think about what RAGE might have done to him.

There was no way of getting rid of the chain round my wrist, so I focused on the RAGE pamphlets again.

Cheaply printed, the leaflet I was holding featured a picture of a puppy with an ear growing out of its back. *Ugh.* The headline read: *Is this the future you want? Genetic manipulation is unnatural and cruel. Join us now and STOP this evil!*

I shook my head.

A puppy with an ear growing out of its back was certainly

disgusting – but genetic engineering meant good things too, didn't it? Elijah had told me before that a lot of his work had meant people who couldn't otherwise conceive could have children – and cloning a human being . . . well, that was really just like test-tube babies, wasn't it? Not good, maybe, but not really bad either.

RAGE might think it was immoral but they weren't much better. There was nothing in these leaflets that suggested the extent to which they were prepared to go to fight genetic engineering.

Anyway, as far as I was concerned, it wasn't Elijah's science that was the problem. It was the way he thought it gave him the right to play God over everybody else that made him dangerous.

Boom.

Was that an *explosion*?

I strained my ears. Water lapped at the hull of the boat. A seagull squawked overhead.

Boom. Boom. They sounded like grenades going off.

Man, this was horrible.

I prayed that Rachel wasn't anywhere near the lab.

I ran my hands through my hair. There *had* to be some way of getting free. For what felt like the fiftieth time I stared at the chain around my wrist. It was fastened with a small but powerful padlock which I had no hope of opening without a key.

I picked the chain up, following its length down to where it was tied round one of the bed's wooden legs. I'd already tugged on it several times, so I knew there was no way of moving the bed leg – the bed was built into the wall, anyway – but what if I tried to separate the bed itself from the leg? Then I could just slide the padlocked chain over the top.

I lifted up the mattress. The bedpost was wooden, held in place by four small screws. If I could just undo them, I might be able to prise the rest of the bed frame far enough apart to make this work.

But what could I use as a screwdriver?

I suddenly remembered Rachel's hairgrip. It was still in my jeans pocket. Hands trembling with excitement, I fished it out and got to work.

49

Rachel

Keeping Grace carefully wrapped up, I grabbed my trainers and a jumper and followed John and Milo outside. It was pouring with rain now. I strained my eyes, looking towards the hill in the centre of Calla. I could see nothing, though shouts and gunfire echoed around us.

RAGE must be attacking the lab. But were Theo and Lewis with them?

My heart pounded at the thought that Theo might be back on the island right now. Was he safe? And what about all the embryos in the lab? I still thought what Elijah was doing was grotesque but each one of those tiny alien shapes in the pods was – nevertheless – a life.

Killing them was wrong.

John led the three of us onto the beach. By the time we reached the shelter of the cave my hair was drenched, though Grace was still dry inside her blanket, under my jacket. John carried Milo over the patch of sand between the path and the cave, then went back for his wheelchair.

I thought about running, but only for a second. Better to wait until John had gone. Milo wouldn't be able to follow me, after all. Except . . . where would I go? RAGE weren't exactly going to welcome me with open arms.

Still, they must have come here in a boat. It was probably moored somewhere near the jetty. If I could just get away from both sides and make it there, I'd surely find a phone or a radio I could use to call home . . . or the police.

I hugged Grace to my chest as John helped Milo into his chair. She was stirring, her little head twisting against my top, her arms and legs wriggling inside the blanket.

'We'll be okay, Grace,' I whispered. Again I felt that fierce tug of love. I thought about what Milo had said . . . *Grace is in Elijah's power. He can do what tests he likes on her. No one even knows she exists.*

'*I* know,' I whispered. 'I'll protect you.'

Grace made that pitiful mewing sound I'd heard before. I headed for the back of the cave and sat down next to a pile of stones. She was probably hungry. I fished out the bottle of formula Milo had prepared.

John was still at the entrance to the cave, giving Milo some last-minute instructions from Elijah.

'Whatever happens, stay here until I come back for you. If I don't appear in thirty minutes, then head for the area just east of Calla Hill. That's where the helicopter's landing, okay?'

John left. As Milo wheeled his way towards me, I put the bottle to Grace's lips, but she turned her head away and carried on wailing.

I looked up. Milo was smiling at me. 'I wish I'd met you a different way, Rachel,' he said, hesitantly.

For God's sake.

'She won't feed,' I said. I had enough problems to deal with without Milo getting all sentimental on me.

Milo wheeled himself nearer. Grace's cries got louder. I gave up trying to make her drink from the little bottle of milk and tried rocking her in my arms.

'Sssh,' I said, soothingly.

Grace just wailed even louder.

'If RAGE hears her, they'll find us,' I said.

Milo nodded. 'We could hide behind that,' he said, pointing at where a piece of rock jutted out at the very rear of the cave. 'There's an opening behind it, into a tunnel. We could go a couple of metres inside – that might muffle the noise.'

I stood up, my heart racing.

'Where does the tunnel lead?' I said.

'Nowhere,' Milo said. 'I mean, it goes along under the rocks, down to the beach near the jetty, but there's no proper exit, just pipes, and it floods at high tide.'

'Is it high tide now?'

'I don't know,' Milo said nervously. 'I just know Elijah said the tunnel was dangerous.'

I snorted. 'Of course he said that.' I walked over to the rock that jutted out. From where I'd been sitting, it had looked just like part of the cave formation, but as I got closer I could see it concealed a low, squarish opening. I peered inside. There wouldn't be room to stand up properly, but the tunnel inside was definitely passable. Maybe the pipes it led to would be big enough for me to crawl through. If I came out on the beach near the jetty, I'd be in a perfect position to make it to the RAGE boat.

'Rachel, we can't go more than a few metres down there. Elijah wasn't lying about that. It's *dangerous.*'

'I get it,' I said impatiently. Grace was almost screaming now – a high- pitched squeal. 'We're just going to take Grace along the tunnel for a little way while she's crying,' I lied. 'You're the one who suggested it. Otherwise if anyone from RAGE comes they'll hear her.'

'Okay.' Milo looked relieved.

I turned and led the way into the tunnel. I had to walk hunched over. Even Milo, sitting in his wheelchair, had to dip his head slightly. The wheels rattled over the uneven ground. Milo's breath came out in uneven gasps. He was clearly having to work hard to manoeuvre the chair. Worried about stumbling myself, I kept a tight hold of Grace as I ventured along in the darkness. Her squeals were deafening now, echoing off the tunnel walls.

After a few metres, Milo let out a frustrated sigh. 'Hang on, let me get my flashlight . . . er, torch,' he said.

I stopped.

A second later a beam of light lit up the tunnel. I peered into the distance. The passageway extended as far as I could see.

This was it. My chance to escape.

Holding Grace with one arm, I turned and reached for Milo's torch.

'You need both hands for the wheelchair,' I said.

I tucked the torch under my arm and took a few more steps. It was easier now I could see the ground in front of me. The tunnel was colder than the cave and it smellled of salt and damp. I sped up slightly.

'Wait, Rachel,' Milo said. 'We've gone far enough.'

'Just a little bit further,' I insisted.

I walked on, my heart hammering. The salty smell *had* to mean that we were close to the sea.

Grace's wail grew more intense. I tucked the blanket around her again. 'Sssh, baby,' I murmured. 'Sssh, Grace, you're okay now.'

'Rachel, please stop.' Milo was several metres behind me now. He sounded breathless from the effort of moving his wheelchair and there was a note of panic in his voice.

Ignoring him, I kept walking. In a minute, I'd make a run for it. I had both the torch and Grace. It would take Milo a while to turn his wheelchair in the darkness and make his way back to the cave. I didn't want to be mean to him, but there was no other option.

We went on, Grace's cries echoing around us. The air grew gradually colder and stiller. I felt like I'd been walking for ages. Surely we were at least half-way to the jetty now?

'That's *enough*,' Milo said. 'Rachel, *please*, no one will be able to hear Grace all the way in here.'

The tone of his voice was more plea than order.

It was time.

'Bye, Milo,' I whispered.

I put the torch in my mouth, then, keeping its beam focused on the bumpy tunnel floor, I clutched Grace to my chest and raced off.

50

Theo

Fumbling, and cursing my clumsy fingers, I undid the fourth screw at last. I forced the bed frame away from the post, making just enough space to slide my chain over.

I raced to the door, the chain trailing behind me. The cabin door was locked, but it looked pretty flimsy. I was sure I could break it down. Except, if I did, then anyone left on the boat would surely come running. I hesitated, but only for a second. I didn't have a choice. I had to take the risk.

I set myself sideways on to the door, took a few steps back, braced myself, then hurled myself shoulder first at the door. It broke with a snap. I stumbled out into the corridor and listened for the sound of footsteps.

Nothing. I crept down the corridor to the engine room where Lewis and I had been held earlier.

I peered round the door. Lewis was lying, slumped, on the floor. His wrists and ankles were bound so tightly with rope, they were blue. I raced over and knelt beside him. 'Lewis?'

He groaned.

'Are you okay?'

He groaned again.

I ran out of the engine room and tore towards the stairs at the end. Up to the main cabin. Still no sign of anyone. RAGE must be using every single person on board for the attack.

I looked round, desperate to find something to release Lewis with. Across the room a cupboard door was ajar, an open padlock hanging from one handle. I yanked it open. This had clearly been some kind of weapons stash, but all that was left now was a broken firing pin from a gun and three rounds of bullets.

Damn. I reached into the far, dark corner of each shelf. As I reached the bottom shelf, my hand closed on a blade. Not sharp – presumably that was why it had been left behind – but a knife nonetheless. I pulled it out and ran back to Lewis.

He was still groaning, curled up on the floor. I dropped to my knees and set to work carving the rope that bound his wrists.

Precious minutes ticked by. Lewis was stifling his moans now, but I could see he was still in pain.

He opened his eyes as I worked away at the rope. The knife was so blunt, it was taking ages.

Another explosion.

I bit my lip. How much longer was RAGE's attack on the island going to go on? Where was Rachel? Was she okay?

At last the knife sliced through the final bit of rope round his wrists. That just left his ankles. Lewis sat up, wincing.

'I think they cracked my ribs,' he muttered, reaching for the knife.

I handed it over and stood up. 'I'm going to find her,' I said.

'No. I'm coming too.' Lewis clutched at the back of his head and let out another groan of pain.

'You're hurt and your legs are still tied up,' I said.

'I have to.' Lewis positioned the knife and started working on the rope that bound his ankles.

'Why? So you can get even with Elijah?' I said. 'This mission is about rescuing Rachel. You need to stay on board and work out how to start this boat up for when I get back with her.'

'You don't freakin' know where she is,' Lewis snarled.

'Neither do you,' I said, turning away. 'Stay here.' I ran out of the engine room and up the stairs, through the main cabin and out on deck. It was still dark, though the moonlight cast a veiled glow over the shoreline, sparkling on the tips of the waves. I could just make out a plume of smoke rising from the part of the island which contained Elijah's lab.

I swallowed down the panicky lump that lodged in my throat. Rachel said she had never been inside the lab and Elijah was hardly likely to have taken her there tonight.

There was no sign of him and his men – or of the RAGE crew. I raced across the jetty and onto the beach. There were two paths. One, to the left, I knew led to the barn with the lab. Surely the other – much stonier and to the right – must

191

lead to other buildings? I still couldn't see anyone, though I could hear distant shouting.

Using the cover of the trees, and keeping the stony path on one side of me, and the coastline on the other, I made my way carefully round the island.

51

Rachel

I ran hard, Grace huddled against my chest, the torch in my mouth. Milo's voice echoed through the tunnel behind us.

'Come back!' he yelled. 'You can't get out that way. *Please.* Or I'll shoot!'

I ran on, my heart thumping. I was certain Milo wouldn't use his gun – that's if he even had one.

The rocky floor was jagged and increasingly uneven. I had to slow down for fear of stumbling. It was colder and damper now. The chill was seeping into my bones. I hugged Grace closer and her cries at last subsided.

I slowed to a jog. The ground was damp now and really slippery, but I couldn't stop. Goodness knows what was going on outside on the island, but this tunnel was my best chance . . . my only chance . . . of reaching the jetty.

Milo was still shouting. I could hear the wheels of his chair bumping over the uneven ground. He was moving more slowly than me, which meant maybe I could slow down myself . . . the rock surface was really treacherous now. Cold water lapped at my feet – and the torchlight showed that it continued as far as I could see.

Was this the flooding Milo had talked about? At least it wasn't deep. I waded on, more cautiously. The uneven surface of the ground was concealed completely. The dark water rose up round my ankles. It was freezing.

'RACHEL!' Milo was still behind me. His voice ricochetted off the rock walls, a booming echo. He didn't sound far away.

I sped up again, splashing as I pounded along the tunnel. Grace wriggled against me as I slid around. She made that mewing sound I'd heard her make earlier.

Sssh. I looked down at her, distracted.

Whoosh. I took another step but my feet met no resistance. Just water . . . more water. My legs burning with the shock of the cold, I lost balance. Screamed. In a single movement I dropped the torch, instinctively raised Grace above my head and sank like a stone into the seawater.

52

Theo

I froze, still under cover of the trees.

The muffled scream echoed in my ears.

It was Rachel. I was sure of it. But *where*?

The sound seemed to have come from beyond the trees . . .
somewhere near the beach. I crept through the patch of
woodland, towards the sea. My steps, crunching on grass and
twigs, sounded loud to my ears, but no one was around to
hear. There'd been no more explosions since I'd left the boat,
though I'd just heard a round of gunfire coming from the
other side of the island.

I reached the edge of the trees, where the stony beach
began to slope down to the shore, and stood still, listening
hard. The wood and the rest of the island was behind me; the
sea in front.

Another round of distant gunfire, then silence. All I could
hear was the wind in the trees and the waves lapping at the
shore.

Had I imagined that scream?

'Help! Help!' The voice came again. It was *definitely* Rachel. And was that an *animal* crying?

It didn't make sense.

I waited for what felt like ages, though it can't have been more than half a minute. Then another yell sounded right beneath me.

Rachel was underground.

I stepped back, wishing I had more than the moonlight to see with. I stood, waiting for more sounds. But there was only silence.

53

Rachel

My head broke through the water. I gasped for breath, shocked to the core by the fall and the cold of the water.

I forced my legs to tread water, though they were already numb with cold. I held Grace above my head. She was screaming like she was being murdered.

Fighting to keep my legs moving, I looked back at the tunnel. The pathway must have shelved very suddenly for me to have fallen so deeply. The torch was lying where I'd dropped it, near the tunnel wall. It was still working, thank goodness, but pointing away from me, which meant I couldn't see how far this pool of water lasted.

Even in my bewildered state, I knew I didn't have much time. My legs were already tired and it was taking a supreme effort just to hold Grace above my head. I couldn't get out of the water without putting her in it – and I knew that the cold of it would kill her, even if she didn't drown.

'Help!' I shouted desperately. 'Help!'

Grace's high-pitched squeal pierced through my brain.

The sound of wheels turning echoed towards us. I squinted into the tunnel.

'Rachel?' Milo wheeled up to the torch. He picked it up and scanned the water. The light glared in my eyes.

'Oh, Jesus.' Milo pointed the torch away from me.

I could only dimly make out his face, but I could hear the terror in his voice.

'Help me,' I gasped, my teeth chattering.

In answer, Milo slid out of his chair.

Lying on his front, he hauled himself by the arms across the wet, rocky ground to the edge of the pool. 'This is where it shelves,' he said, shining the torch across the water. 'I can't see where it ends.'

'Please help,' I gasped.

I was sinking lower in the water, the freezing brine splashing against my lips. My arms shook uncontrollably. I was going to drop Grace in a moment.

'Let me take her then I'll get you out,' Milo said.

He laid the torch on the ground beside him and reached across the water. I held Grace up to him, kicking as hard as I could to get closer. I could barely feel my legs.

Milo took Grace. She stopped crying straight away. He picked up the blanket that trailed in the water and felt along its length.

I let my arms fall into the water. They were so cold, *so cold.*

Milo found a dry bit of blanket and wrapped it tightly round Grace.

'I'm going to put her in my chair,' he said, 'then I'm coming back for you.'

I tried to speak but my teeth were chattering too hard. I seriously couldn't feel my legs now, but they must be moving, or I wouldn't still be afloat, though now my arms were helping, weren't they? I looked down, unable to connect my brain giving the instruction with my arms trying to obey it

I *was* moving, though very slowly. My mouth was completely underwater now, so I was breathing through my nose, my whole body shaking with cold.

Milo was crawling, commando-style, back to his wheelchair, Grace firmly in his grasp. At least she wasn't crying any more. At least she was safe.

And then my legs stopped moving altogether. I flailed with my arms, panicking, tipping my head back. Mouth above water. One last yell.

And then I sank beneath the water.

The shock of the water on my face roused me for a second. Enough to register that I *had* to move.

Swim, my brain screamed at my limbs. *Swim.*

Somewhere, somehow I managed to move, clawing back the water, fighting the urge to sleep. I was running out of breath now.

Give up, said a little voice in my head. *It's the easier choice.*

No. My hands banged the side of the tunnel. I reached along the mossy wall, pulling myself through the water. Which way was up? I couldn't breathe.

And then a huge hole appeared in the wall. I could feel it with my hands. The water was even colder here.

Swim there, my brain shrieked at me.

I had no idea if I should. I'd lost all sense of where I was or who I was or what I was doing here.

All I knew was that I had to keep moving.

My lungs were going to burst. I kicked myself into the hole. Another kick. Darkness forcing itself into my closed eyes.

And another. The darkness was overwhelming.

And then the water seemed to tip me downwards and I slid down a metal pipe . . . down, down, and suddenly there was cold air around me and hard, wet ground beneath.

I took a single conscious breath, then gave myself up to the darkness.

54

Theo

I forced myself to walk slowly down the beach, away from the trees, my whole body tense as I listened out for more sounds. Rachel was here somewhere ... why didn't she shout again?

'Rachel!' I called as loudly as I dared. 'Rachel, where are you?'

The gunfire in the distance was intensifying. Above the island I could hear a helicopter lowering, its lights shining out.

Ahead of me, the beach sloped right down to the sea. The tide was out. I strained my eyes into the darkness. I could just make out the curve of a metal pipe emerging into the stones at the very edge of the water. Was that a *body* slumped on the ground? I raced towards it. Behind me, the helicopter was getting louder.

'Rachel?' I shouted, throwing all caution to the wind.

No movement. I reached the body. It was her.

I pulled back her hair, lifted her up. Her body sagged against mine.

'Rachel, *please*,' I hissed at her. '*Rachel, wake up!*'

She spluttered. A dribble of water trickled out of her mouth. She gave a low moan, but didn't open her eyes.

In the distance the helicopter's engine slowed. Jesus, had it *landed*? Footsteps pounded along the path I'd been following. Crouching lower against the sand, I covered Rachel's body with my own. A crackling radio message drifted faintly across the night air:

'*Lennox says the lab is destroyed. Get to the helicopter. Elijah Lazio is on board.*'

'On my way.' The footsteps disappeared.

'Can you walk?' I whispered.

But Rachel was still only semi-conscious.

I hauled her up and over my shoulder. Weighed down by all the water in her clothes, I could barely carry her.

RAGE wouldn't be busy with this helicopter for long. Either they'd take it or it would take off. And whoever won the fight, Lennox and her men would be back on their boat within minutes.

I set off along the beach, walking as fast as I could, soaked now from Rachel's clothes.

She was still moaning lightly under her breath, though I couldn't work out what she was saying. *Ace?* No, *Grace.*

What was that? Some kind of prayer?

I made my way along the beach. There was the jetty. Looking round as I approached, I hurried onto the wooden walkway and along to RAGE's boat.

It looked deserted. *No.* There was a man on deck.

He'd seen me. He raised his knife.

I held my breath. How was I going to defend myself *and* Rachel?

And then the man lowered his knife and shouted out, 'Theo?'

'Lewis!'

Overwhelmed with relief, I rushed on board as Lewis limped to the hull and threw off the rope that bound the boat to the jetty.

'You got her,' Lewis said, as I deposited Rachel on the couch that ran along one side of the main cabin. 'Is she okay?'

The noise of the helicopter taking off made us both look round. Through the door of the cabin I could see it rising into the moonlight.

'Where's Elijah?' Lewis took an unsteady step to the door. I grabbed his arm.

'He's on that copter,' I said. 'I heard a RAGE soldier say so. Which means *he's* got away, but RAGE will be back any second. We need to get out of here, fast.'

Lewis hesitated a second, then nodded. He raced over to the back section of the cabin where the boat's controls were situated.

A moment later the engine fired and we were away.

Part Two

The Aphrodite Experiment

55

Rachel

I came round to the sound of muffled voices above my head.

I lay still, completely disoriented.

Where was I? Who was talking?

Why was my bed moving?

The cloth under my hand was rough and scratchy.

I was warm, my limbs heavy.

I registered these things slowly, as the voices above me grew stronger and clearer. I stroked my finger across the coarse blanket that tickled my chin. Even that small movement was an effort.

'She moved her finger.' It was Theo, his voice full of relief. 'Rach, we're here. Me and Lewis. We've got you. You're safe.'

My heart skipped a beat at the sound of his voice.

'I told you she was just asleep.' Lewis. As he spoke, a hand stroked a wisp of hair off my face.

I wrinkled my nose, trying to open my eyes, but the effort was too great.

'Where am I?' I whispered through parched lips.

'On a boat,' Theo said.

Well, that made sense of the way everything was moving – a gentle rocking motion that was somehow both soothing and vaguely nauseating.

'I found you unconscious on the island . . .' Theo went on. 'I brought you back . . . this is RAGE's boat. We escaped on it about six or seven hours ago.'

The memory of last night stabbed me like a knife.

'Grace?' I moaned, remembering how I'd been forced to hand her to Milo before we both sank under that freezing water. 'What happened . . . Grace . . .'

'What's she talking about?' Lewis sounded concerned.

'Dunno, she said something like that before, last night.' Theo hesitated. 'Maybe she banged her head.'

'No.' I forced my eyes open.

I wasn't on a bed. I was lying on a large padded bench in what looked like the main cabin of the RAGE boat. Lots of dark, scuffed wood. Theo was sitting beside me, Lewis standing next to him. They were both peering down at me with anxious eyes – Theo's a warm deep brown, Lewis's a piercing blue.

I gazed at Theo, the joy of seeing him shot through with the desperation of losing Grace.

'Baby . . . tests . . . Elijah . . .' I said, trying to make them understand. *God*, my whole body ached. Every word was an effort. 'Tried . . . rescue . . .' The memory of how I'd sunk into the water – unable to move, panic surging through me – flashed into my head. I shivered.

208

Theo and Lewis exchanged looks.

'Whatever it is, you can tell us later – you should rest right now,' Lewis said. He moved closer and I realised for the first time that his face was cut and bruised. Had RAGE done that?

'Get her another blanket, Theo. I need to check where we are.'

They both disappeared, Lewis limping. I struggled onto my elbows. Apart from my underwear, all I had on was a large checked shirt. My clothes – or, rather, the men's top and trousers I'd been given on Calla – were draped over a chair on the other side of the cabin.

I blushed as I realised that must mean that either Theo or Lewis had removed my soaking wet clothes last night.

Theo came back, another blanket in one hand, a glass of water in the other. I took a sip from the glass, draped the blanket over my shoulders, and sat up. We stared at each other.

It was funny. For the past nine months the thought of seeing Theo again had pretty much been all that had kept me going. And yet now we were face to face with each other, I felt self-conscious.

'What was that stuff about a baby?' Theo asked gently.

I sipped again at the water, my head clearing. Taking a deep breath I explained about the clone embryos in the lab.

'Elijah calls it the Aphrodite Experiment but there's one proper baby – one *actually born* – Grace – and . . . and Elijah's going to do tests on her to find out about this special thing in my blood . . . my DNA . . . which is presumably going to be in *her* blood too . . .'

209

Theo frowned. 'What tests?'

'I don't know, but he doesn't have *me* any more, and the embryos were killed, so he's only got Grace now.' Tears welled up as I realised how much danger she was in. 'Oh God, Theo, I left her behind.'

'What happened?'

I told him how I'd tried to escape with Grace. As I talked, Lewis limped back into the cabin.

'. . . then Milo took Grace from me and he had a torch and I know he could make it back to the cave and I'm sure Elijah would have sent someone to get us from there so Milo should have made it to the helicopter but I'm so worried he'll hurt her,' I said breathlessly, tears trickling down my face. 'I mean, Elijah was telling me to keep her safe so he could do tests on both of us but she's so tiny and he's capable of . . . of *anything* . . .'

Theo leaned forward and took my hand. 'Maybe Elijah will just let her go, like he did Daniel.'

I looked away. 'He didn't let Daniel go.'

'What d'you mean?'

My heart thudded. I couldn't bear to tell him.

But I knew I had to.

'What, Rachel?' Lewis said.

'Daniel's dead,' I said, looking up.

'*No!*' Theo's face paled. 'How?'

I explained as briefly as I could, stressing there was nothing any of us could have done to save him. 'Elijah said he had the operation . . . the heart transplant . . . ages ago . . . last year, before he left the States.'

Theo sat quite still for a moment. In the background, Lewis let out a frustrated sigh, but I kept my gaze on Theo, wishing I knew what to say to him.

A year ago I know I'd have blurted out something . . . the wrong thing . . . trying to make him feel better. But now I knew that sometimes there's nothing you can say. Sometimes you just have to let people be . . . let them sort stuff out for themselves.

After a few moments, Lewis cleared his throat.

'Are you sure you're feeling okay, Rachel?' he asked. 'I mean, physically?'

'I'm just tired now,' I said. 'What about you?' I added, indicating his bruises.

Lewis made a face. 'That was RAGE.' He explained everything that had happened to him and Theo since last night. Theo continued to sit silently beside us.

'So did Elijah get away in the helicopter?' I asked as Lewis finished.

'We think so. Theo heard one of the RAGE soldiers say he was on board,' he said. 'His lab on the island was definitely destroyed.'

No. It was weird – I hated the idea of Elijah breeding clones . . . creating a baby farm where the children didn't have proper mums and dads. But the reality was that once those children existed – however tiny they were – each one of them deserved to live. I couldn't bear to think about that, so I tried to focus on Grace, on the way her little fingers had tightened round my own . . . on her perfect, tiny face.

My baby sister.

'So, what's this special thing in your DNA that Elijah's after?' Theo said at last. 'Is it something he wants for himself? Like . . . like with me and Da—' His voice cracked as he tried to say Daniel's name.

'I don't know,' I said. 'That's what I'm saying. Elijah wasn't sure. He wanted to do more tests . . .'

Theo shook his head and stood up. I watched him pace across the cabin, his shoulders hunched over. After the adrenalin rush of reliving last night I felt totally exhausted again. And defeated. Sure, I'd got away, but only to cause Theo pain by telling him about Daniel.

And – worse – without rescuing Grace.

'Are you hungry?' Lewis asked.

I nodded absently, and he fetched some bread and cheese from the kitchen area of the cabin. I tried to eat, but it was hard to force anything down. I couldn't stop thinking about Grace and whether she was okay. Had Milo saved her? Had Elijah got her off the island?

If Elijah had her, he was going to do these awful tests on her, not caring about the consequences. If RAGE had her, they would kill her for being a clone. Either option filled me with horror.

As we went on deck, I knew that I had to find out where Grace was and try to save her from whatever she was facing. It was bitterly cold outside, despite the presence of a fierce sun high in the sky. The boat was moored in a small cove. Lewis said we were south of Calla, on the mainland – just a couple of hours' drive from Roslinnon.

I kept my blankets round me as protection against the strong wind. No one spoke for a while, then, eventually, Theo folded his arms.

'I suppose you want to find this baby, Rachel.' It was more of a statement than a question. His voice was even.

I stared at him, unnerved that he'd seen so exactly into my head – and wondering if he understood why it mattered to me so much.

'That's ridiculous,' Lewis said, his forehead creased into a deep frown. 'We've all just risked our lives to get away from Calla. Rachel nearly *drowned*. There's no way she's putting herself in *more* danger.'

Theo stared stubbornly at him. 'She needs to find this baby.'

'Excuse me, I can speak for myself,' I said.

They both looked at me.

'I want to get you home, Rachel, that's the priority,' Lewis said firmly.

'You want to get even with Elijah, *that's* your priority,' Theo snapped.

'That can wait,' Lewis said. 'We—'

'We can't go home,' I said. 'Once people know I'm still alive, the press will be desperate for a picture of "the girl who came back from the dead". It'll be like we've sent out a signal to both Elijah and RAGE telling them how to find us. I'd like to tell my parents I'm okay, but I can't go home just yet,' I said. 'Which is fine, because Theo's right . . . I have to find Grace.'

'*We* have to.' Theo put his hand on my shoulder. 'We couldn't save Daniel, but we're not going to let anyone else die.'

I smiled and looked up, grateful for his support. Theo's dark eyes were serious and intense. They were the same eyes as Elijah's and Milo's, of course, but somehow they seemed warmer and stronger in Theo.

'Why does this baby matter so much?' Lewis said, his voice bitter.

I opened my mouth to answer, but Theo got there first.

'Grace is her clone . . . her *sister*,' he said. 'Like Daniel was my . . . my little brother.' His voice cracked again. I could see he was trying not to cry and I reached up to touch his hand. Theo squeezed my fingers hard.

'Okay,' Lewis said, more gently. 'But we've got no idea where RAGE or Elijah *are* right now.'

'Actually, we do,' I said. 'The man who sent the helicopter was Elijah's backer, Don Jamieson. I saw him on a video cam. I reckon that if we track *him* down, we'll find Elijah. Elijah will either have Grace, or he'll know where she is. Either way, we'll get closer to finding her.'

'Or finding out what happened to her,' Lewis said. 'You do realise if RAGE got her, she's probably . . . not made it.'

I looked him straight in the eye.

'I have to try,' I said.

'What about the police?' Theo asked.

'We can't risk that until we know more,' I said. 'Elijah said Jamieson had very powerful friends. There are obviously

214

people in the government or the police force . . . senior people . . . who're prepared to turn a blind eye to whatever Elijah's doing.'

'What about going back to our contacts . . . the agents we were given when we relocated?' Theo suggested.

'How do you think Elijah found me in the first place?' I said. 'He told me that an agent from the original team who resettled us "sold me out". We can't trust anybody.'

'Jesus.' Lewis sighed.

There was a long silence. Theo wandered away from us, to the very front of the boat. He stared out to sea.

I knew he was thinking about Daniel.

I looked down at the deck. The wood was scratched at the top of the steps down to the cabin.

'I think this is yours.' Lewis handed me my silver chain with the tiny 't' at the end. 'It broke when I was getting you out of your wet clothes.'

My eyes widened. I'd been so caught up in losing Grace and having to tell Theo about Daniel that I hadn't even noticed it was missing.

'Oh, thank you.' I took the chain and examined it. One of the links had snapped off, but I was sure a jeweller could repair it. I glanced round at Theo. He was still looking away, thank goodness. I blushed. How embarrassing would that have been, if Theo had seen I wore his initial round my neck?

Lewis smiled. 'You like him, don't you?'

I swallowed, my face burning.

'Rachel?'

I glanced at him, knowing my expression was totally giving my heart away.

'Okay, well come and help me get our stuff together,' Lewis said, now sounding slightly embarrassed himself. 'There's a town a few minutes' walk away. We can buy a couple of pay-as-you-go phones and call your parents, then see what we can find out about this Mr Jamieson.'

Lewis disappeared down the steps to the cabin. With a last look at Theo, who was still gazing out over the dark water, I shoved the broken chain into my pocket and followed him.

56

Theo

We abandoned the RAGE boat and walked in silence along the coastal path to Lamerdeen – a dull, dirty town full of grey stone buildings and run-down-looking shops. The sky clouded over as we arrived, as dark as my mood.

Elijah only killed Daniel because I got away.

The truth of this was so awful I couldn't bring myself to face it head on. Daniel was an innocent little boy. The same little boy I had once been. And by escaping myself, I'd left Elijah with nowhere to turn for a heart but his younger clone. The guilt of it washed over me in waves.

Rachel hovered beside me. I knew that she sensed what I was going through, but I couldn't bear to look her in the eye. I didn't want to make the whole thing any more real. She started talking about Milo, the other clone of Elijah's who was in a wheelchair. Reading between the lines it sounded like he was well into her . . . though it was hard to tell how Rachel felt about him. She was most concerned about whether he'd have the bottle to stand up to anyone and protect Grace.

Beside me, Lewis made an inventory of everything we had with us.

'Enough money to pay for two cheap phones and a few meals . . . maybe even a couple of nights in a B&B . . . some rope off the boat, and the clothes we're standing up in.'

'What about the knife we used to cut you free?' I said.

'Too blunt to be of any use,' Lewis said. 'It took me nearly half an hour to cut through the last rope.' He hesitated. 'Anything else?'

I shook my head. The small bag I'd brought with me from America was still in the B&B back in Roslinnon.

'These clothes are as bad as the ones they gave me on Calla,' Rachel complained.

She was still in the outsize shirt Lewis had found for her last night, plus a pair of jeans rolled up at the ankles and a sweatshirt we'd found in one of the cabins.

'Well, there's nothing we can do about that,' Lewis said distractedly. 'Our first priority should be to get the phones so you can call your parents and find an internet café to start tracking down Jamieson.'

It was midday by the time we found a café. Lewis ordered some food while I dialled Mum's number. It was only seven a.m. at home in Philly, but Mum should be up.

She answered on the first ring.

'Theo?' Her voice cracked. 'Oh my God, are you okay?'

'I'm fine,' I said. 'Did you get my other messages?'

'Yes, but what the hell are you doing? Where are you? Who are you with? Why didn't you—?'

'I'm in Scotland,' I said. 'I came here because Rachel was in trouble and I had to help her.'

'*What?*' Mum shouted. 'You little *idiot.*' She started ranting on at me about how stupid I was being, and how much danger I'd put myself in. 'And how did you even get over there?' she shouted.

'I had help,' I said, not wanting to dump Lewis in it.

'I'm calling the police,' Mum shrieked. 'You can't do this, Theo. Don't you see, the only reason Elijah would want Rachel is to try and use her to bait you.'

'I don't think so. He's managed to find himself a new heart . . .' I paused, unable to bring myself to explain about Daniel, '. . . he doesn't need me any—'

'Don't be ridiculous,' Mum yelled. 'You don't know *what* he's thinking . . . what he's after . . . For goodness' sake, Theo, you *have* to come home. The government went to a lot of trouble to hide us. You're risking *everything.*'

'I can't come back yet,' I said. I could feel all my old, stubborn anger at Mum rearing up. *Why did she have to treat me like I was a little kid who couldn't look after myself?*

Mum shouted some more.

'I'm sorry, Mum, but I'm nearly sixteen,' I said in the end. 'I have to do this.'

I rang off and went back to the others. Lewis was still queuing at the food counter. Rachel had found a stool by the window and was leaning against it, frowning.

'Did you speak to your parents?' I asked.

'Yeah,' she said. 'It was awful. They cried and asked

masses of questions, then cried some more. They want me to come home.'

'My mum shouted at me, she wants me home too.'

We looked at each other. Rachel shrugged. 'They don't understand.' She paused. 'I've been thinking. I'm sure Milo will do everything he can to protect Grace. He's a good person, basically, and—'

'*Milo?*' I interrupted, unable to believe what I was hearing. 'Elijah's henchman is a *good person*?'

'He's not a henchman,' Rachel insisted. 'He's sweet and Elijah treats him really badly.'

'Right,' I said, feeling unsettled. How could Rachel seriously think anyone who worked for Elijah was 'sweet'?

I pointed to the nearest computer terminal. There were several arranged in two rows on a long trestle table. A few were occupied. Most were vacant.

'Let's Google Mr Jamieson,' I said.

Rachel pushed herself up from the stool and went over to the computer. She sat down, logged on and began the search. I went over to help Lewis with our plates of food.

As we came back, Rachel looked up, all excited.

'Look,' she said, pointing at the screen. 'That's him.'

57

Rachel

The picture on the screen was definitely the same Don Jamieson – balding and round-faced. But he didn't look like a villain. In fact, he looked like your average middle-aged businessman with a pleasant smile *and* a CV full of charity work.

'What's his connection with Elijah?' Theo asked.

I ran my finger down the screen, stopping at an entry halfway down the page. '*There*. It says he runs a company called Amarta Pharmaceuticals.'

'So?' Theo said.

'Maybe this special thing in my blood . . . these tests Elijah wants to do on Grace . . . maybe Jamieson is hoping he can turn whatever Elijah finds into a product he can sell.'

Lewis nodded. 'That makes sense.' He leaned forward and typed the name *Amarta* into an open Google search box. He rubbed the back of his head.

'Are you okay?' I said.

'It's just this headache,' Lewis said. 'I've had it for a while, now. It won't go away.' He clicked on *search*, then scrolled down the list of hits until he came to a news story.

We read the item together – it was about Amarta's development of a controversial drug used in fertility treatments.

'That's the connection,' Lewis said.

I nodded, adrenalin rushing through me. 'We've got to find Jamieson . . . fast,' I said, clicking back to the original list of hits.

'Here's the main office address.' Theo pointed to another link. The office was based on the outskirts of Glasgow.

'We'll get a cab as soon as we've eaten.' Lewis rubbed his head again, wincing. 'It'll take most of the money we have left, but it's the fastest way to get there.'

I smiled gratefully at him.

'But how are we going to get Jamieson to talk?' Theo said. 'He's not going to take us to Elijah just because we ask.'

'We *won't* ask,' I said. 'In fact, he won't even know we're there. We don't want him tipping Elijah off that we're after them.'

'So what are you thinking we should do?' Theo stared at me. 'Break into Jamieson's office?'

'We won't need to break in,' I said. 'It's a workday afternoon. We can just walk through the door and find Jamieson's computer. There's bound to be something linking him to Elijah on that. Don't you see? It's our best lead to Grace.'

Now both Lewis and Theo were staring at me.

'What?' I said.

'Just walk in?' Theo said faintly.

I clicked onto another news item which referred to Jamieson's charity work for an organisation called Kidsbeat. It offered deprived children a chance to get involved in musical clubs, where free instruments and lessons were provided.

'Kidsbeat are very grateful for Mr Jamieson's help,' I said, glancing from Lewis to Theo. 'This is how they're going to show it.'

58

Theo

We'd taken a cab to the outskirts of Glasgow and found a café on a high street where Lewis insisted we cleaned up a bit before we headed off to Jamieson's office.

Lewis had gone to buy the balloons that were part of Rachel's plan, while I waited for Rachel to come out of the Ladies. She'd already taken more than three times longer than either Lewis or me. I wondered what on earth she was doing but, to be honest, it didn't matter. I was happy to sit on my own, glugging back a hot chocolate, and trying to work out how I was going to phrase what I wanted to say to her.

And then she walked out.

She was still wearing the shirt from the RAGE boat, but she'd knotted it at her waist and belted her trousers at her hips.

I couldn't take my eyes off her as she came over.

'I borrowed some girl's make up in the toilets,' she said, matter-of-factly. 'And her hairbrush.' She looked round. 'Has Lewis got the balloons?'

At that moment, Lewis appeared in the doorway, a bunch of silver helium balloons clutched in his hand.

Rachel rushed over. 'They're perfect,' she said.

'You look nice, too.' Lewis smiled approvingly.

Rachel smiled back. She whispered something to Lewis. He nodded. Rachel handed him something. I caught a flash of metal, but couldn't see what it was. Lewis slipped it into his pocket and Rachel kissed him on the cheek.

I followed them out of the café, frowning. What had she given him? *And why*?

I mean, I wasn't after any gifts, but I couldn't help feeling a bit left out.

'What was that?' I said as we fell into step with each other on the pavement.

'Nothing,' Rachel said. 'Hey, you know, this is going to work.'

I remembered what I'd been intending to say to her.

'Yeah, it will work but *I* want to do it, not you . . . the first part of the plan, I mean,' I said. 'It's safer that way. If there's anyone in Jamieson's office who was on Calla they'll recognise you.'

She stared at me. 'Well, they'll recognise you too, won't they? You look just like Milo, remember?'

This hadn't occurred to me. 'But still—'

'No, Theo.' Rachel's expression hardened. 'The Aphrodite Experiment is something to do with *me*. And so is Grace. I'm not staying behind.'

She stalked off.

I shook my head. Well, at least I'd tried.

I tipped my face to the sun. It was still a beautiful day – except that it wasn't. Somewhere across the Atlantic my mother was insanely worried about me. And with good reason. RAGE was still out there – and so was Elijah. And Daniel was dead. A little boy with my genes had been murdered so that an ageing man could live. Worst of all, I could have prevented his murder.

If Elijah had taken *my* heart, he wouldn't have needed Daniel's.

I closed my eyes against the glare of the sun. I couldn't let myself feel the pain of that. I couldn't let myself feel anything but anger, which I had to channel into helping Rachel. She was the only thing that mattered. And she wanted to save Grace.

I was going to help her do that, or die trying.

I opened my eyes, startled by the sudden realisation that I was prepared to die.

It would be better than living with the guilt I felt over not saving Daniel.

Ahead of me, Lewis staggered slightly as he walked, stumbling into the road for a second. I caught his arm.

'Are you okay?' I said.

Rachel was at his side in an instant, her face full of concern. 'Lewis?'

'I'm fine.' Lewis rubbed the back of his head again and handed the balloons to Rachel. 'Take these.'

Rachel took the balloons.

'You don't *look* fine,' I said.

There were beads of sweat on Lewis's forehead and his eyes looked a little unfocused.

'Maybe you should get yourself checked out,' I said. 'Like at the hospital?'

'No,' Lewis snapped. 'It's just a headache. Now come on.'

Rachel shot me a sympathetic smile then hurried after Lewis, the helium balloons bobbing along behind her.

I followed them, a deep feeling of foreboding in my gut.

59

Rachel

We stood outside Jamieson's business headquarters while I went over the plan one more time.

'Is it clear?' I said, feeling anxious.

'Sure.' Theo gritted his teeth. 'Let's get on with it.'

I glanced at Lewis. His face was clammy and there were dark rings under his eyes. He'd just bitten Theo's head off for asking if he was okay, but it was obvious something was really wrong with him. He kept rubbing the back of his head and every now and then he seemed to stumble as he walked.

Still, there was nothing I could do about that. And, right now, I had to focus on getting inside Jamieson's office.

'Good luck,' Lewis said.

Theo squeezed my hand. He looked like he wanted to say something. I'd kind of snapped at him when he offered to go into the office in my place. I hadn't meant to, it was just hard to carry on pretending I was really cool about what I was doing, when the truth was I was totally freaking out inside my head.

I squeezed Theo's hand back and smiled, then took a deep breath and walked through the main office front door.

It was a small, gleaming reception area – lots of white surfaces with a bunch of lilies on the reception desk. I went up to the middle-aged lady behind the counter. She was groomed and lipsticked and smartly dressed in a blouse and what my mum refers to as 'slacks'.

She smiled as I indicated the balloons.

'These are from Kidsbeat as a present for Mr Jamieson after his party last week,' I said.

'Thank you, dear.' The receptionist reached out for the balloons, but I held them away.

'We all gave money for them ourselves,' I said, with a frown. 'Me and some of the others. I want to give them to Mr Jamieson personally. He said it would be okay if I ever came to see him.'

'Of course, dear,' the woman said in a conciliatory tone. 'Just sign in and you can take them up to his office on the third floor. His PA will meet you up there.'

I quickly signed myself in, using a false name, and headed for the lift. I clocked the security camera focused on its doors and held the balloons between me and the lens as I stood waiting for the lift to arrive. I gripped the bunch of balloons more tightly, my palms sweaty around the nylon string.

I reached the third floor, the lift doors opened and a smiling woman in a navy suit appeared. 'Hello there. I'm Mr Jamieson's PA. Reception phoned up to say you were coming. His office is this way.'

As we crossed the open-plan office, I gazed around, carefully holding the balloons close to my face. With its desks and chairs and shelves and filing cabinets this looked like a totally normal office. Several people looked up at me and my huge bunch of balloons as I passed. For the first time since I came up with my plan, I started to doubt if it could possibly work. There were just so many people around . . .

I sent Theo a text showing the number '3' as the PA led me out of the open-plan area and into a short corridor. She turned into a small ante-room complete with a desk and two sofas. It led through to another office.

'Mr Jamieson is through there,' she said. 'I'll tell him you're here.'

I breathed a sigh of relief. At least this office was private. Maybe there wouldn't even be a security camera. I looked around. Damn it, there was. Just to the right of the door, a lens was trained on the entrance to Jamieson's private office.

The phone on the desk rang as the PA passed it. If everything was running to plan, that phone call was from reception . . . The PA answered, her fingernails tapping impatiently against the desk as she listened.

'What?' she said, sounding exasperated. 'He's already up to his eyes . . . he wasn't in the office until . . . Fine, I'll tell him . . .' She put the phone down and turned to me. 'Wait here.'

I leaned against the arm of the small sofa opposite the desk. I was gripping the balloons so tightly my knuckles were white.

I watched the PA cross into the inner room. A balding, round-faced man was sitting inside at a glass table, going over some papers. He looked up, blinking behind his glasses. It was the Don Jamieson from our internet search.

'There's a man downstairs,' the PA said. 'He's complaining about something . . . says he's got a message from an Elijah Lazio.'

Don Jamieson's mouth dropped open. His eyes flashed with shock . . . and recognition.

My heart thudded.

'He won't come up and he won't pass this message on to anyone but you personally,' the PA went on. 'Reception are asking what you want to do.'

Jamieson stood up, banging into the table. His face had lost all its colour.

'I'll go down,' he said.

They both came back into the outer office. Jamieson scurried past me and out of the door. I ducked my head, hiding behind the balloons, but he was so intent on leaving the room, he didn't even seem to register I was there.

The PA sighed and went to her desk. 'Sorry about that,' she said. 'Hopefully he won't be too long.'

I held my breath, waiting. *Come on, Theo.*

At that precise second, the fire alarm rang.

'For goodness' sake,' the PA muttered. She stood up and picked up her handbag. 'Come on, we have to go downstairs.'

'I'll leave the balloons here,' I said, looping the strings round the sofa cushion.

231

'Right.' The PA ushered me through the door. We walked back to the open-plan office. The people inside were all heading for the stairs. As the PA joined the crowd, I hung back. A few seconds later she turned, looking for me, but by then there were at least twenty people between us.

I gave her a thumbs up and pointed towards the stairs, to show I was right behind her. She nodded distractedly from across the office. Keeping my face turned away from the security camera, I headed back towards Mr Jamieson's office.

'Didn't we have a drill last Monday?' I heard one man say, as he headed for the stairs.

I moved further away, round the corner. The fire alarm was still blaring out, a harsh screech above my head. I counted to ten in my head then crept back inside Mr Jamieson's office. Keeping my head bowed, I raced across the room, grabbed the balloons and let them float up towards the security camera that was trained on the door into Jamieson's private room.

I checked the camera was totally covered, so no one would know I'd come back, then scurried into Jamieson's office myself.

How long did I have? Five, ten minutes?

I needed to make every one of them count.

60

Theo

Setting off the fire alarm had been easy. I'd waited outside the building, my hood pulled low over my head to avoid any security cameras outside, while the receptionist was busy with Lewis. He stood at the desk insisting he had a message for Jamieson from Elijah.

Loud, rude and aggressive, with glassy eyes and his face all pallid and sweaty, he looked convincingly unhinged. He thumped his fist against the company logo, a pattern of swirling lines around the name *Amarta*, which was embossed on the front of the reception desk. A moment later he started gesticulating wildly, then began pulling wires out of the security panel on the wall beside the desk.

'It's all "Big Brother is watching you",' he was shouting, as the screens showing the view from all of the security cameras in the building fizzed into darkness.

As the receptionist rose from her chair, looking alarmed, I slipped inside, past the reception desk and into the corridor beyond.

The receptionist was so intent on making Lewis leave the building that she didn't even notice me.

'I'm calling the police,' she shouted.

I reached a fire alarm and swiftly smashed the glass to set it off. A harsh screech filled the air. Seconds later, people started milling towards me along the corridor.

I glanced over my shoulder. In the distance Lewis was limping out of the front door. I slipped into the toilets for a minute, then, when it sounded quiet outside, came out and raced along to the stairs at the end of the corridor.

Rachel's text had said '3', which meant Jamieson's office was on the third floor. I pounded up the stairs two at a time then flew through the open-plan office. Jamieson was too senior not to have his own private room, wasn't he?

I saw a door and raced through it.

There. Along the corridor, glancing around, I spotted the dangling balloon strings several doors down. Rachel looked up as I ran into the room.

She was seated at what must be Jamieson's desk, in an anally-tidy room, examining his computer.

'Found anything?' I said.

'Yes,' she said. 'Look at this.'

61

Rachel

'What is it?' Theo said, peering over my shoulder. He wrinkled his nose. 'I don't get it, that's just a medical report.'

The shriek of the fire alarm was still piercing through my head. Ignoring it, I pointed to the name and date at the head of the report. *Lab Three. Aphrodite.*

'It's *her* medical report. Grace's. It says these are preliminary tests. Done this morning.'

Theo's eyes widened.

'Does it say *what* tests? Has Elijah hurt her?' he said.

'I don't know . . . I don't think so.' I scanned the report again. It was written almost completely in medical jargon. I only recognised a couple of references – one to blood type, which was 'O positive', the same as me, and the other to Grace's date of birth – which was given as yesterday evening.

As I stared at the report, the fire alarm stopped. The sudden silence seemed to buzz in my ears. Panic rose in my chest. This document might prove that the connection between Jamieson and Elijah went right to the heart of the

Aphrodite Experiment. But I was no closer to finding out what that experiment was about . . . or how my DNA was involved . . . or where Grace was . . .

'Listen.' Theo moved to the door.

Desperate now, my eyes raced over the medical report. There had to be something here . . . some clue . . .

'*Rachel*,' Theo hissed. 'There's someone coming.'

I looked up, as the unmistakable sound of footsteps raced towards us.

62

Theo

Rachel stared at me, her eyes wide. I rushed over, grabbed her arm and dragged her under the desk. We sat, squashed against each other. I could feel the frantic thump of Rachel's heart vibrating through her back.

The footsteps grew closer and slowed.

'I've left the screen open showing that report,' Rachel whispered.

'*Sssh.*' I peered out through a crack in the desk. Two men were standing in the doorway. I could only see their legs, but it was obvious they were examining the balloons, which Rachel must have placed over the surveillance camera.

'I told you I saw something moving.' One of the men tugged at the strings and Rachel's bunch of helium balloons drifted into view. 'It must have been these.'

'We're supposed to be looking for the girl who brought them, remember?' Another male voice.

The two men moved closer to Jamieson's inner office door. There was a pause while they looked into the room.

Rachel and I froze under the desk. Seconds passed. They felt like minutes.

At last one of the men spoke. 'There's no one here,' he said. 'She must have gone down a floor. Let's go.'

I held my breath as their footsteps died away.

As soon as they were gone, Rachel crawled out from under the desk and peered at the medical report on the screen again.

'We should go,' I said. 'It's obvious there's no fire, everyone will be coming back in any second.'

She nodded. 'But we haven't found out anything.'

An idea struck me. I pointed to the medical report. 'Does that say where the tests took place?' I asked.

'Just "Lab Three", wherever that is,' Rachel answered.

I clicked on Jamieson's address book. 'Look.' I pointed to the 'labs' folder in Jamieson's contacts list. There were five – all with addresses in the Glasgow area.

Rachel peered intently at the details for Lab Three. 'Holloway Street,' she said. 'Number 55.'

We stared at each other.

'That's where Grace is,' Rachel said, excitedly.

'It's where she was this morning.' I corrected her.

'Then she might still be there.' Rachel grabbed my arm. 'Come on, we have to go *now*.'

We raced out to the stairs. I pounded down them, two steps at a time, Rachel right behind me. We made it to the first-floor landing before a deep male Scottish voice echoed up towards us.

'It's too much of a coincidence,' he said. 'I mean, hopefully it's just kids messing about, but if they're still in the building . . .'

Rachel stopped in her tracks, yanking me back by the shoulder.

'That's Jamieson,' she hissed.

I looked round. The door to the first-floor offices was right beside us.

'In here.' I raced through the door and along the corridor, Rachel following right behind.

I stopped at the nearest window. It was shut, but opened easily when I pressed on the window lock.

We scrambled outside, onto a flat roof that appeared to jut out from the side of the building. I lay prostrate on the roof, then crawled forward commando-style and peered over the edge. Below us, a narrow passageway ran along the side of the building, leading to a metal gate a few metres away. Beyond that was an empty stretch of pavement.

I eased myself down and turned, holding out my arms to help Rachel as she jumped.

She landed softly, stumbling against me, then looked up into my eyes.

My breath caught in my throat. She was right there, in front of me, closer than at any moment since I'd picked her up off the beach on Calla.

I wanted to kiss her. But I couldn't. Not here. Not now.

We pulled away from each other and raced over to the metal gate. I gave Rachel a leg-up and she climbed onto the

239

gate. She straddled the top for a second then jumped down onto the pavement on the other side.

I clambered after her, glancing anxiously over my shoulder as I reached the top of the gate.

No one was following us.

I jumped down and started running after Rachel, the thrill of success surging through me.

We ran hard for a couple of minutes, heading for the place where we'd agreed to rendezvous with Lewis. As we neared the meeting point, Rachel slowed to a jog. I took her hand and she smiled up at me.

'We're going to find Grace,' she said. 'I can feel it. And I was thinking . . . there's bound to be stuff in this Lab Three that will explain what Elijah's found in my DNA . . . this special thing in my blood . . .'

'Maybe it's just some little quirk that means your clones can survive in an artificial womb?' I said.

Rachel shook her head. 'There has to be more to it than that. That's why Elijah wanted to do more tests . . . to see how he could use whatever it is. He won't stop until he's got all the answers, I'm sure of it.'

We reached the junction where Lewis had told us to meet him – a crossroads beside a patch of wasteland, complete with scrubby bushes and a broken-roofed bus shelter.

Lewis wasn't there.

Rachel looked frantically up and down the roads that led to the junction. I peered across the patch of wasteland. A jacket lay crumpled on the grass, just visible past the bus shelter.

Except it wasn't just a jacket. It was Lewis.

And he wasn't moving.

63

Rachel

I dropped to the ground beside Lewis, my heart in my mouth. He was totally still, his eyes shut. I held my trembling hand against his nose . . . at least he was breathing. I shook his shoulder gently.

'Lewis?' I whispered.

No response.

'What's happened to him?' Theo said.

'I don't know.' I gently lifted Lewis's jacket and then felt round the back of his head. 'There's no blood . . . I don't think he's been hit . . . at least not since last night . . .'

We stared at each other for a moment, then Theo fished his phone out of his pocket. 'We have to call an ambulance,' he said.

'But Elijah could be watching the hospitals . . .'

'Elijah's not after Lewis, he's after you. And we'll give the paramedics a false name.' He paused. 'Anyway, we can't just leave him here.' He stared at me, his gaze steady.

'Okay.'

Theo dialled 999. He was amazingly sorted on the phone,

giving false names for all of us and explaining that Lewis was a guy we knew vaguely who we'd heard had been beaten up the night before. Afterwards, we went through Lewis's pockets. We took some money and the rope from the boat. Then we hid behind the bus shelter – watching out for Jamieson – until the ambulance crew arrived.

We got the name of the hospital Lewis was being taken to, but said we couldn't travel with him, telling the paramedics we had to get home to our parents. They told us they didn't know what was wrong with Lewis . . . that the doctors needed to check him over. I noticed they carefully avoided saying that he was definitely going to be all right.

I felt like crying as they drove away. Lewis had always been there in my fight against Elijah. Without him I felt really vulnerable.

I didn't speak as Theo checked for directions on his phone, took my hand and led me away. We walked for five minutes, neither of us saying a word. Theo led me down a series of small roads, finally stopping on the edge of an industrial estate. The sky had clouded over and was as grey as the squat modern buildings ahead of us. In the distance lay a range of greeny-brown hills. I guess they should have looked attractive, but everything now seemed dull and depressing.

How could we carry on without Lewis?

'Lab Three is in there.' Theo pointed into the industrial estate.

I nodded, turning away so Theo wouldn't see my eyes fill with tears.

'Rachel?' His voice was uncertain.

I turned back. 'I don't know if I can do this.' The words came out without me meaning them to, in a tiny whispered voice.

I blushed, hating that I'd shown Theo how vulnerable I felt.

'You're not alone.' He put his hands on my arms. 'I'm here. We can do this together, yeah?'

I looked up into his dark brown eyes. They were so beautiful – warm and strong and with a certainty . . . a self-belief . . . that hadn't been there last year.

I suddenly felt overwhelmed by how much I loved him. Tears welled up again – this time with relief. Sobbing, I flung myself into his arms.

He held me for a minute while I cried, then leaned down and kissed me.

It was a different kiss than the one on Calla – more tender and protective. As we pulled apart I knew that all the months apart hadn't made any difference.

Theo and I were meant to be together.

'When this is over,' I said, croakily, 'I don't want to go back to Roslinnon.'

'I'm not going back to the States, either,' Theo said.

'They'll have to let us live nearer each other . . . be able to see each other . . .'

Theo smiled. 'They won't be able to stop us,' he said. 'Now, are we going to find this lab or what?'

I smiled back. 'Come on, then.'

244

We edged slowly round the industrial estate, stopping at each pre-fab building to check its name.

Jamieson Labs was clearly signed – an ultra-modern concrete construction on two floors with steps down to a basement. A man was standing outside the basement door, smoking. We hid behind a wall, then peered round it to get a better look.

'That's one of Elijah's men . . . Paul,' I whispered.

'Looks like he's guarding the basement door,' Theo said.

'That's good.'

Theo stared at me as if I were mad. 'What's good about it?'

'Well, Paul works for Elijah. If he's guarding the basement I bet that's where Lab Three is.'

'Let's find out.' Theo gritted his teeth. 'Though it's going to take both of us to deal with an armed guard. We're going to need everything we've got.'

I glanced at him. 'Which is what, exactly? We don't have any weapons.'

'A good attack technique and the element of surprise.'

I smiled, knowing that Theo was referring to the way I'd learned to fight last year. But that memory brought me back to Lewis, unconscious on his ambulance stretcher, and the smile slid from my face.

Lewis had risked so much for me. He *had* to be okay. I couldn't bear it if he wasn't.

But there was no time to think about that. Theo was explaining his plan for getting past Paul – it was risky, but definitely do-able. And it was our best shot for finding Grace.

245

We got as close as we could to Paul without being seen, then Theo stayed hidden while I walked into plain view.

Paul saw me straight away. He gasped, his hand reaching automatically for his gun. He pointed it at me as I walked down the short flight of concrete steps to the basement yard where he was standing.

I clocked the sign on the door. *Lab 3*.

So far, so good.

'Stand still,' Paul ordered.

Ignoring him, I headed for the door to Lab Three, forcing Paul to turn so he was still facing me.

'Stand *still*,' he said again.

This time I stopped. I'd done what I needed to do. Paul had his back to the street now. He'd never see Theo coming.

Paul stared at me, his mouth agape. 'Milo said you'd drowned.'

My heart bumped against my chest. 'I nearly did,' I said.

I forced myself not to look up, above Paul's head. I mustn't warn him that Theo was about to approach from behind.

Paul shook his head. Still holding the gun in one hand, he reached for his radio with the other.

This was Theo's cue. I kept my eyes fixed on Paul's gun hand. Behind him, I could see the faintest flicker of movement.

And then Theo leaped, knocking Paul down. Both the gun and the radio clattered to the ground as Paul instinctively used his hands to break his fall. He landed heavily on his side, but used the momentum to roll over, trying to get up again. Theo flung himself at Paul's chest, pinning the man's arms to the ground.

Paul was yelling and kicking out.

I rushed over and kicked the gun and the radio into the far corner of the basement yard. Paul was pushing Theo back. He was broader and stronger. On his knees now. No longer yelling. All his energy concentrated on Theo. His hands round Theo's neck.

I stood beside him, steadied myself and took my stance. The whole weight of my body went into the roundhouse kick I aimed at Paul's ribs.

He flew backwards, releasing Theo, who lunged for him again.

They were on the ground, fighting. I reached between the flailing arms and felt in Theo's pocket for the rope we'd taken from Lewis.

Theo forced Paul's arms behind his back and I wound the rope round his wrists. Paul was still kicking. He yelled out – a furious roar.

Theo immediately clamped his hand over Paul's face. I ripped a length off the end of my shirt and we wound it tightly round his mouth. Now the cries were muffled.

Theo sat back, panting. He had a cut on the side of his lip and a red mark on his cheek, but otherwise he looked fine. I ripped another length of my shirt off and we bound Paul's ankles then fastened him to the stair railing with a tight knot.

Paul was still thrashing about, but he couldn't move far.

No one passing by would see him now unless they looked right over the wall.

Theo breathed out a relieved sigh.

'D'you think those knots will hold?' He grinned. 'Maybe you should take off the rest of your shirt so we can make sure?'

I blushed, looking down at my ripped shirt. At least I had a little vest top on underneath. 'Very funny.' I shot him a quick smile. 'But if we need any more substitute rope I think we'll be using *your* shirt. Come on, let's get going.'

I tiptoed up the stairs and glanced around the industrial estate. A small group of people were leaving another building, a hundred metres or so away. They stood in the road, chatting. They clearly hadn't heard us. The rest of the estate was empty.

Paul was still issuing muffled roars as I went back down the stairs.

I turned to the door of Lab Three. 'Ready?'

Theo nodded and I pushed the door open.

We were in a dark corridor. Halfway down, two doors led off on either side. We crept closer to them, my heart pounding. The building looked and sounded deserted, but it couldn't be, not if Paul was guarding the outside. We reached the left-hand door and I pushed it open slowly. Inside was a research room, full of scientific equipment. I glanced round at the shelves, which were covered in bottles and tubes and boxes.

Several microscopes were ranged across the countertop beneath them. There was no sign of any people.

I pointed to the door on the other side of the corridor and we crossed over to it.

Holding my breath, I pushed it open.

Another, similar, room.

Theo frowned. 'No one's here.'

I shook my head. It didn't make sense.

'I'm going to check no one's found Paul,' Theo whispered. 'If there's nobody about we can have a good look around.'

He vanished and I tiptoed across the room. Halfway over and I noticed it – a tiny perspex cot at the end of the room. A yellow blanketed bundle moved inside.

I raced over.

Grace's tiny face peered up at me.

My heart gave a jolt. I reached into the cot and gently drew her out.

'Grace,' I whispered, holding the baby tight against my chest.

She made a nuzzling noise, then closed her eyes.

A clatter behind me. I spun round. Milo was wheeling himself through a door I hadn't even noticed before.

We stared at each other.

Milo's eyes filled with relief. 'Rachel, I thought you were . . . How did you . . .?'

'I got washed out onto the beach,' I said, backing away. 'But I'm back for Grace.'

'No.' Milo's eyes filled with alarm. 'You can't take her.'

I glared at him. 'She's less than a day old, Milo and she's been abandoned in a lab. Elijah's doing *tests* on her, it's obscene.'

'No . . . I mean, yes, but the tests are over. Elijah's furious. He's tried it every which way and he's not getting the results he wanted.'

'What results?' I said, still backing towards the door.

'Grace doesn't have the same protein in her blood that you do.'

I stared at him. 'The same *protein*?' Was that what it was?

'Yes, Elijah just found out. '

'You mean it's only in *me*?'

'Yes. Rachel, you have to leave Grace and get out of here. If Elijah finds you . . . if he knows you're here . . .'

'What exactly *is* this protein?' I said, still holding Grace close.

'I don't know exactly but Elijah says it's amazing. That . . . that it could save peoples' lives. Rachel . . . it's not in *anyone* else. Elijah thinks you're dead but if you take Grace then he'll know—'

'He'll know anyway,' I said, thinking of Paul. 'I have to take Grace. We both know what he does to clones he doesn't have any use for.'

'He'll kill me if he knows you were here and I let you go,' Milo said.

Arm trembling, he raised his hand from his lap and pointed a gun at me.

Oh God.

'You don't know how to use that,' I said.

'Yes I do,' Milo said. 'Elijah taught me years ago.'

I took another step back.

'Well, even if you *do* know, you won't use it,' I said. 'I know you, Milo, you're too much of a coward to pull the trigger.'

Damn. That was a stupid thing to say.

Milo's mouth set into a firm line. His eyes hardened.

'You don't know *what* I'm capable of,' he said.

64

Theo

I raced outside, anxious that Paul had somehow managed to work his way free from his bindings. I needn't have worried. Paul was still tied safely to the railing. He kicked out when he saw me, his expression furious. I ignored him and ran up the steps. I could see quite a long way up and down the industrial estate from here.

The place was deserted.

I jogged back inside, feeling more confident. Now all we needed was a clue to Grace's whereabouts.

As I ran down the corridor back towards Rachel I heard her voice. She was talking . . . No, arguing . . .

I froze. Someone was with her. Moving as slowly as I could, I reached the room she was inside and eased the door open.

Rachel had Grace in her arms. She was talking to a guy in a wheelchair. He was pointing a gun at her.

Oh, crap.

They both turned as I entered.

252

With a jolt, I realised that the guy in the wheelchair looked like me. This must be *Milo*. My mouth fell open. I mean, his hair was more off his forehead than mine and his face was a bit fuller but, even from this distance, the similarity was obvious.

I stared at him for a second, shocked. So this was the other clone of Elijah. It was the weirdest thing, seeing his face, like looking at a mirror in reverse – or maybe into the face of some long-lost brother.

That thought sent Daniel flashing through my head – with his big brown eyes and innocent smile. Fury filled me.

Milo was staring at me, open-mouthed. I guess my face was as much of a shock to him as his was to me.

'*You?*' he said.

'You need to put down that gun,' I said. 'Because Rachel and the baby are coming with me.'

65

Rachel

Milo stared at Theo, his mouth open in a totally shocked 'o' shape.

'*Jesus*,' he said.

'Not quite,' Theo said, coming up behind me. 'My name's Theo.'

'I see you've got his sense of humour . . .' Milo said. 'Elijah's, I mean.'

'Whatever.' Theo put his arm round me and leaned closer. His breath was hot on my neck as he whispered, 'Will he shoot us?'

'No.' As I said it, I knew it was true. It didn't matter what Milo said, I could see in his eyes that he wouldn't shoot. And it wasn't because he was a coward, either.

'Come on, then,' Theo whispered again.

'Stop.' Milo's arm was still shaking. 'Stop or I'll shoot.'

'No you won't,' I said. 'I'm sorry I said you were a coward, Milo. You aren't. You're a good person. You're just caught up with a bad person and you don't know how to get out of it.'

Clutching Grace, I took another step back. Theo's arm was round my shoulders. Another step, then another.

We reached the door.

'Rachel, please . . .'

I took a final look at Milo – at all the loss and longing in his face – and I knew there was another reason why he wouldn't shoot me, or the people I cared about.

He liked me too much to risk hurting me.

And then we were through the door and running for all we were worth, along the corridor, out of the lab and past Paul who was still tied to the stair railing.

I raced up the steps and followed Theo down the street, clutching Grace tightly to my chest.

Now that I had her back, I was never going to let her go again.

66

Theo

Everyone agreed that without knowing more about Elijah's backer and his government links, it was too risky to call the police.

Nobody agreed about anything else.

'We can't keep her, Rachel.' Mr Smith's gaze shifted from his daughter to the baby in her arms.

I looked away.

It was late afternoon and we were in a hotel room. As soon as we'd got clear of the lab, Rachel had called her parents and arranged for them to meet us.

The hotel had been Mr and Mrs Smith's suggestion. They booked us into a room as soon as they heard that Elijah would almost certainly be on our tail again, so we could talk somewhere privately.

It was kind of funny, being with Rachel in a hotel room while we waited for her parents to arrive. Not that there was any chance to take advantage of being on our own together. We couldn't even talk properly – Grace made sure of that.

I couldn't believe how much noise one small baby could make. As soon as we got inside the room – a huge suite with two double beds – Grace started bawling and she didn't stop until Rachel took off her very smelly nappy.

Neither of us wanted to call down to reception to ask if they had any nappies, so Rachel cleaned her and wrapped her in one of the soft white towels in the hotel bathroom.

At that point her parents arrived. I stood back while they showered Rachel with hugs and kisses. I'd never been their favourite person and neither of them seemed inclined to pay me much attention now.

I think they both completely forgot I was there when Rachel announced she wanted the three of them to take Grace home – as a family. It was clear to me from the start that Mr and Mrs Smith thought this was a mad idea, but Rachel wouldn't listen to their arguments.

'But she's my *sister*. Genetically, she's *my* sister and *your* daughter.' Rachel's eyes filled with tears. She held Grace up towards her mum and dad. They were both standing by the bed, arms folded. Mr Smith was wearing a dark suit. Mrs Smith was in a smart, fitted dress with a huge beaded neck-lace that reminded me of the one I'd seen in Rachel's room a few days earlier.

They looked like they'd just wandered out of a church coffee morning.

'Sharing your genes with someone doesn't make you a parent,' Mr Smith said.

'No,' Mrs Smith added. 'We didn't plan her or try to

conceive her. I didn't carry her in my womb. There's *nothing* that makes me her mother. I don't *want* her.'

At this, Rachel started weeping. She walked over to where I was standing by the window and I put my arm around her.

Still holding Grace, she buried her face against my chest. I stared over her head at her dad.

'Theo, will you give Rachel and me a moment?' Mr Smith's voice was calm, but the tone was icy.

I opened my mouth to speak, but Rachel got there first. She was properly crying now.

'I want Theo to stay here,' she sobbed. 'He's the only person who cares about me. Are you going to take *him* away from me too?'

'For God's sake, Rachel,' her mother shrieked. 'Theo's the reason we're all in this state right now.'

What? Was she serious?

'How is *any* of this Theo's fault?' Rachel demanded, turning to face her mother again.

'He found you last year – RAGE didn't even know about you until then. If Theo hadn't come looking for you back then, RAGE wouldn't have known you existed and Elijah would have left you in peace and—'

'Well, if Dad had never taken a job working for Elijah, then none of this would have happened either,' Rachel shouted. 'In fact, *I* wouldn't have happened. Is that what you want? That I'd never been born?'

'Don't be ridiculous, Ro,' Mr Smith cut in. 'Anyway, we're talking about Grace, not Theo and—'

'You're the ones being ridiculous,' Rachel yelled.

I looked at the floor. The hotel had a greeny-brown carpet which matched the curtains in the room. I stared at the swirly pattern that ran across it. I badly wanted to leave the room, but Rachel needed me, so I stood still, hoping neither she nor her parents would drag me any further into their argument.

My mind went back to the way Milo had looked at Rachel earlier in Lab Three. *Man*, he was *really* into her. Jealousy rippled through me. Rachel had spent several days in his company on Calla. Had he tried anything on? Rachel hadn't said, but then we hadn't had much time to talk . . . about anything.

'Look, Ro,' Rachel's dad said, more softly. 'Please try to see things from our point of view. Mum and I are in our *sixties*. We don't have the energy for a baby. And even if we did, it's not fair on Grace. We'll be in our *eighties* before she's grown up.'

'I could look after her,' Rachel said, sullenly.

I stared at her. Was she mad?

'You're too young,' Mr Smith said. 'And we're too old and all of us are known both to RAGE and Elijah which means that even if we relocate again they might find us. But if we do the *right* thing and hand Grace over to social services then she will be adopted into a good family – a vetted, solid family who want her – where she'll be safe.' He paused. 'You want her to be safe, don't you, Rachel?'

Rachel bit her lip. I wasn't sure what she was thinking, but it was obvious to me that her dad was right. I mean, don't get me wrong. One day, when you're older, kids and stuff are

259

fine, but if Rachel's parents weren't prepared to look after Grace, she was far too young to be dealing with a baby on her own.

'What do you think, Theo?' Mr Smith said. 'Do you think us taking on a baby makes sense?'

I shrugged. 'It's what Rachel wants,' I said. 'Grace is her sister. Genetically, more like her twin. That's family.'

Mr Smith's face clouded with impatience. 'Right, well, like I said, maybe you'd give us a moment, Theo?'

Rachel opened her mouth to protest again but I put my hand on her arm to stop her.

'You should talk to your parents on your own,' I said quietly. 'I'm just annoying them.'

Rachel followed me into the corridor. She lifted her face up to mine.

'Thanks for backing me up in there,' she breathed.

I kissed her and she smiled. 'See you soon.'

'Definitely.' I grinned. 'In fact, there's a juice bar downstairs . . . just along from the lobby. Why don't you meet me there in, like, ten minutes?'

'Sure.' Rachel kissed me again and disappeared back into the room.

I went downstairs and out to the juice bar, feeling suddenly hopeful. Maybe if Rachel and I could just get some time on our own, everything would become clear. I was pretty sure she still liked me as much as ever . . . and it certainly wasn't like I wanted some big conversation about it – just a bit of time to let things feel normal again.

The juice bar was heaving, so I got myself a strawberry smoothie and stood outside. The drink reminded me of Cheri's diner – and my life back in Philadelphia. The weather didn't. It was really cold now, with the sun hidden behind a bank of grey clouds . . . After the past few months in sunny Philly, I wasn't used to how biting the wind could be – and this was *July*.

I didn't hear the footsteps until it was too late. Someone stopped, right beside me. Too close.

I spun round. Whoever it was turned with me. A large hand came down behind me . . . clamped itself over my mouth.

Something bad-smelling was shoved under my nose and before I even had time to struggle, I was sinking into blackness.

67

Rachel

Everything was wrong. Everything was awful.

I mean, I could see what Mum and Dad were saying. All the logical, rational stuff about Grace being safer . . . better off generally . . . with some nice young couple. But couldn't they see how it felt for me? Grace was the closest thing to a sister I'd ever known. She was far more real to me than Rebecca, the dead sister I had been cloned from.

Anyway, it was done now. Dad had called social services . . . told them some made-up story about finding a baby round the back of the hotel.

And now someone was on their way to pick Grace up. Mum was holding her. She'd asked the hotel for formula milk and a proper blanket.

I sat beside them, gazing down at Grace's tiny, perfect face. Insane thoughts raced through my head – maybe I could run off with Grace . . . find a place to stay . . . a job to support us . . .

But in my heart I knew that was just a fantasy. I had no job and no money and no idea how to get either. Plus, I couldn't possibly guarantee keeping Grace safe if we were on the streets. There'd be all sorts of threats out there – not least RAGE and Elijah.

Dad was right about that. If Grace got taken in by a solid family, then she *would* be safe. I knew that was what counted most.

But my heart still felt like it was breaking.

It was well past the time I'd said I'd meet Theo, but Grace would be gone soon and I didn't want to leave her. I sent him a couple of texts but he didn't reply.

I could see Dad was feeling sorry for me. He even called the hospital where Lewis had been taken. The nurses said he was in surgery – that the beating he'd had last night had caused some sort of swelling in his brain. It didn't sound good, but at least he was holding his own.

A few more minutes and reception called up to say that social services were here to pick up Grace. Mum let me cuddle her for a moment.

I stared into Grace's eyes. She'd stopped crying and was nuzzling against me again. She felt so fragile in my arms.

'Come on, Ro,' Dad said gently.

'Just one more minute,' I pleaded.

He sighed. I could sense him and Mum exchanging looks, but I kept my gaze on Grace . . . trying to memorise exactly how she looked.

Seconds passed. Then Dad cleared his throat. 'Ro, please?'

I shook my head.

'That's enough, Rachel,' Mum said.

She reached down and took Grace from my arms. I watched the three of them cross the room, keeping my eyes on Grace right to the last second.

And then they were gone.

I'd agreed that Mum and Dad should take Grace downstairs alone, so they could tell their lie about finding her outside . . . and how they'd sent Theo and me inside to get a room while they searched for any sign of the baby's mother.

I sat on the huge hotel bed, feeling numb.

Suddenly I was overwhelmed by a desire to see Theo. I jumped up and headed for the door. Even if Mum and Dad saw me in the lobby, they wouldn't be able to stop me going to the juice bar.

As I reached the hotel room door, my phone rang.

Theo calling.

I snatched the mobile up to my ear.

'Oh, Theo—'

'Ah, Rachel,' Elijah interrupted.

My breath froze in my throat.

'I have Theo's phone and I have Theo,' Elijah said, smoothly. 'If you would like to see him again, you need to listen to me very carefully.'

68

Theo

I could dimly hear my own voice moaning. It sounded like it was coming from a long way away. I came round. My head hurt badly. I was freezing. There was a splash of strawberry smoothie down my shirt. I raised my aching head. I was in the back seat of a car in a completely deserted car park. On one side was a narrow stretch of water – a canal – on the other a patch of wasteland with industrial-looking buildings beyond.

What the hell had happened?

My hands were free. And my feet. But moving anything hurt – especially my head.

I tried the car door beside me. Locked. I reached for my phone. It was gone.

Panic rose inside me. Who had taken me? Why had they left me here in the middle of this car park?

I looked around for something to smash the car window with. Nothing.

At the opposite end of the car park stood a small hut.

A man was standing beside it. He was speaking to some-one on the phone.

'Hey!' I battered my fists against the car window. Each thump sent a shooting pain through my skull, but I had to get his attention. 'HEY!'

The man turned round.

Shit. It was Elijah. He flicked his little finger. The guard from Lab Three walked into view. He was heading in my direction, his gun held at his side.

I sat back, my heart racing.

What was going to happen now?

69

Rachel

Hands trembling, I gripped the mobile.

'What do you want?' I said.

'Call it a ransom,' Elijah chuckled. 'A payment for Theo's release.'

'A payment?' My mouth was dry. 'I don't have any money. Neither do my mum and dad.'

'It's not money I'm after, Rachel.'

'Grace isn't here any more. I don't have her,' I said, quickly. 'She's somewhere safe.'

Elijah chuckled. 'Oh dear, do you still understand so little, Rachel?' He sighed. 'Tell me, why do you think I was trying to clone you?'

'It wasn't about me. You said that you just ended up with clones of me because I've got this special . . . protein that helped them live in the artificial wombs.'

'But why would I want to create new life at all? For what reason?'

'Because you can?' I said. 'That's what you always say

when anyone asks you about your scientific work. The Aphrodite Experiment's the same as everything else. You do it because you want to and you don't care who gets hurt!'

There was a pause. Elijah sighed. 'You are quite wrong, Rachel, on every count. I know I told you all my other clones died in the artificial wombs. Only the clones of you survived. Well, that was not true. I was only *trying* to clone you. You were . . . are . . . all that matters.'

'Me?' I stared at the flowers on the wallpaper of the hotel room. 'Why?'

'Because of this unique quality in your blood, Rachel. I was hoping to copy it. Why else would I clone so many babies? I'm a geneticist – not the head of some surrogacy clinic manufacturing babies. No, the Aphrodite Experiment was all about *you*. It was an attempt to re-create the protein that your blood contains. And it failed. None of my embryos ever contained the protein. I was hoping that with a fully-developed, living baby the protein might be present, but Grace proved this hypothesis wrong.'

My head spun as I tried to process what he was saying. 'You said you wanted a ransom for Theo,' I said.

'That's right.' I could hear the thin smile in Elijah's voice. 'And *you* are that ransom.'

'Me?'

There was a pause. The hotel bedroom was so still, suddenly. The silence pressed down on me.

'You mean you want me to give myself up, to save Theo?'

'Yes, your co-operation is the price of his freedom.' Elijah

268

said. 'I could have kidnapped you directly, of course. But this way I can ensure you leave a note for your parents *and* sound like you mean what you say when you speak to Theo.'

'What I say to Theo?' I frowned. 'I don't understand.'

Elijah made an impatient clicking noise at the back of his throat. 'It's simple, Rachel. I have Theo. In a few moments I will give him the opportunity to "escape". He, of course, will take that opportunity and, as soon as he is free, he will phone you . . .'

'But—'

'When you speak to him you have to make him believe you are leaving him and your family through your own free will. You have to make him believe you want to be alone. Without him. Without your parents. It shouldn't be too hard . . .'

'But no one's going to believe I've run away—'

'Then make them,' Elijah snapped. 'That's what I'm giving you the opportunity to do . . . make it feel real to them. Write a note they'll believe.'

Seconds ticked by. 'What happens to Theo if I refuse?' I stammered.

'My guard, Paul, has a gun trained on him right now,' Elijah said, and there was real menace in his voice. 'Paul will follow Theo until you are with me. It's a clear choice, Rachel. Leave everyone and come with me – and Theo lives. Refuse – and he dies.'

I hesitated, my heart pounding.

'I don't want to hurt you, Rachel. You know I can find you if I want to. I found you before, when you were hidden away.

All I want is a month or so of your time, so I can continue my research into this protein.' He paused. 'I know Milo told you that this unique quality in your blood can save lives. Do you not want to be a part of such amazing research?'

'*How* does it save lives?'

Elijah clicked his tongue impatiently again. 'I can't explain a complex chemical process like that over the telephone. Please, Rachel. I've called it the Eos protein. Eos is the goddess of the dawn. You know my protocols. You *know* I would not use such a name unless this was a truly miraculous discovery. Believe me, with this protein the lame will walk and the blind will see.'

What? I couldn't believe any of this was true. I didn't trust Elijah an inch.

But what did that matter?

He had Theo. Which meant I had no choice.

'I'll need to speak to Theo,' I said.

'Of course. He'll phone you after his "escape". You need to head for the Bressenden shopping centre right now. Get a taxi outside the hotel. Milo will pay when you get there. Theo will call you in about thirty minutes. Remember, it's imperative he thinks you're running away from your life and from him. Imperative that neither he nor Lewis nor your parents come after you. If they do, I will kill them.'

I swallowed.

'Deal?' Elijah said.

'Deal,' I whispered.

70

Theo

Elijah finished his phone call and strode across the car park. The guard, Paul, was watching me through the car window.

Cold air swept over me as the door opened and Elijah got into the back seat beside me.

'Are you all right, Theo?' He smiled. 'I'm sorry we had to chloroform you. It's a very old-fashioned method.'

I shivered. My head still felt horribly fuzzy. 'Where am I? Why have you taken me?'

Elijah sat back, his expression thoughtful. Outside the car, Paul still hadn't taken his eyes off me.

I shivered.

'So many questions, Theo,' Elijah said softly. 'Let me reassure you, you've only been unconscious a few minutes. You're just a mile or so away from the hotel we found you outside.'

I stared at him, my head clearing.

'How did you know where we . . . I . . . was?'

'I was guessing Rachel would call her parents and that they

would tell her to meet them in the safest place they could think of. We phoned all the public areas, then all the local hotels, asking if you'd been seen. You're quite a memorable trio . . . two young teenagers and a tiny newborn baby . . .'

'So why take *me*?' I said. *Man*, was Mum's warning true? Was this whole business of coming after Rachel really a cover for getting hold of me?

'I see your ego is as strong as ever.' A smug smile curled round Elijah's lips.

Fury roiled inside me.

Outside, Paul tapped on the window. As Elijah rolled it down, Paul's gun was visible inside his jacket.

'Yes?' Elijah said, imperiously.

'Transport will be ready in one hour, sir,' the guard said.

Elijah nodded then closed the window. He checked his watch. He gave a sigh, eyes half closed as if he were deep in thought.

'Shame you have to wait,' I said, sarcastically. 'Guess you're missing your private jet, eh, Elijah?'

Elijah's head jerked round, his eyebrows raised in shock. And then he laughed.

'I forget how like me you are, Theo,' he chuckled.

'Don't start that again,' I said. Last year, in Washington, Elijah had often commented on the similarities between us – how we were both impatient and aloof . . . I knew there was some truth in what he said and I didn't want to think about it. 'Where are you going in one hour? Are you taking me with you?'

'What do *you* think, Theo?' Elijah said. 'Now, please excuse me, I still have arrangements to make.' He got out of the car.

I gritted my teeth. Why did that man always have to talk in riddles?

The car doors locked with a click. I peered through the window. Elijah and the guard were speaking in low voices. Elijah placed something on the roof of the car, then walked away. I strained my eyes to see what he was doing, but he had his back turned to me. More of his bloody arrangements, presumably.

A moment later and Paul reappeared. He leaned against the bonnet, casting occasional vicious glances in my direction.

Long minutes passed. I couldn't work out what was going on. Why was Elijah holding me? Where was he planning on taking me?

At last Paul pulled a pack of sandwiches out of a small rucksack. My stomach rumbled and I suddenly realised how hungry I was.

The same thought seemed to have occurred to Paul.

He came round to the far door and unlocked the car. I glanced at his gun as he passed one of the sandwiches across the back seat towards me.

'Any chance of a drink?' I said.

Paul swore and slammed the door shut, relocking it with a sharp click.

I ate greedily. After another few minutes, Elijah

appeared by the hut on the far side of the car park. 'Paul!' he shouted.

Paul straightened up from the car. 'Sir?' he yelled back.

'Inside!' Elijah shouted. 'Now.'

Now what was happening? I strained to see beyond Elijah, to the interior of the building, but it was too far away. Muttering under his breath, Paul chucked the remains of his own sandwich onto the floor and jogged off. As he ran he reached behind him, pointing the car's centralised locking device towards me. I heard the click.

I froze in mid-chew. Paul had already locked the car when he'd handed me my sandwich. Which meant that click had surely just *unlocked* it? I reached for the nearest door. *Yes.* It opened.

Swallowing the bread in my mouth, I got out, keeping low behind the car. Paul was already inside the brick building at the end of the car park. There was no sign of Elijah – or anyone else.

And the phone Elijah had been using earlier was *still* on the car roof. Unable to believe my luck I snatched it up and ran as fast as I could across the wasteland, towards the buildings in the distance.

I reached the edge of the wasteland, vaulted over the low fence that separated it from the pavement and sped along the street. I could see another road up ahead – cars racing along it. I didn't know where I was or where I was going . . . I just wanted to get as far away as possible. I turned onto the busy street. There were shops at the end. Another street. I dashed along, my breath coming in rasping gasps.

I stopped at last in the shadowy gap between two buildings. At least there were people about now.

Think, Theo.

I needed to get further away, but where . . .?

I glanced down at Elijah's phone. With a jolt I realised it was *my* phone. Which meant that Rachel's number was programmed into it.

As I thought of her, my stomach flipped over.

And in an instant I knew that it didn't matter if Rachel did things I didn't understand, like obsessing over keeping Grace. She and I were bound together in a way that I could never have imagined before.

Whatever she did, I loved her.

I scrolled down to her number and pressed *call*.

71

Rachel

I wrote the note and left it by the bed, then slipped out of the room. I left the hotel via the fire escape then cut round to the front of the building where the taxi rank was situated.

'Where to, hen?' My driver had a thick Scottish accent and a friendly smile.

'Bressenden shopping centre, please.' I settled back into the taxi, realising as I did so that I'd left the hotel without a thing – no spare clothes, not even a toothbrush.

It didn't matter.

Nothing mattered now. I'd lost Grace. And in a few minutes I was going to have to tell Theo that I didn't want to see him any more.

I couldn't see how my life could get much worse.

The taxi reached the shopping centre. Milo was clearly visible out the front of the mall, wheeling back and forth in his wheelchair. Even from this distance he looked nervous.

As I directed the taxi driver to pull up beside him, Milo smiled with relief.

No, it was more than relief.

'Hi, Rachel,' he said, reaching out to open my door.

The cold air was like a slap in the face.

Milo didn't take his eyes off me.

'It's so good to see you,' he said.

My insides gave a sickening lurch.

'Hi, Milo.' I looked round. No sign of Elijah's bodyguards at least.

Not that it made any difference.

Milo turned to pay the taxi driver, just as my phone started ringing.

I stared down at the screen where his name was flashing up at me: *Theo*.

I swallowed, taking a beat before answering.

I had to make this work.

72

Theo

Rachel answered on the third ring.

A wave of relief washed over me at the sound of her voice.

'Rach? It's me. Elijah took me but I got away.'

'You're kidding,' she gasped. 'God, are you all right?'

Something was wrong. I could hear it in her voice.

'I'm fine,' I said. 'Are you still at the hotel?'

'Yes, oh thank goodness you're all right.' Rachel stopped.

There was definitely something wrong.

'Rachel—?'

'Go back to the hotel. My mum and dad can pay for a cab if you can find one.'

There was a pause. My mind was careering about, desperately trying to work out what was going on.

'What's the matter, Rach?' I said.

'Noth—'

'I can hear it in your voice. What's going on?'

There was a long pause. Cars zoomed past me.

'Mum and Dad sent Grace away,' she said.

'I'm sorry,' I said.

'And I'm going away, too,' she said.

'What d'you mean?' My voice rose in alarm. 'Going where? When will you be back?'

There was a long silence.

'Rachel?'

'I won't be back,' Rachel said, her voice carefully even. 'I'm sorry.'

'What are you talking about?'

I could hear Rachel take in a deep breath. Then she said it. 'I'm going away . . . with Milo.'

For a second I couldn't work out who she was talking about. Then I remembered.

'Going with *Milo*?' I said. 'Why? Where?'

'We're running away from Elijah,' Rachel went on, her voice strained.

'You're not making sense,' I said. 'You already *have* run away from Elijah. We both did. And Milo's the one who tricked you into *going* to him . . . Man, he *works* for Elijah, he—'

'Elijah made him trap me,' Rachel said. 'Milo only did it because he was scared. But since then we've got to know each other and Milo knows Elijah better than anyone. He knows all about his work . . . the way he thinks . . . he's in the best position to keep me safe.'

I stood in the chill of the shadowy wall, sweat prickling at my neck.

'Is someone there?' I said. 'Someone *making* you say this?

Because I don't get it, Rachel. Why would you go with *Milo* to be safe?'

'You're just saying that cos he's in a wheelchair, aren't you?' Rachel said, accusingly. 'God, Theo, you're so immature sometimes. Milo might not be able to use his legs but he's really kind – look at the way he looked after Grace. And he's really smart too. He's older than we are . . . he *knows* stuff . . .'

'I didn't mean that,' I said, stung. 'I just mean there are loads of people who can keep you safe. There's your mum and dad and Lewis, when he's better, and . . . and *me*.'

'I hate Mum and Dad. They've stopped me being with Grace. They don't care about me. And Lewis might not *get* better. Anyway, you don't understand.' Rachel's voice grew even more tense. 'I *want* to be with Milo.'

Want?

'You mean you . . .?' I couldn't bring myself to finish the sentence. My stomach was twisting into sick knots.

'I like him,' she said at last.

In the distance, traffic roared past but all my focus was on what Rachel was saying.

'I *really* like him,' she went on. 'More than anyone, *ever*.'

More than me?

'I'm sorry, Theo. I'm really sorry, but I want to be with him. He . . . he told me how he felt at the lab, while you were outside. I've had a chance to think and . . . and I want to be with him.'

I couldn't believe it. I mean, I'd seen with my own eyes how Milo felt about Rachel, but . . .

'You hardly know him,' I said.

'You and I hardly knew each other either before we got separated nine months ago. It didn't stop us staying in touch . . . *wanting* to stay in touch . . .'

That was true, but it still didn't make sense. For the past nine months Rachel had been this constant presence in my mind – my secret girlfriend, the one person who knew me, who *understood* me . . .

And now she was saying none of that mattered. I couldn't speak.

'Like I said, I'm sorry. But you must have felt it yourself. I mean, I really care about you, Theo. But not like that. We don't really know each other . . . us . . . being together . . . it was a mistake . . .' Her voice was cold now. Hard.

'*What?*' I couldn't believe it. Maybe we'd both felt a bit self-conscious for the first few minutes back on the RAGE boat, but after that we'd been fine. And at the hotel, just now, she'd smiled at me . . . kissed me . . .

'I have to go. When you get to the hotel, please explain it to my parents. I left them a note but I know they'll freak. Tell them I'll be in touch when I can. And tell Lewis too.'

I stood there, my mouth open, the world turning circles in my head.

'Theo?'

'Yes.'

'Thanks for everything. Goodbye.'

She rang off and I stood, staring out at the cars still zooming past, wondering how the world could still look exactly the same, when everything that mattered had just fallen out of it.

Part Three

Operation Eos

73

Rachel

The next few hours were the longest of my life. After saying goodbye to Theo, I was in a total daze. I ditched my phone so I couldn't be traced – at Milo's request – then took a cab with him to a heliport a few miles away. I didn't notice where, exactly.

We'd taken off straight away – Elijah, his guard Paul, Milo and me.

I tortured myself for a while that Elijah had ordered Theo to be killed before we left. Paul certainly looked murderous enough – he was clearly still furious about Theo and me tying him up outside Lab Three.

But I knew that didn't make sense. Elijah might be an ego-maniac but he wasn't stupid. He never acted without a reason. Mel died because she chose Lewis instead of him – that was revenge. Daniel died because Elijah wanted his heart, and there was no one to stop him taking it.

Elijah had no reason to kill Theo. In fact, murder would simply invite the authorities to come after him.

I was what Elijah wanted now.

And what Elijah wanted, he got.

As we banked over the buildings below, I thought about Mum and Dad in the hotel – and how Theo would tell them I had gone . . . how they would find my note . . . how Mum would get all hysterical and Dad would worry and then, later, Lewis in hospital would find out and turn it all over and over in his mind as he got better . . . If he got better . . .

And Theo. I'd heard the hollowness in his voice when I'd told him we were over. The misery. I couldn't bear him to believe that . . . to move on . . . to forget me . . .

And yet, I knew this was the only way to keep him from following me . . . to keep him safe.

Tears trickled down my face. I closed my eyes and turned my head further away from the others.

I couldn't tell which direction we were heading in, but we were over water very quickly. After twenty minutes or so, Elijah shifted across the row of seats and positioned himself next to me.

'You should sleep, Rachel. I want you well.'

I shook my head. No way was I going to be able to sleep. Not tonight.

Elijah sighed. 'I must insist,' he said, moving away again.

I found out what *that* meant a few minutes later when he reappeared with a syringe.

'This will help you relax,' he said.

'*No.*'

Elijah ran his hand through his hair. 'Please don't make me get Paul over here to restrain you,' he said.

Over his shoulder I could see Paul watching. *God*, he looked *really* pissed off.

'It's just to help you sleep, Rachel. I realise how traumatic today has been.' He paused. 'Please.'

What choice did I have? I nodded, and he injected me in the arm. I felt the stab of the needle, then the coldness of the liquid entering my vein. Moments later I sank back, reality obliterated.

It was morning when I woke. I was in a bright, sunny room. The central heating was gurgling as I blinked myself awake. I was in my clothes still, but in a proper bed. I sat up and looked around. Not a large room – or a fancy one – but clean and very white. White walls, a white duvet and white curtains.

I got out of bed and tiptoed across the wooden floor to the window.

Whoa. The view that met my eyes was the last one I expected to see at the beginning of July.

Snow. Snow *everywhere*. A beautiful landscape of fields and distant mountains. Snow-covered pine trees lined the area immediately below the house, which sloped down to a frozen lake. The sky was a clear, bright blue – the sun a fiery orange disc, well above the trees.

Where on earth was I?

I looked round the room again. Someone had laid a blue

towel and a change of clothes on the chair next to the bed. The clock on the wall said it was seven a.m. There was a white wooden wardrobe – empty – and an open door in the corner leading into a small shower room.

The other door was shut. I walked over and pulled on the handle. Locked.

Despite the radiator below the window belting heat into the room, I shivered. I went back to the bed. A blue blanket had been folded up at the end of it. I wrapped this round me and sat down, my mind running over the possibilities.

Provided I hadn't somehow lost an entire day, there was no way I could have travelled all the way to the southern hemisphere since leaving Scotland, which meant that I must have come north. A long way north, like maybe somewhere in Scandinavia? That would explain why the sun was so high in the sky, even though it was only seven a.m.

After a few minutes, I heard a key turn in the lock of my door. Elijah came in. He looked tired but was neatly dressed, as usual, in what looked like a very expensive suit.

'Good, you're awake,' he said.

'Where am I?' I said.

Ignoring this, he indicated the shower room and the clothes on the chair.

'Wash and change. I'll be back in ten minutes.' He left.

I did as he said. To be honest, despite the anxiety gnawing away at my guts, it felt good to feel the powerful jets of warm water on my back. I hadn't had a proper wash since nearly drowning on Calla. The little shower room had been set out with a range of bottles. I couldn't read most of the labels – they were in a foreign language – but it was easy enough to work out which was shampoo, and I scrubbed at my hair til it squeaked.

The clothes were nothing special: a long-sleeved top which was too old for me, and some leggings and warm boots.

Elijah returned, as promised, when the ten minutes were up. He ushered me through the door without speaking. My room was at the end of a corridor. Two doors led off on either side.

'Other bedrooms and a bathroom,' Elijah said, when I asked what they were.

The house we were in was a sort of chalet. Bare and minimalist, the furniture was almost all made of wood, as were the floors and stairs. These led down to an open-plan living/dining area with a TV and two sofas at one end, a wooden table set against the window and a galley kitchen beyond. Milo was at the hob, bent over a frying pan. He was wearing a black beanie hat that made him look younger, even more like Theo than usual.

The smell of bacon wafted towards us.

I suddenly realised how hungry I was. I hadn't eaten since I'd been in the café with Lewis and Theo. That seemed a million years ago now.

As Elijah and I walked over to the table, Milo glanced nervously at Elijah.

'I'm cooking pancakes and bacon and there's maple syrup too,' he said.

'Where's my coffee?' Elijah demanded.

'Just coming.' Milo shot a swift smile at me and wheeled himself back to the kitchen.

We sat down at the table. I was still struggling to take everything in.

'Where are we?' I asked.

Elijah sat back in his chair and sighed. 'Okay, Rachel, some answers. But first, here are the things you should know. The nearest village is over a mile away, with very limited transport facilities and the temperature outside is sub-zero, so please do not think about attempting to leave. I do not intend to keep locking you in your room and you are free to walk around the house and the grounds, though please be careful of the electric fence. It will knock you out if you touch it. We left John behind in Scotland, of course, but Paul is still with us to provide security. He is resting upstairs in one of the bedrooms right now, but he will be patrolling the grounds at night. Milo has the chalet maid's room.' Elijah pointed to a door next to the kitchen area.

'So where's your clinic . . . your lab?' I said. 'Where do you work?'

'Nearby,' Elijah said, with a vague wave of his hand.

I looked down at the smooth wood of the table. 'You said you'd give me answers and you're not,' I said, anger mounting inside me. I'd agreed to Elijah's stupid deal but he wasn't even prepared to give me the most basic bits of information. 'I asked where we were.'

'I *am* giving you answers – to the questions that are

290

important right now.' Elijah sighed again as Milo trundled over with a cup of black coffee.

He waited till Milo set the cup down on the table and turned away then spoke again, a note of irritation in his voice. '*Clearly*, Rachel, we are not in the UK any more. But it doesn't matter exactly where we are. In fact, it's better that you don't know. What's important is that you don't think about running off. Not just because of the consequences to Theo, but because you won't get very far.'

'So what are you going to do with me?' I said, trying to control my temper. There was no point losing it with Elijah. 'You said these tests wouldn't take long, but I don't understand what it is you're trying to do . . .'

'Okay.' Elijah took a swig of coffee. 'I already told you that my cloning experiment was an attempt to recreate the Eos protein in your blood, but that none of the clones I created *contained* it.'

'And this Eos protein supposedly saves lives?' I said.

'It *does* save lives,' Elijah said. 'At least, it will.'

'How?' I said.

'Okay.' Elijah cleared his throat. 'The Eos protein mimics the actions of a set of known proteins called sirtuins.'

'Sir . . . *what*?'

'Sirtuins. We already know that these are activated by the chemical resveratrol, but . . . anyway . . . the Eos protein is far more powerful than these sirtuins. My early research suggests that Eos has the potential to strengthen the body's resistance to the degenerative diseases of ageing.'

'Will it protect *me* from ageing?' I asked.

'No, you're just a carrier, but if I can extract it from your blood successfully then the scientific benefits will be enormous.'

And the financial rewards. I thought this, but didn't say it.

I kept my gaze on Elijah. It suddenly crossed my mind just how was weird it was that his face would be Theo's face when Theo was much, much older. Elijah ran his hand through his hair. The same gesture I'd so often seen Theo make.

'I've told you everything I know, Rachel,' he said earnestly. 'I will perform my tests. You will be safe. No one will suffer. And the world will benefit beyond anyone's wildest dreams.'

He was lying. I couldn't be sure exactly which part of what he said was the lie but I was sure there something else . . . some catch he wasn't about to reveal.

I sat back. 'I still don't see why you need me *here*,' I said. 'I mean, you took loads of my blood back on Calla. You could easily have brought that with you and done more tests on it.'

'I need fresh blood,' Elijah explained. 'The Eos protein in your blood is one of the most unstable materials I've ever worked with. Once I've taken it from you, it's only potent . . . viable . . . for about two hours. After that, the protein mutates . . . stops working in the same way. I need a regular supply of fresh blood in order to give myself time to work out how to synthesise . . . copy . . . the protein.'

292

I stared at him. 'So you're going to keep taking blood from me?'

'Yes, just a few drops at a time.' Elijah produced a small box from which he drew a little disc with a pin attached. 'This is an easy, pain-free way of doing just that. Diabetics use these all the time to test their blood sugar levels.'

He took my hand and pressed the pin on the disc into my finger. It stung for a second. He held my finger so the blood dripped into the empty box. Two . . . three drops. Then he let go.

I sucked on the tip of my finger. The sting had already gone.

Elijah stood up as Milo wheeled over with a plate of food.

He looked at Milo and the plate dismissively. 'Keep mine hot, I'll have something in an hour or so.'

Milo nodded, his face expressionless. He set the plate down in front of me.

'I'm sure I'll be able to achieve what I'm aiming to do here, Rachel,' Elijah went on. 'Then you will be free.'

My heart seemed to constrict in my chest. It didn't matter how many times Elijah tried to reassure me, I didn't . . . couldn't . . . believe his plan was as straightforward as he made out.

'How long will your tests take?' I asked.

'This I cannot say. I would hope no more than a week or two. Then you can return home to your parents.'

But not to Theo. He won't ever want me back, not after what I've just put him through.

'You'll really let me go?'

'Once I've produced a working synthesis, yes.'

Right. Again, I couldn't trust what he said. I mean, he sounded so reasonable, but he'd told me about the Eos protein . . . and I could identify his chalet . . . surely I knew too much for Elijah to ever let me go?

'In the meantime,' Elijah went on, 'I'm afraid there's no phone and no internet access, but there are some wonderful books in the library next to the sun porch which I think you are of an age to enjoy. Plus there is Milo to entertain you. I'm sorry, but you will have no contact with the outside world for a while.' He paused. 'I came to this place a long time ago, when I was first on the run from RAGE. It has always brought me good luck before . . .'

As he left the chalet, Milo wheeled over with his own plate of food. We ate in silence for a minute or so.

'Was that true about there being no internet connection?' I said.

'Yeah, and the TV isn't wired up either.' Milo made a face then smiled gently. 'It's real nice to see you again, Rachel.'

I nodded. Oh *God*, I was going to have to resume my pretence at friendliness with Milo in the hope that it would win me more information. I glanced at Milo's black beanie.

'Your hat looks good on you,' I said, biting into a piece of bacon.

Milo smiled, his face reddening a little.

I swallowed the bacon. 'Er . . . so where's this library?'

'Through there.' Milo pointed beyond the kitchen area, to

where the room angled round in an L-shape. Taking another piece of bacon, I went over. Here, the room narrowed into a dark corridor lined from top to bottom with shelves full of books. I walked along, peering at the titles. A lot of books in a foreign language I didn't recognise. Then a whole section of classic English writers: people I'd done – or heard of – at school, like Charles Dickens and Charlotte Bronte, plus loads of others. A shelf of modern paperbacks stood at the end.

The corridor bent around again, in another L-shape. I followed it and the room suddenly opened up into what, I realised immediately, must be the sun porch. Floor-to-ceiling windows – and a French door that opened onto a balcony – looked out over acres of white snow. A stream ran through a pine forest over to the right – presumably leading round the chalet and down to the lake on the other side.

In the distance I could just make out Elijah, hands deep in the pockets of his greatcoat, trudging towards what looked like some sort of concrete bunker rising up out of the ground.

Was that where he was carrying out all his tests?

With a jolt I realised that maybe Elijah was telling the truth about not hurting me, but lying about what this Eos protein did. He'd said it would 'save lives' but maybe it was actually harmful . . . even evil.

Oh God. It hadn't even occurred to me before that by sacrificing myself to save Theo, I might end up condemning far more people to some awful fate.

Trying not to think about this, I looked round the sun porch. Like everywhere else in the chalet it was warm and bright and comfortable, full of red padded armchairs and a long brown couch, with ornaments on the tables and an art deco clock on the wall.

A squeaking noise sounded behind me, and Milo appeared, my breakfast plate in his hand. 'Here.' He offered it to me, shyly.

'Thanks.' With a great effort I smiled at him. 'Why don't you bring your food in here too?'

'Sure.' Smiling, he wheeled himself off.

I sank into one of the armchairs. Outside, in the distance, Elijah had reached the concrete bunker. He stood by the door. After a few seconds, it slid open and he disappeared inside.

One thing was for sure: somehow I was going to find a way inside that place myself and discover all I could about the Eos protein and exactly how Elijah was planning on using it.

74

Theo

I couldn't stop thinking about her. How could she have fallen for Milo so soon? Maybe it was that syndrome I'd read about where, after a while, kidnapped people develop feelings for their captors. Except Rachel had only been on Calla a few days.

Of course Milo did look a lot like me, and Rachel had liked me once, so maybe that made everything happen faster . . .

I wandered around for a couple of hours, unwilling to go back to the hotel. In the end a combination of gnawing hunger and lack of money sent me back. As I trudged in through the lobby doors, I tried to force myself to accept what had happened.

It didn't matter how much I agonised over it – Rachel didn't want me any more. She'd chosen someone else. And I was just going to have to get used to that fact.

I still felt worse than I'd ever felt in my life.

I took the lift straight up to the room we'd checked into

earlier. Rachel's parents answered the door together when I knocked.

Rachel's dad grabbed my arm, his face desperate.

'Have you seen her?' he said. 'Do you know where she's gone?'

I stared at him. 'She said she was leaving you a note.'

'She spoke to you? When?' Mrs Smith gasped. Her eyes looked red and sore. 'Oh, Richard.'

She reached for her husband's arm, but he had turned away to pick up a piece of paper. He thrust it in my face. I was still standing in the doorway.

'This is what she left,' Mr Smith said, angrily. 'What else do you know, Theo?'

I glanced down at the note.

Dear Mum and Dad

If you don't want Grace, you can't really want me. I know that you love me and I love you too. And I know that you've been through so much thinking I was dead, then getting me back, but I don't belong at home any more. I want to be with someone else. Milo is another clone of Elijah's. He's lived with him and worked with him and he knows everything about him. Please believe that Milo loves me. He only wants to help me and keep me safe. I will get in touch when I can – and I will see you both again soon.

Please look after yourselves and tell Lewis the same.

Lots of love to you both. Rx

'Well?' Mr Smith stared accusingly at me.

I shuffled from foot to foot. A chambermaid walked along the hotel corridor past us. She cast us a curious glance.

I suddenly felt completely humiliated. How could Rachel do this? How could she just up and turn her back on me?

'What she says in the note is what she said to me,' I mumbled, my face burning. I looked down at the carpet. 'I don't know any more.'

Mr Smith sighed, slumping sideways against the wall. His wife turned on her heel and stalked away across the room. Mr Smith stepped back, giving me room to walk inside, and when he spoke again, his voice was softer.

'Come in, Theo.'

He shut the door after me and indicated I should take one of the chairs by the window. I sat down and he sat opposite me, on the bed. Mrs Smith paced up and down.

'I thought you and Rachel were . . .' Mr Smith hesitated, clearly trying to find the right phrase, '. . . er, going out together?'

I shook my head. *Apparently not.*

'Who is this Milo?' Mrs Smith snapped angrily. 'How does Rachel know him?'

I told her what I knew.

'Why on earth does Ro think she can trust this guy?' her dad asked, an expression of complete bewilderment on his face.

I thought back to the way Milo had looked at Rachel in Lab Three . . . how he'd let her walk away without shooting.

'He thinks he's in love with her,' I said.

Mrs Smith snorted. 'And how would you know that?'

Because I am too.

I said nothing.

Mr Smith sighed again.

'What are you going to do?' I asked.

'I've been onto the police,' Mr Smith said.

I opened my mouth to protest that this could lead Elijah straight to us, but he silenced me with his hand.

'I deliberately haven't gone to the people who organised our relocation. Rachel told us it was one of our own agents – a government contact – who gave her new identity away in the first place,' he said. 'We don't know who we can trust there yet, so I've just told the local police that our daughter is missing again. Of course they all thought she was dead, so I'm having an uphill struggle getting anyone to believe she's run away.'

'Frankly, I don't think they're that bothered,' Mrs Smith snapped. 'You were far too conciliatory on the phone, Richard.'

'I was trying to be diplomatic,' Mr Smith protested.

'Is that what you call it.' She turned to me. 'When they heard about Rachel's note, they strongly implied that if she'd gone of her own free will and was less than two months away from her sixteenth birthday that finding her wasn't really a top priority.'

'I know, but—' Mr Smith started.

'But it *should* be a top priority, Richard,' Mrs Smith

300

shrieked. Her mouth was set in a thin line. 'You should be *pushing* them to make it one.'

They started arguing, Mrs Smith slinging insults at her husband and Mr Smith trying to calm her down. After a minute, Mrs Smith turned on me.

'Did you do something to upset her?' she demanded.

My mouth fell open. '*No*,' I said. 'Lewis and I *found* her . . . we *rescued* her.'

'So what are you saying?' Mrs Smith went on. 'That her father and I didn't do enough?'

I stared at her.

Mr Smith stood up. 'Sweetheart, I think—'

'Get out!' Mrs Smith shouted at me. Spit flew out of her primly lipsticked mouth. 'Get out of my sight.'

I stood up. That was fine by me.

'Wait.' Mr Smith turned to his wife. 'We can't just turn him out onto the streets—'

'It's fine,' I said.

'Well, if you won't send him away, then I'm leaving.' Mrs Smith stalked across the room and walked out, slamming the door behind her.

Mr Smith sank down on the bed, his head in his hands.

Several moments passed.

'Er . . . I should go,' I said.

Mr Smith blinked as if he'd forgotten I was in the room. He looked at me with a rueful smile.

'You can't just walk out, Theo. We need to get onto your mother in the States. Organise getting you home,' he said.

I made a face. Going back to Philadelphia was the last thing I wanted.

And yet . . . what was to keep me here any more?

Mr Smith called Mum, who was still furious with me. It was too late to book me on a flight to Philly that day, but she and Mr Smith arranged a ticket for me for a plane the next evening. Mum made it quite clear I'd be spending the rest of the summer doing chores to pay her back for the ticket.

I said nothing, but the more I thought about it, the less I wanted to go.

Rachel or no Rachel, I didn't belong in the States.

But then I didn't belong anywhere.

I didn't much like thinking about it, but being Elijah's genetic twin meant I was biologically the son of his parents: two Nazis who had fled Germany at the end of the Second World War and settled in Argentina, where they'd brought up their only son.

I couldn't imagine a heritage much worse than that, to be honest.

Anyway, I didn't belong in America or Germany or England or Scotland or Argentina.

Suddenly I saw what that meant . . . that the upside of not belonging anywhere was that I was free to choose where I wanted to be.

All I had to do was decide.

Mr Smith sorted a different room for me to stay in and told me to order food from room service. As I was moving there, Mrs Smith returned and the two of them went for 'a walk'.

Which I understood to mean a continuation of their argument.

That was okay with me. I was happy to sit alone with my thoughts.

It was fairly late by then and dark outside. I was exhausted and yet it still took me ages to fall asleep and when I did my dreams were full of visions of Rachel and Milo together.

I was woken, late the next morning, by the phone beside my bed.

It was Mr Smith.

'There's still no news of Rachel,' he said. 'But Lewis has called from the hospital. He's recovered okay from the operation and knows about Rachel. He says he wants to see you and I'd like to talk to him too. Could you be ready in ten minutes? We'll take a cab all the way there – and Lewis is registered under a false name. I think you'll be safe.'

'Sure.' Lewis was just the right person for me to speak to. Like me, he had no real home. He'd understand my situation. Help me decide what to do next.

I hurried down to the lobby where Mr Smith was waiting.

But when I got to the hospital, Lewis told me something that changed everything.

75

Rachel

My first full day in the chalet passed quietly.

I spent most of my time in the sun porch. Milo bustled around in his beanie hat, offering me food and a choice of some old copies of *National Geographic* magazine which he'd found in a kitchen cupboard. I was torn between my natural instinct to tell him to get lost and the knowledge that encouraging him to think I liked him was a sensible tactic.

I tried to read a little, to keep my mind off Theo and Grace and my parents, but the day seemed to stretch on forever. I kept an eye on the bunker. Elijah emerged after a couple of hours, came to the house and took more blood from me, then went back.

I felt like I was on Calla again, but in a proper house with snow instead of an old farmhouse surrounded by the sea.

Elijah came and went again.

I went outside myself. Elijah had provided me with a jumper, hat and scarf. I hated wearing them, I didn't want to have anything to do with his handouts, but it was freezing in

304

the icy air and I was determined to explore the entrance to the bunker at the back of the chalet.

I walked past the frozen lake and round to the wood at the back of the house. It only took a couple of minutes to reach the concrete bunker. In the distance I could clearly see the high electric fence covered with 'danger of death' notices, but there was no sign of Paul.

Taking my courage in my hands, I approached the entrance.

The bunker door, also made from concrete, had no handle, though I knew from watching Elijah that it slid open when he did something to the tiny screen beside it. Trouble was, I couldn't work out *what* he did to open it. The screen was mounted on metal but contained no intercom and no keypad. My first guess was that it was some kind of retinal scanner, like the one in the lab on Calla. However, it was positioned at waist height – so more convenient for hands than eyes.

Whatever it was, it was impossible to get past.

76

Theo

Lewis was asleep when we arrived at the hospital. He looked terrible – even worse than when he'd collapsed – with his skin grey and pallid and a huge bandage round his head.

The nurse who showed us where he was said that he was actually doing really well, but that he got tired quickly, so we shouldn't stay long.

We sat on either side of the bed for a few minutes. Then Mr Smith's phone rang.

He jumped up, guiltily, and rushed out of the ward to take the call.

I leaned forward.

'How are you?' I asked.

'Awesome,' he whispered.

We looked at each other for a moment.

'Who took Rachel?' he said.

'No one.' I looked down, at the weave of the white blanket on his bed. 'She left by herself. She went with Milo.'

'No.' Lewis's voice rose slightly. 'Doesn't make sense.'

I looked up, angry at having to go over this again.

'I'm telling you she went with Milo,' I said bitterly. 'She told me. She *wanted* to. She wanted *him*.'

Lewis's blue eyes met mine. He frowned then shot a sideways glance at his bedside locker. 'Look in there.'

I bent down, wondering what he wanted. The locker was virtually empty – all I could see were the clothes Lewis had been wearing yesterday, when he'd collapsed.

'Pocket,' Lewis ordered.

Grunting, I dug in the trouser pockets. Nothing. I tried the jacket. My hand grasped fine metal. A chain. I pulled it out and held it up.

A silver chain with a tiny 't' on the end. Broken.

I looked at Lewis.

'It's Rachel's,' he whispered. 'She gave it me before we went to Jamieson's office . . . to look after . . . to keep safe . . .'

I stared back at the necklace. It was elegant and simple – a far cry from the chunky beads and gold leaf chain I'd seen in Rachel's bedroom.

This was exactly the kind of jewellery Rachel would wear.

I held the 't' in my palm.

'It's you, man,' Lewis whispered with a smile. 'She told me. I *saw* it. She's got it real bad for you. No way is there anyone else.'

He closed his eyes. I gazed at the 't'. Rachel's name didn't begin with 't'. Her cover name in Roslinnon hadn't begun with 't' . . .

A smile crept over my face.

Lewis' eyes flickered open. He was clearly exhausted at having to force the words out.

'There's something wrong . . .' he said. 'Rachel . . . Elijah . . . don't underestimate Elijah . . .' His eyes shut. Within seconds his breathing had become steady and even.

He was asleep.

Mr Smith reappeared, his eyes full of worry, his mobile in his hand.

'Just had a call from the police,' he said. 'They say two people answering Milo's and Rachel's descriptions were seen yesterday getting into a cab at Bressenden shopping centre. No sign of any force. But they were dropped on an ordinary street. The driver thinks they may have got into another car, but he's not sure.' He glanced at Lewis. 'Did he wake up?'

'For a few seconds,' I said, shoving Rachel's necklace into my pocket. 'He doesn't think Rachel went off with Milo.'

'Well, this latest police report suggests she did, doesn't it?' Mr Smith sighed.

A nurse bustled over to tell us we could only stay another couple of minutes.

Lewis didn't wake up again.

As we left the hospital and travelled back to the hotel, I kept going over what Lewis had said, trying to make sense of all the conflicting bits of information.

Mr Smith came with me up to my room. He took off his jacket and paced up and down.

I got the distinct impression he was avoiding going back to

his wife. Then she rang . . . I could hear her shouting on the other end of the line . . . and he rushed out, leaving his jacket still on the back of my chair.

I took Rachel's silver chain out of my pocket and held it up to the light. It sparkled – as pretty as she was.

I thought about what Lewis had said in the hospital, then went over my phone conversation with Rachel again . . . she'd sounded strange . . . different . . . not just what she was telling me, but the way she was speaking . . .

I closed my eyes. Maybe the truth was staring me in the face and I just couldn't see it because I was still in shock after escaping from Elijah. I'd been lucky to get away from him, though why he'd suddenly tried to kidnap me I couldn't imagine.

At least I'd spoilt his plans.

Or had I?

With a jolt, my eyes shot open. Lewis's parting words echoed in my head.

Don't underestimate Elijah.

I'd escaped from Elijah, at the same time as Rachel was leaving the hotel.

Was that really a coincidence? What if the two things were connected?

What if I hadn't escaped at all? It was hardly like Elijah or his men to be as careless as Paul had been, not locking that car door.

What if they'd *let* me escape?

Adrenalin surged through me as the pieces fell into place.

Rachel *was* with Milo. But she was with Elijah too.

309

She'd sacrificed her own freedom to buy mine.

That's why her lies about Milo made no sense. *That's* why I'd got away from Elijah so easily myself. And *that's* why she'd asked Lewis to look after this 't' on a chain like it was her most treasured possession.

How could I have been so stupid?

I paced across the room. If Elijah still had Rachel, then I *had* to find her . . . and fast.

The last time I'd let him escape with someone I cared about, an innocent little boy ended up dead.

I caught sight of Mr Smith's jacket hanging on the back of my chair. Should I wait for him to come back and tell him what I was now sure of?

I hesitated. The Smiths just wanted to be shot of me. And even if they believed what I was saying, they couldn't do more than they were already doing to find Rachel through the police. Why worry them futher?

I would have told Lewis, but he was still so ill . . . and clearly in no position to help me.

No. Whatever I did now, I would do on my own. I didn't have much to go on, but maybe I could make a virtue out of operating on a small scale.

I knew where Elijah had been holding me. I'd go back there, see what clues I could pick up. Mr Smith had said that the trail on Rachel and Milo went cold when they left their cab. Supposed they'd switched to one of Elijah's cars . . . maybe even that car I'd been held in at the deserted car park? At least I could see if it was still there.

I walked to the door, past Mr Smith's jacket, still hanging over the chair.

I wouldn't get anywhere without money. I hesitated for a second then fished his wallet out of his inside pocket. I took all his cash – £250 – then scrawled I.O.U. in big letters with the pen and paper from the hotel room desk.

It was a start.

I shoved the money into my pocket, and headed out into the morning.

77

Rachel

I'd spent the rest of the day wandering down by the frozen lake. I'd realised that my broken silver chain was missing. I'd left it for safe keeping with Lewis before going into Jamieson's office. I had no idea what would have happened to it in the hospital or if I'd ever see it again.

Stupid, I know, but that little 't' had become like a security blanket to me and I felt lost without it.

Elijah reappeared, stomping round to the back door, at about midday. Milo called me inside for some food soon after. He was still wearing that black beanie hat. He hadn't taken it off, in fact, since I told him he looked good in it.

Elijah was already munching away at his lunch – pasta with tomato sauce. I fetched a plate for myself and sat opposite him. He looked drawn and tired and was clearly in a foul mood, snapping at Milo to bring him a glass of water.

After he'd eaten, he took more blood from me, then went back to the bunker. I sidled up to Milo, who was stacking our plates in the dishwasher. I leaned down to insert my glass in the top tray. Our heads collided.

'Ow, sorry,' I said.

Milo rubbed his forehead and smiled. 'My bad – I should have looked where I was going.'

He shut up the dishwasher. We were uncomfortably close to each other now. I looked away, feeling his eyes on my face.

'How're you doing?' he said gently.

I shrugged. Maybe this was an opportunity to get him talking.

'It would help if I knew why I was here . . . what this Eos protein in my blood is really all about,' I said.

There was a pause. Milo's eyes were still fixed on my face.

'I told you what I know, that it will "save lives",' he whispered. 'But you know Elijah doesn't talk to me. He just said it's big. *Really* big. As big as his cloning experiments.'

'Is that what he's doing in that bunker of his?'

'You don't want to know what he's doing in there.' Milo shuddered.

'What does that mean?'

Milo turned away and wheeled across to the sink. I followed him.

'Milo? Talk to me.'

He ran the tap and washed his hands. 'I can't tell you any more,' he said softly. 'But as far as Elijah's concerned the Eos protein's potential completely justifies what he's doing.'

'Which is *what*?' I said.

Milo shook his head.

'Please tell me,' I said, my mind racing. What on earth could Elijah possibly be doing with a few drops of blood in a sealed bunker that was so awful? 'Milo?' I went on. 'Do you think what Elijah is doing is justified?'

But Milo refused to say another word.

78

Theo

I traced my route back to the car park easily enough, but the car I'd been held in was no longer there and I couldn't find any clue to Elijah's whereabouts either in the little hut in the corner or outside it. As I crossed the empty tarmac, I realised just how hopeless my situation was.

A couple of hundred pounds might be a start, but it wouldn't get me very far . . . and it certainly wasn't going to buy me the information that I needed. The truth was, Elijah could have left the area on any kind of transport and gone in any direction.

And I had no idea about either.

The sky clouded over as I reached the patch of car park nearest the canal. This was where Elijah's car had been parked. I looked round. The tarmac was clear, right up to the kerb that marked the boundary with the canal path on one side and the wasteland beyond. I wandered over to the water and stared in. It was stagnant and slimy by the bank, smelling of damp and mould. I trudged along the path to the wasteland, following the kerb along to the exact parking space Elijah's car had used before. There was nothing here, just a load of litter – crisp packets and cans, mostly – alongside some dried-up dog poo.

It was a depressing place and I was now thoroughly depressed myself. I'd been so sure I'd discover a clue here. It was hard to accept I was no closer to finding Rachel.

There was a roar in the air nearby. The wind swirled around me and some of the litter scudded into the canal and across the stagnant water.

I looked up. A helicopter was rising into the air nearby. I was close enough to make out the logo on the side – it showed a number of swirling lines, with the name *Amarta* printed across the middle. I'd seen the logo before somewhere . . .

Of course.

It was Don Jamieson's company logo. I'd noticed it on the front of the reception desk when I'd followed Lewis inside.

Why hadn't I thought of that before? Elijah had used one of Jamieson's helicopters to get off Calla. Maybe he'd used one to get away from here, too.

I raced across the car park towards the place I thought the helicopter had come from. Past the hut was a row of fairly run-down warehouses. No cars. I could see more traffic in the road beyond, where three women with pushchairs had stopped for a chat in the street.

I raced over and asked them if there was a heliport nearby. They looked at me as if I were mad and said they had no idea.

I ran on, up and down the nearby streets. I tried to be systematic, but it was hard without any kind of map. In the end I stopped a couple of workmen who pointed me in the right direction, and a few minutes later I arrived, panting, at Charnhill Heliport.

The man on reception wasn't very helpful at first, but when I persisted, another guy and a woman came out. I spun them a huge sob story about my disabled brother . . . bla, bla, bla . . . and in the end the second guy admitted seeing Milo boarding a copter late last night.

They refused to tell me where the copter had gone, of course, but I waited outside the heliport and when the guy's shift was over, sometime around four p.m., I approached him, and explained it was really important I found Milo because he'd left home after an argument with our dad and now my dad was seriously ill and I was just desperate to reach my brother before our dad died so they could be reconciled in time.

A load of bollocks, I know, but my desperate 'brothers in crisis' story did the trick – though probably only because I did look so incredibly like Milo.

Eventually the guy went back inside, checked the log and told me that the copter had been heading for a place called Tromstorm in Norway.

Yes.

Almost as soon as I'd felt the sensation of triumph, it faded. How on earth was I going to get to some remote place in a country I knew nothing about? For a moment I strongly considered going back to the hotel and telling Rachel's parents what I'd discovered. After all, Rachel had said she was with Milo. Surely they'd want to follow the lead?

Maybe, but they'd still insist on sending me back to Philadelphia.

In fact, *crap* . . . I checked the time. I was supposed to be on a flight bound for Philadelphia right now. Which meant that not only had I stolen Mr Smith's money, I'd also wasted the ticket Mum had bought me.

They would both be furious. Which settled it.

I was on my own.

I found an internet café and worked out my route. It wasn't straightforward. I needed to take a bus, which I knew would be cheaper than a train, across Scotland to Aberdeen, then two ferries – one from Aberdeen to a remote island called Lerwick and from there another ferry to Bergen in Norway.

I had no idea how I was going to get up to Tromstorm once I arrived in Norway but at least now I knew where I was going.

79

Rachel

I still had no idea exactly where I was, though I knew it had to be somewhere really far north. At night it had stayed light until about eleven p.m. and the sun was always high in the sky whenever I woke, even at four or five in the morning.

Two more long days had passed in much the same manner as the first.

The only change was in Elijah's mood. He was becoming increasingly irritable, liable to snap at someone just for walking past him.

He was rude to me, and to Paul, but he saved his worst behaviour for Milo, never missing an opportunity to criticise him or put him down.

We all avoided him as much as possible.

On the evening of my third day, I was searching the bookshelves in the corridor between the kitchen/diner and the sun porch. If I had to be here, then I might as well find something interesting to read. Raised voices drifted up from the lake. I rushed through to the kitchen, where Milo was already staring out of the window.

It was late – nearly eleven p.m., but still light. Paul was down by the lake, gun in one hand, radio mic in the other.

He was pointing his weapon at a red-haired woman in a long brown coat. She was talking fast. I could only catch the occasional word . . . *must speak . . . Elijah Lazio . . . important . . .*

'What's going on?' I said to Milo.

'No idea,' he said. 'Paul caught her trying to cross the lake just now. Not that I think she was sneaking around, particularly. And that coat isn't exactly spy wear.'

'I'm going to find out what she wants,' I said. And, before Milo could say anything, I was out of the door and racing across the sloping garden, down to the lake.

Paul looked alarmed as I approached. 'Go back inside,' he ordered.

I ignored him. Let him manhandle me back if he wanted to. There was no way he was going to hurt me; Elijah wanted me – and my blood – in good health.

The woman in the brown coat looked at me with intense interest. She was maybe in her late twenties and strikingly beautiful – her red hair streaked with natural highlights and her eyes a bright, emerald green. She wore warm designer boots and had a large brown leather satchel looped over her shoulder.

'Rachel?' she said.

'Who are you?' I said.

'Get inside, Rachel,' Paul ordered.

I shook my head.

The woman smiled – a soft smile, though it didn't reach her eyes.

'My name's Amanda Lennox,' she said. 'I've heard a lot about you, Rachel.'

Paul was speaking into his radio mic now – his voice low and menacing – but I kept my gaze on the woman.

'Yeah?' I said. 'What have you heard about me?'

'Well,' Amanda Lennox said. 'I know that you're a clone and that Elijah Lazio created you. And I know about his current work – and how that involves you too.' She paused, patting the leather bag.

'What do you know?' I said, my throat tightening. 'Why are you here?'

Amanda Lennox just smiled.

Paul came off the radio mic and turned to the woman. 'Elijah's coming.'

'Good,' she said. 'I'll explain everything properly when he gets here. It's about RAGE . . . I've been working for them, but I'm not any more. Elijah Lazio is going to want to hear what they know about his plans.'

80

Theo

It had taken me a long time to get here, but I was in Norway at last.

I spent my first night of travelling – the second since Rachel had disappeared – on the coach to Aberdeen. I was horrified to discover when I arrived there at six the next morning that there was only one ferry a day from Aberdeen to the island of Lerwick – and it didn't leave until five p.m.

I bought a ticket for later and wandered off to find food, then shelter from the rain which had just started drizzling. I spent part of the morning huddled on a park bench. Well, maybe 'park' is a bit of an exaggeration. More like a patch of dry grass with a few bushes and a couple of trees.

The worst part of being in the park was remembering how Rachel and I had hidden out somewhere similar – though smarter – in Washington D.C. last year. We'd had Daniel with us and I'd been hurt but somehow it had brought Rachel and me together, which was all horrible to remember because now Daniel was dead and Rachel was gone and I was on my own, shivering and imagining that I'd got it all wrong and Rachel really *was* with Milo after all.

At last it was time to get the ferry, but we weren't due to arrive in Lerwick until the following morning. I was frustrated at the amount of time that was passing – but at least I was able to spend my second night away travelling on a warm ferry instead of sleeping rough outside.

I kept myself to myself on the ferry. My phone battery had long since died, not that there was anyone I wanted to call. There weren't many people about to talk to either. Working guys mostly, who looked tired and who paid me no attention.

I slept a bit and ate another burger. The next morning I had to wait again, for a ferry to Bergen in Norway. By now I was getting quite good at handling the transactions and answering any questions I got asked. I made sure that I kept my face washed and my hair slicked neatly back, so I didn't look like some homeless person. And I still had the fake passport that Lewis had organised for me. That said I was two years older than I really was, which helped.

I wasn't too worried about anyone other than Mum trying to track me down. Elijah clearly had only used me to get to Rachel and, though I was sure RAGE would still love to kill me given half a chance, it seemed unlikely they were expending any resources looking for me while Elijah was still at large.

I arrived in Bergen late in the evening of my third day's travelling. I wandered out of the ferry terminal, suddenly filled with anxiety.

323

For a start, I had hardly any money left. That was bad enough, but I was up against far more than that. I was in a country I didn't know, where they spoke a language I didn't understand – and I had no idea where Tromstorm was, let alone how to get to it.

I walked down to the busy main road. Despite the fact that it was nearly midnight, the sky wasn't properly dark. That was something, I supposed. Cars and lorries were roaring past. No one gave me a second glance.

Well, I was just going to have to make them.

It was my only option.

I stuck out my thumb and started hitching for a ride.

Rachel

Elijah had been interrogating Amanda Lennox for hours. He'd ordered Milo and me upstairs while they talked in the sun porch. I'd crept onto the landing but couldn't hear anything from there and I didn't dare go any closer, what with Paul making regular patrols round the chalet.

One thought kept going through my head. If Amanda Lennox was connected with RAGE, did that mean the organisation knew where we were?

In the end I gave up trying to work out what was going on and went to bed. I fell asleep surprisingly quickly, but was jolted awake by shouts about an hour later.

I raced to the top of the stairs. Elijah and Amanda Lennox were in the kitchen area below. Elijah was holding Lennox's brown leather shoulder bag.

'You can't *keep* me here,' Amanda Lennox cried. 'I came to *help* you.'

'And I'm grateful for your help, Ms Lennox,' Elijah said,

'but I can't possibly let you go now you know where we are. There's too much at stake.'

Amanda Lennox blinked rapidly. She looked totally shocked. 'But I'm offering to destroy all the data.'

What data? I kept my gaze on Elijah. He sounded calm, in control as usual.

'You are an excellent actress, Ms Lennox,' he said. 'However you can't seriously expect me to believe there are no copies?'

I gripped the banister at the top of the stairs. Copies of *what*?

'Why should there be copies?' Lennox protested. 'I'm the head of RAGE. Everyone there thinks I'm going to the police with that stuff.' She pointed to the brown leather bag. 'No one at RAGE suspects I've come here.'

Elijah shook his head. 'There's a room upstairs where the guard sleeps during the day. You will stay there tonight. I'll decide what to do with you in the morning.'

Amanda Lennox rolled her eyes. 'I came here in *good faith* and—'

'Maybe.' Elijah ran his hand through his hair. 'Maybe you did. But you also betrayed your own organisation and tried to blackmail me with the information in this . . .' he glanced down at the bag, '. . . which makes you fundamentally untrustworthy.' He smiled. 'And I am not a trusting man at the best of times.'

My hands tightened round the banister. *Blackmail?* What was Amanda Lennox trying to blackmail Elijah over? Could it have something to do with the Eos protein?

I had to find out.

Elijah called Paul and told him to lock Amanda Lennox in his room. Paul obeyed without speaking. I scuttled into my room as their footsteps sounded on the stairs. Amanda Lennox protested the whole way.

'This is outrageous,' she kept saying. 'You can't *do* this.'

I heard the door opposite mine lock, then Paul's heavy footsteps going back down the stairs. I crept out onto the landing but by the time I could see downstairs there was no sign of either Elijah or the brown leather bag.

I tiptoed across the landing to the locked room.

'Hello?' I whispered, crouching by the door.

There was a short pause, then a scuffling noise.

'Rachel?' Lennox's voice was anxious. 'Is that you?'

'Yes.' I paused. 'What are you doing here?'

'I'm trying to help Elijah but he won't listen.' Lennox launched into a garbled, panicky, self-justifying explanation of her decision to betray RAGE and blackmail Elijah. 'You have to help get me out of here. *Please*, help me.'

'What's in the bag you brought? You said it was data . . . information of some kind?'

'Yes, it's the data Elijah left behind on Calla,' Amanda Lennox said quickly. 'RAGE took samples from Elijah Lazio's clinic and office on Calla. They found the hard drive he'd tried to destroy and managed to hack into his notes. I was tasked with taking them to the police, but I brought them here instead.'

'RAGE wanted to go to the police?' I frowned. That didn't

make sense. RAGE were usually more into blowing up Elijah's work than exposing it.

'Yes, we realised that whenever we attack Elijah Lazio he just moves on to another location. We know Lazio has some kind of government support for what he's doing, but until now we had no idea who was involved. This time we've got proof of his business relationship with Don Jamieson . . . which starts a trail that should lead to the really high level collusion. Once the police arrest the corrupt bastards who're supporting Lazio, his work will lose its funding and stop.'

I nodded. As a strategy it made sense. In fact, it was the most sensible move I'd ever heard of RAGE making – a way of defeating Elijah without innocent people getting killed.

And now this woman had blown everything. 'But you were too greedy to let that happen?' I said, filling up with anger. 'That's disgusting.'

There was a short silence inside the room. Then Lennox spoke again – a desperate whisper.

'I know it sounds bad, but I need the money to help my sister. She's dying of cancer in the UK but there are treatments in the States that could save her.' Lennox paused.

Was that true? I hesitated, wondering what I would be prepared to do if Grace were dying. Or Theo.

'Listen, Rachel,' Lennox went on. 'RAGE will get Elijah in the end . . . me selling him back these notes will just be a setback, and . . . and you have to help me, Rachel. Out of common humanity, if nothing else.'

'I thought I wasn't human to you,' I shot back. 'I thought I was just a clone.'

'No, *no*.' Amanda Lennox insisted. 'No, we don't . . . we're not targeting clones any more . . .'

Yeah, right. 'Suppose RAGE realised what you were up to and followed you?' I said, struggling to keep my voice low.

'There's no way,' she said. 'D'you think they'd be hanging back now if they knew where Elijah was? No, I'm alone. *Please*, I'm begging you, help me get out of here.'

I stared at the locked door between us. 'I don't see how I could do that, even if I wanted to.'

'You have to try . . . for your own sake. *Please.* I've seen Lazio's notes . . . his files . . . there's information about the Aphrodite Experiment . . . and the Eos protein. You're in terrible danger.'

My heart skipped a beat. 'You know what Elijah's planning to do with me?' I said. '*Tell me.*'

'Only if you help me escape,' Lennox hissed.

I had no idea if I could trust her. Still, I needed to hear what Lennox knew about Elijah's plans for me. Should I help her?

Before I could make up my mind what to do, there was movement downstairs.

Floorboards creaked and a flurry of cold air whooshed up the stairs. It was either Paul or Elijah – and I didn't want either of them catching me here.

A heavy footstep sounded on the bottom stair. Someone was coming.

I scuttled into my room just as Paul reached the landing. He paused outside my door. I held my breath, as he turned the key in the lock.

I was locked in. *Oh, God.*

Tonight, sleep was never going to come.

82

Theo

'I'm eighteen,' I lied.

The lorry driver tilted his head to one side.

'This is dangerous for you,' he said. 'Even if you are eighteen.'

'I know, so will you give me a lift?'

I was on the road just outside the Bergen ferry. Finding someone prepared to take me to Tromstorm hadn't been easy. I knew, from the other drivers who'd rejected my plea for a lift, that it was going to take several hours to get there – and the town wasn't on any of the major roads. I'd been standing on this corner for hours now. It was bleak and cold and, though I wouldn't have admitted it to anyone, I was terrified of every aspect of what I was doing . . . Even if I managed to find my way to wherever Elijah was holding Rachel, I had no idea how I was going to face him down and rescue her.

The lorry driver pursed his lips. 'If you were my son . . .'

I looked away. I wasn't anyone's son. Not properly. Elijah might have called me Apollo, the son of Zeus (his own code name), but he had never been a real father to me. Anyway, he was genetically more like my twin, which made *his* father my dad. *That* was a horrific thought. An imagined image of Elijah's Nazi parents drifted through my mind. I shook myself. I couldn't let myself get distracted. I had to think of something to say to persuade this driver to give me a lift. I looked at him, searching for the right words. But nothing came. I could feel the desperation rising inside me.

The lorry driver's eyes softened.

'OK,' he said. 'I cannot take you all way to Tromstorm, but I take you closer.'

Smiling with relief, I got into the lorry and we set off. The roads were clear and the landscape wide and flat with mountains in the distance. Bizarrely, despite the fact that I'd adjusted my watch to the local time and it was only two a.m., the sun appeared to be rising. Rolf, my lorry driver, explained.

'The further north you go, the shorter the night in summer. In winter the night is very long. Only a few hours when the sun shines. Summer is much better.'

How weird was that?

The sun was fully up by the time Rolf dropped me off at some petrol station. I found a local map in the concourse shop and studied it hard, much to the annoyance of the shop-keeper.

I guess I could have bought it, but I didn't have much money left. Anyway, the map showed that I was just ten miles from Tromstorm. The main roads were clear and the route straightforward. I decided to walk it.

As I got further north I reached higher ground and, unbe-lievably – seeing as this was early July – even some snow. At first it was just a sprinkling of white flecks on distant moun-tain tops, but pretty soon the air cooled and the snow lay thick all around me.

I zipped my jacket up, pulled the hood over my freezing ears and trudged on.

I arrived in Tromstorm, cold and exhausted, towards the end of the afternoon and immediately started asking if anyone had seen two men meeting Elijah's and Milo's descriptions.

It wasn't a huge town and actually quite pretty – though that may have been all the snow. All the shops were shutting, so I trailed round the bars, noting the names of the streets I was checking out.

I pretended I was looking for my grandfather and brother who were staying somewhere in the area and who'd arrived by helicopter three evenings ago.

Two hours later I'd exhausted all the bars I could find and had found out nothing. I was on the verge of letting myself give way to panic when I passed a small supermarket. It was open, with a *24 hr* sign flashing above the door.

I went inside and began my usual conversation. 'Hi, do you speak English?'

'Mmm, ja.' The lady behind the counter looked at me sus-piciously.

I wondered whether, after all my travelling and that long walk into Tromstorm I was starting to look – and smell – like a homeless person after all.

'I'm looking for my brother,' I said. 'He looks like me, but in a wheelchair?'

The woman shook her head.

'Or my grandfather? He's a bit taller than I am . . . greyish hair . . . brown eyes. He speaks English and Spanish and German. They came in a helicopter three days ago and they're staying nearby, but I've lost the address and phone number.'

'Mmm, ja,' the lady said with a sniff.

'So have you seen them?' I said, fully expecting the answer to be no.

'The brother in the wheelchair, no.' The lady sniffed again. 'But an older man, ja. He comes twice.'

She told me, in broken English, that Elijah had visited on two occasions in the past three days – once to buy a brand of commercial cleaning fluid and a second time to purchase some sort of powerful acid, which she said he'd told her was in order to clear his drains.

'This one is special chemical,' she said. 'Ja.'

I didn't like the sound of that.

'So do you know where he lives?' I said. 'Is it nearby?'

'Oh, ja,' she said, with another sniff. 'It is near. Everyone knows this place. It has a special fence all around the property to stop burglars.'

'A fence?' I said.

'Ja.' Another sniff. 'They call it the . . . how would you say? Ja, the death fence.'

334

83

Rachel

I'd tossed and turned all night.

I badly wanted to know about Elijah's plans for me. And yet, why should I trust anyone from RAGE, let alone offer them help? Last year – and in the recent attack on Calla – RAGE had proved just how brutal they were. And Amanda Lennox was not just the head of that vicious group – she was also a selfish blackmailer who – if she'd been telling the truth – was putting the needs of her sister ahead of a whole bunch of innocent people. Not that anyone who had anything to do with RAGE truly thought that most people were innocent – especially clones. I could still remember that guy, Franks, from last year, telling me that I was a freak . . . that I shouldn't exist . . .

I'd finally fallen asleep at about six a.m., then woken several hours later to find I was still locked in my room. Paul came up with some food and drink, but refused to answer my questions. There was no sound from the room opposite, where Lennox was being held.

I had no idea what was going on . . . or why I was being treated differently all of a sudden. I could only assume Elijah was trying to keep me and Lennox apart. Which surely meant she *did* have some knowledge about Elijah's plans for me.

By early evening, when Paul finally unlocked the door and brought me downstairs, I was totally freaking out, though trying hard not to show it. Paul, still refusing to answer my questions, went outside for a smoke.

I turned to Milo, who was stirring a saucepan on the hob.

'Why've I been locked in my room all day?' I said, the words blurting out of me. 'What's happening? Why am I out now? What's Elijah doing?'

Milo shook his head. He ladled some soup from his saucepan into a bowl, then wheeled himself across the room and placed the bowl on the table.

'Eat it while it's hot,' he said.

I stared at him. 'Why won't you talk to me?' I said.

My voice cracked as I spoke. I couldn't stop it. Tears threatened to well up.

Milo placed a roll on the table beside my steaming soup bowl. I noticed his hand trembled slightly as he did so.

'You act like you care about me,' I said, 'but if you really did then you'd tell me what's going on.'

Milo stared up at me, his brown eyes so like Elijah's and Theo's but without the former's haughty confidence or the latter's gentle strength.

'Elijah's rattled,' he said quietly. 'He knows Lennox came to blackmail him with those files, but he didn't believe

336

RAGE would really let her go without keeping copies. And he was right.'

'How does he know?'

'He hurt Lennox . . . forced her to tell him where RAGE were based.'

I nodded. 'Then what?'

'He got John, the other guard from Calla, to go round there with some back-up and find and destroy the copies. He just received news that it was done.'

I closed my eyes. Another defeat.

'What's he doing now?' I said.

'Elijah? He's upstairs having a shower then he's planning to take some blood from you and go back to the bunker to work. He's in a terrible mood. Says he's wasted nearly a whole day.'

I picked up the roll beside my bowl of soup and nibbled a little. It was soft and warm, but it tasted like cardboard in my mouth.

'What about Amanda Lennox?' I said.

'She's still upstairs.' As he spoke, Milo's eyes flitted across the room to the front door of the chalet.

Elijah's greatcoat was hanging on the hook on the back. Peeking out from underneath it was Amanda Lennox's brown leather bag.

Was it possible that Elijah had left the contents in the bag? No, *surely* he wouldn't have done that. And yet I *had* to check.

I glanced upstairs. No sign of Elijah. I jumped up from the

337

table. Through the window I could see Paul, still puffing on his cigarette down by the lake. He wasn't looking towards the house.

I headed for the bag.

'Rachel, stop,' Milo hissed.

I ignored him. Reached the bag. Opened the flap and thrust in my hand. *Nothing*.

I hadn't seriously expected Elijah to have left incriminating and revealing notes about his work lying around on the back of the kitchen door, but even so – after being cooped up in my room for the whole day, it felt like the last straw.

'Rachel, please.'

I dug my hand right into the far corners of the bag. It was totally empty.

'What the hell are you doing?' Elijah roared.

I jumped. Spun round, my cheeks burning. Elijah was at the top of the stairs, glaring down at us.

He strode downstairs, his furious gaze fixed on Milo.

'You *useless* idiot,' Elijah shouted. 'What are you doing letting her look in that bag?' He advanced on Milo, who shrank back in his wheelchair. Elijah reached him in two strides. He slapped him across the face with the back of his hand.

I gasped. Milo yelped, his hand shooting up to his cheek.

'You're unbelievable,' Elijah went on. 'What do you have to say for yourself?'

Milo gaped at him. 'I didn't . . .'

'You didn't *what*? *Think*? *Care*?' Spittle flew out of Elijah's mouth. 'Words fail me.'

338

I stepped away from the bag, my heart thumping.

Milo was totally shrunk down in his chair now. Despite my earlier irritation with him, I felt a wave of pity rise up. Elijah had never given him a chance.

'I'm sorry,' Milo muttered.

Elijah's lip curled with scorn. 'You're *pathetic*,' he said. 'But I *will* make a man of you today, whatever it takes.'

I stared at him. What on earth did that mean?

Milo looked similarly horror-struck.

Ignoring us both, Elijah stormed across to the kitchen door and yelled out to Paul. 'Fetch Amanda Lennox down here now!'

Paul jogged in and disappeared up the stairs.

Elijah was still fuming, his arms folded.

Long, tense seconds ticked by. Lennox appeared, glancing anxiously round as Paul brought her down to the kitchen. She looked visibly shaken – a different person from the confident, stylish woman who'd turned up at the chalet the day before.

As soon as she saw Elijah, Lennox clasped her hands together in a gesture that was both emphatic and beseeching. 'Please, just listen to me, Elijah,' she said. 'I didn't know RAGE kept copies of the files I brought with me. You have to believe me.'

'Really?' Elijah said, his voice dripping with sarcasm. 'I don't think I *have* to do anything.'

'But nothing's really changed,' Lennox protested. 'You've destroyed the copies of my files. The situation is exactly as I said it was. Do a deal with me, and you'll be safe forever. Please, just think about it.'

'Oh, I have thought about it.' Elijah snorted. 'In fact, let me tell you what I *think*. I think RAGE knows you're here. I think you're working undercover with no real intention of blackmailing me. I think that you thought that once you were inside and we were talking and my guard was down, you were banking on finding and destroying my work. As RAGE has attempted to do at least twice before, under your predecessors.'

I stared at Lennox. Was that true?

'No,' she said, her whole face tensing up. 'No, they—'

But Elijah wasn't listening. 'What RAGE didn't count on was that I'm far better at this game than they are.' He took a deep breath. 'Now, where's your gun, Milo?'

Milo patted his jacket with trembling fingers.

Oh, God.

'Good.' Elijah paused. 'Now, the truth, please, Miss Lennox, or I'll make sure this is very slow and very painful.'

'I've told you the truth,' Lennox spat. 'If you don't believe me and you're not going to pay me for the data I've brought you, just let me go.'

'I don't think so,' Elijah snarled.

I stared at him. If he wasn't planning on letting her go, what *was* he going to do with her?

'You don't have another choice,' Lennox persisted. 'If anything happens to me, people will come after you.'

'How will anyone know you were here?' Elijah said

340

nastily. 'I thought you came here under your own steam to blackmail me?'

Amanda Lennox's mouth opened, then shut again. For a split second I could see the defeat in her eyes, then they hardened again.

'You'll be caught,' she spat. 'This is stupid.'

'I'll take my chances.' Elijah's voice was icy. 'Gun, Milo.'

He was going to kill her. My heart thundered against my throat.

'Okay.' Lennox gritted her teeth. 'Okay, you're right about why I'm here, but that makes killing me even more stupid. Other people know about Eos – about your foul agenda . . . the evil work that you do. You'll never be free of us.' She held her head high.

'I've been living as a refugee for fifteen years,' Elijah snarled. 'I'm not scared of your pathetic threats.' He turned to Milo. 'I told you to get out your gun.'

Reluctantly, Milo drew the pistol out of his jacket. He offered it to Elijah.

I stared, transfixed, at the small black weapon. This wasn't really happening. It *couldn't* be.

'No, not me.' Elijah waved the gun away with a flick of his little finger. 'I already said, Milo, today we make a man of you.'

I gasped. Surely he couldn't mean . . .?

'Go on, Milo.' Elijah narrowed his eyes. 'Kill her.'

I froze. He couldn't do this.

Milo's mouth gaped open. 'I can't,' he stammered.

'You have no choice,' Elijah sneered. 'Either you kill this woman, or I kill you – and then her.'

I stared at them both. Milo was clearly totally over-whelmed, his hands shaking as he grasped the small gun. Elijah could barely contain his fury, his hands clenching and unclenching as he stood there, waiting.

And then I looked at Amanda Lennox, standing defiantly in the middle of the room. She was a woman who, by rights, I should have wished dead. She worked for RAGE, which believed I shouldn't even be alive. She stood for prejudice and bigotry and hatred. As I stared at her, my mind flashed back to the moment last year in Washington D.C., when Theo had stood in front of me, to protect me from Elijah's bullet.

I didn't have to think about it any more. Whatever Lennox had done, Elijah had no right to take her life.

Or anyone's.

Or to force Milo to do it for him.

I stepped in front of Lennox.

'If you want Milo to shoot her,' I said, looking straight at Elijah. 'You'll have to make him shoot me first.'

84

Theo

I stared at the lady in the shop. 'What's the death fence?'

'You will see when you arrive. It is well-known around here . . . but you will have no trouble getting through. You will just ring at the gate and they will let you in, ja?'

'Ja,' I lied. 'So, how do I get there? To the house, I mean?'

The lady gave me the directions. It sounded like a fair walk away, but adrenalin was coursing through me now.

I set off, walking fast, trying not to dwell on how on earth I was going to get past this fence the woman had talked about. Despite the fallen snow, the sun was shining. The roads had clearly been properly swept with snow ploughs and there was little traffic.

The lady in the shop had told me the house was hidden from the street, but the long gravel drive, surrounding woodland and huge fence made it easy enough to spot if you kept your eyes open. After about thirty minutes, I found it – a drive in the middle of a pine forest, with a tall metal fence visible through the gaps in the trees.

I headed cautiously up the drive. Rounding a short bend, I could see a set of large metal gates in the distance. The house must be beyond those.

I'd been feeling hungry as I walked, but the pangs in my stomach vanished as I stood, staring at the huge fence next to the gate. It was high. *Really* high. Far higher than any tree I'd ever climbed. But that wasn't what terrified me.

I suddenly understood why the woman had called it the 'death fence'.

Strapped to the fence and bounded with a thick black line, was a sign with the outline of a man and a lightning bolt shape.

I didn't know exactly what the words underneath said, but I certainly understood what they meant.

This was an *electric* fence.

I followed it round, away from the gate, to where the woodland was most dense. I was hoping there would be a gap, or a hole . . . something that I could wriggle through without touching the sides.

But the fence was completely intact.

How on earth was I going to get past it?

85

Rachel

So much for grand gestures.

Elijah just laughed when I stood in front of Amanda Lennox, though I noticed he did turn and check that Milo wasn't pointing the gun anywhere near me.

'I'm astonished by your stupidity, Rachel. Do you not realise that this woman would cheerfully see you dead?'

'That doesn't make killing her right,' I said.

'We don't target clones now,' Amanda Lennox said behind me. 'I know I lied about certain things, Rachel, but that part of what I told you was true. Since Simpson . . . he was the old head of RAGE . . . since then we've got a new policy. We don't blame the people cloned for the work of the cloner.'

'What about all the embryos in the clinic?' I said. 'You killed them.'

'They were only a few weeks . . . for Christ's sake, it wouldn't be illegal to have an *abortion* at that stage.'

'So abortions are okay, but clones can't exist?'

'They're completely different things. Anyway, whatever

crimes RAGE may have committed in the past, Lazio's done *far* worse. You should see what he's got in that bunker outside. Do you know what he's using Eos for? What he's planning to do to you?'

I stared at her.

'Quiet, both of you,' Elijah snapped. 'Rachel, please move out of the way.'

I stepped closer to Amanda Lennox. 'What's he doing with Eos? What is he planning for me?'

Elijah swore under his breath. 'Move her, Paul.'

As Paul strode over, Lennox darted closer.

'Stop him, Rachel.' She gripped my arm, her fingers digging in so hard they hurt. 'For your own sake.'

'What—?' I started.

But before I could say more, Paul grabbed Lennox by the wrist and wrenched her away. She clutched me with her other hand. Paul reached to stop her, but instead of pulling away from him, Lennox stepped backwards, into him. This unbalanced Paul, who stumbled for a second.

In that tiny moment, Amanda Lennox lurched forward again, so her mouth was right by my ear. She flung her arms round me, as if clinging on for dear life, which, I suppose, she was.

'The code is 2509,' she whispered. 'Find it and kill it. That's why I'm really here . . . to *stop* Elijah . . . and to *kill* it.'

I froze. What was she talking about? Code for *what*? Kill *who*?

But Paul had already regained his balance and was stepping forward, fist raised.

His arm swung past me. *Wham.* The punch hit home. Amanda Lennox went flying across the room. She fell against the far wall, winded and gasping for breath.

Elijah pointed to Milo's gun and said something quietly that I couldn't hear. Then he looked up at Paul.

'Take Rachel upstairs.'

'No,' I yelled.

But Paul had already picked me up and slung me over his shoulder.

'NO!' I kicked and punched with my legs and arms, but Paul just tightened his grip.

As we climbed the stairs I lifted my head. Below us, Amanda Lennox was still sitting, slumped, against the wall. Opposite her, by the table, Elijah was talking – low and insistent – to Milo.

Milo wheeled himself over to Amanda. She sat, arms wrapped round her knees, staring defiantly up at him.

I stopped yelling. Stopped kicking.

Milo raised his arm and held the gun against Amanda's temple.

The gun shook. Elijah put his own hand on Milo's arm to steady it.

Still slung over Paul's back, I reached the top of the stairs. I could no longer see what was happening, but I held my breath, waiting.

Surely Milo couldn't pull that trigger. Not in cold blood.

Surely Elijah wouldn't make him.

The gun went off as Paul dumped me in my room. He turned without a word and left, locking the door behind him.

I stood still, listening for more sounds. Nothing. I pressed my ear to the door. I could hear voices downstairs – a dragging movement. Was that someone moving a body?

A few minutes later, the door downstairs slammed. And, a few moments after that, Milo's sobs drifted up to me.

God, he really did it. He really killed her.

I took a deep breath, trying to get my head round it.

Amanda Lennox was dead.

I couldn't believe it.

I sank down on the bed trying to make sense of what I'd just seen and heard. Always before, RAGE had gone to attack Elijah's labs mob-handed. And, while they'd managed to destroy most of his work, Elijah himself had always slipped through their fingers.

I could see why they'd try sending in a lone agent with a cover story.

My mind went back to Lennox's last words – about the code 2509, and the instruction to '*find it and kill it*'.

I still had no idea what she was talking about – but I was certain I knew *where*.

Elijah's bunker – that was the only place that could possibly need a code to open it. I *had* to reach it. Maybe there was someone inside who was helping Elijah do whatever terrible things he was doing . . . maybe that was the 'it' Amanda Lennox had referred to?

348

My mind careered about, trying to figure everything out.

Lennox had said I was in danger too. A danger connected with the Eos protein Elijah was trying to copy from my blood.

What *kind* of danger?

I shook my head. I couldn't let myself get distracted worrying about that.

Anyway, it didn't matter *what* the danger was. RAGE's mission had failed. I was the only person left who could stop Elijah. *That* was the priority.

I got up and pushed at my bedroom door. It was firmly locked. There was no way I could break it down. I turned to the window. I'd already examined it, of course. It was double-glazed, and looked out over a first-floor drop made deeper because the garden of the chalet sloped so steeply away from the house.

As if that wasn't enough, the ground below my window was covered with shrubbery, punctuated by a series of sharp rocks that spread at least a metre from the house. The chances of me not impaling myself on one, even if I managed to land without breaking my legs, were minuscule.

But I had to try. Elijah had to be stopped.

In the distance, a car engine revved. Was Elijah going out?

It was a chance . . . I might not get another.

I took the lamp beside my bed. Like almost everything else in the room it was made of white-painted wood. I rammed it against the window. The glass shook, but didn't

349

break. I tried again. Still nothing. I cast my eyes round, desperate for something else to use.

I picked up the chair, shoving the clothes on top of it onto the floor.

It was much heavier than the lamp. I gripped it by the back and swung it up and against the window. It slammed against the glass. A tiny crack appeared. *Yes.* I swung it back and rammed it into the window again. With a satisfying smash, glass shattered outwards, onto the shrubbery. *Damn*, another hazard.

There was no time to think about it. If Paul had heard the crash he'd be upstairs in seconds.

I put one leg over the sill. In the distance I could dimly hear Milo calling my name. Ignoring him, I looked down. *God*, it was a long way to the ground. My heart pummelled at my chest. It was too far . . . too lethal . . .

Go on.

I crouched on the sill for a second, poised . . . ready . . .

I flung myself as far as I could away from the house, hurtling through the air.

Wham. I landed on my feet, making sure I rolled forwards as Lewis had taught me. *Ow.* Pain shot through my right leg. I glanced down. One of the sharp rocks had sliced through the side of my calf. Blood poured out.

Panting, I scrambled up. *God*, it wasn't just the cut . . . my ankle felt twisted as well.

'Rachel! RACHEL!!!' Milo's yells were close. He was outside.

I hobbled away. *Get round to the bunker. You have the code.*

'Rachel, stop.' I heard his gun click.

I stopped and turned. Milo was on the path behind me, holding his gun outstretched in front of him. His hands were shaking, his face under the beanie hat was ashen.

We stared at each other for a second then he put the gun down.

'You killed her,' I said.

'Come back inside, please, or I'll call the others.'

'Elijah's gone out,' I said. 'I heard the car.'

'He's only gone into town for something,' Milo said. 'He'll be back in twenty minutes.'

'What about Paul?'

Milo looked away. 'He's dealing with . . . with the body . . . down by the lake.'

'How could you have killed her like that?' I said. 'Just because Elijah told you too?'

'I didn't,' Milo said. 'In the end I couldn't . . .'

'Elijah did it?'

Milo nodded. 'He put his hand on mine . . . then he pulled the trigger.'

We stared at each other. I was suddenly aware of the silence all around us – the way the snow muffled everything.

'Please come back inside, Rachel,' Milo said. 'It's cold out here and you know that you can't get over the fence. There's no way you'll escape.'

'I'm not trying to escape,' I said. 'I'm trying to make right what Elijah's made wrong.'

Milo's eyes widened. 'You mean the bunker? Getting into the that's harder than getting over the fence,' he said. 'Elijah uses three different types of security.'

I thought of the code *2509* Amanda Lennox had given me. 'I'll be okay,' I said.

'But Elijah will win. He *always* wins.' Milo's voice cracked. 'You've got no idea what he's capable of . . . what he's doing in there.'

'That's why I have to try and stop him,' I said. 'I've been hiding from him for nearly a year. I'm not hiding any more.'

I hobbled away, through the trees.

'Rachel!'

I could hear Milo on the path, his wheels clattering over the stones. That path took a longer way round to the bunker than my route through the wood. If I walked quickly I'd reach the bunker well ahead of him.

I sped up, trying to put as little weight as I could on my foot, and hurried on across the snow.

86

Theo

I picked up a large stick lying on the ground and threw it at the fence.

The metal sparked – a loud, bright flash. Lethal.

Man, no wonder the woman in the shop had called this the 'death fence'. How on earth was I going to get over it without getting electrocuted?

I wandered along, looking for a gap or a break in the thick metal bars, but the fence remained sturdy and unbroken. Typical Elijah. I followed it round for a few minutes until I was as far away from the gate as I could get. Despite the densely wooded area I was now in, the pine trees had been cut back so they were set several metres away from the fence on either side.

There was only one option. It was crazy, but I couldn't come this far and give up now. I was going to have to climb a tree and then jump from its highest branches to the nearest tree on the other side of the fence.

I looked for a suitable tree. It needed to be big enough for me to climb – and close enough to a tree on the other side of the fence so that the jump was merely insane, rather than completely suicidal.

There, that one would do. The pine tree I'd picked was slightly stubbier than the others around it. If I could just climb it to a metre or so above fence level, then I was sure I could clear the fence when I jumped. What was less certain was whether I'd manage to reach the nearest pine tree on the other side of the fence. It was set nearly two metres back from the wire but it was particularly bushy, with lots of dense branches.

I grabbed hold of my stubby pine tree and hauled myself up. I was used to clambering up trees – last year I'd even climbed one to get out of the back of school.

That was before I knew about being a clone. Before I met Rachel.

I hooked my knee over the next branch. And the next. The tree was sprinkled with snow that slid off as I disturbed it. My jacket was soon covered. An icy trickle ran down my neck. I was sweating now. The tree was harder to climb as I got higher. Would the thinner branches hold my weight? I pushed on, wanting to get as far above fence level as I could.

I stepped onto a branch. It snapped. *Damn.* I swung for a second from the branch above then hauled myself up, testing the next branch more carefully.

A couple more branches up and I stopped. The top of the fence was at least a metre below me. The ground several metres below that.

Trying not to think about the dangers of what I was about to do, I peered through the dense woodland beyond the fence. I could just make out the roof of a wooden house. It wasn't all that far away. Maybe Rachel was inside.

As I braced myself, ready to jump, a muffled shot rang out.

I froze. Was that a *gun*shot? Panicking, I stood on my branch, breath misting in the air, straining my ears to hear another sound. But nothing came. No voices . . . no more shots . . .

I prepared to jump, flexing my legs, focusing on the tree on the other side of the fence.

Go. I pushed off, legs tucked under me. For a second I was flying through the air. I cleared the fence . . . reached out for the bushy pine tree beyond.

I'm not going to make it.

The thought flashed through my head. In the split second that followed I reached out my arms, clawing for the pine branches. My hands closed on fragile pine needles but nothing firm enough to hold me. I was panicking now, arms flailing, desperate to grab hold of something, anything. Pine branches slapped at my face.

Down. Falling. *Thump.*

I landed on my arse in the snow.

I sat there, getting my breath back for a moment, testing out my legs and my back. I appeared to be fine, apart from a couple of cuts on my face from the pine branches and what I was sure was going to be a whopper of a bruise on my bum.

In the distance I could hear a car engine start up. I couldn't tell which direction it was coming from, so I lay low, close to the tree where I'd jumped, until the car drove off and the noise faded away. There was silence now. Even the wind had died down. The snow was only patchy here, under the trees.

I set off in what I hoped was the right direction to reach the wooden house I'd seen earlier. As I walked, the faint sound of breaking glass drifted towards me. I had no idea how that connected to the gunshot or the car driving away, but there was no time to think about it. I had to reach the house, then find a way in without anyone seeing me and look for Rachel.

The wood thinned out suddenly and I could see the outline of the house. At the same time I heard faint voices. One male. One female. I couldn't work out what they were saying. Was the girl's voice hers?

Stomach tight, throat dry, I edged closer to the sound. Then the talking stopped.

I stood still, straining to pick up any noise at all. Someone was walking through the wood, feet cracking over the loose sticks and stones between the trees.

I crept nearer, my whole body tensed with anticipation. The woodland grew thicker again. I kept close to the trees, using them as cover. After a few moments I came to a small concrete hut. I ducked behind it, as the footsteps grew louder. And stopped.

I waited a second, my breath fast and shallow, then peered round the corner.

It was her. She was standing, staring at the entrance to the hut. Her face was flushed and her hair scraped back in a rough ponytail.

I'd never been so pleased to see anyone in my life.

'Rachel?'

She turned, her eyes widening as she saw me.

'Theo!' And she burst into tears and flung herself into my arms.

87

Rachel

I wiped my eyes and pulled away from him. There was no time. Anyway, if I let myself feel everything I was feeling for Theo, I'd never let go of him.

'You lied to me,' he said. He didn't sound angry.

'I'm sorry,' I mumbled, unable to meet his eyes.

Theo took my chin in my hand and lifted my face. It felt like he was seeing straight through me.

We stood, looking at each other. For a moment I forgot everything else: Elijah and his sinister research . . . Milo and Paul nearby . . . even the bunker we were standing next to . . .

'Want to know how I know you lied?' Theo said.

I nodded.

Theo pulled my silver chain out of his pocket. He handed it to me. 'This.'

I blushed. The tiny 't' nestled in my palm. So he knew, then. He knew exactly how I felt about him. My blush deepened.

'You gave yourself up . . . for me . . .' Theo said.

I nodded again.

'That's the bravest, most stupid . . .'

I reached up and touched a dark red line on his face.

'You're hurt,' I said.

'Could have been worse.' He shrugged, then slid his fingers off my face and took my hand. 'Come on,' he said. 'We have to get out of here.'

'No.'

Theo stared at me, his expression incredulous. 'You want to *stay*?' he said. 'Listen, don't worry about protecting me any more. I'll take my chances. We can hide from Elijah. You and me. We'll find somewhere he can't reach us. We'll—'

'It's not that.' I explained quickly about the Eos protein. 'Elijah's doing something really bad in here.' I indicated the bunker beside us. 'He just got Milo to kill that woman from RAGE because she found out about it and came here to destroy his work.'

'The woman with red hair? Amanda Lennox?' Theo blew out his breath. 'Man, I thought I heard a gunshot.'

'Yeah, well, before she died she told me Elijah was doing something evil in here. She said to "kill it" but I don't know what she was talking about. I've never seen anyone apart from Elijah coming in and out of here.'

Theo looked at the bunker door. He frowned. 'How do we get inside?' He dug in his pocket and took out a hairgrip. 'I've been using this to open doors recently, but it's not going to work on this one.' He offered me the grip.

With a jolt I realised it was one of my own, with a tiny diamante arrow at one end.

'I got it from your house,' Theo said gruffly. 'Now, how do we get inside?'

I smiled at him, pocketing the hairgrip. 'It's okay, Amanda Lennox gave me the entry code.'

'A code?' Theo stared at the concrete bunker door and the small blank screen beside it. 'You mean like a pin number?'

'Yes.'

'But where do you input the numbers?' he said, frowning. 'Rach, I understand you wanting to stop whatever Elijah's doing, but we can take all this to the police.'

'No,' I insisted. 'Elijah always gets round the police. He's got people in the government who protect him. It's up to us to stop him. For good. Right here. Right now.'

Theo stared at me. The look of shock in his eyes gave way to determination. 'Okay,' he said. 'Where *is* Elijah?'

'Out for the next fifteen minutes or so. With the guard,' I said, examining the screen by the door again. Theo was right. There was absolutely nowhere to input the numbers Amanda Lennox had given me.

'Maybe it's a retinal scanner,' Theo said. 'Like the ones Elijah's used before.' He walked right up to the screen, but it was level with his waist, not his eyes. He crouched down, so the screen was at eye-level. He waited a second, but nothing happened.

I reached round him and prodded the screen.

Still nothing.

'Try your palm print,' I said. 'That's how they did it in *Avatar*.'

Theo pressed his fingertips against the screen.

It remained blank.

'Maybe my fingerprints aren't the same as Elijah's – just because we've got the same DNA doesn't mean all the tiny marks are identical.'

He removed his hand. As he did so, the screen flickered for a fraction of a second.

Theo looked at me. 'Did you see that?'

I frowned. What kind of scanner *was* this? 'Try waving your hand in front of it.'

Theo did as I suggested, holding his palm a few centimetres away from the screen.

Nothing happened. *God,* this was frustrating. I tried to clear my mind. What had Theo done when he took his hand away from the screen that he wasn't doing now?

'Turn your hand round,' I suggested.

Theo presented the back of his hand to the screen. 'I can't see how this would work—' He stopped, his mouth agape, as the screen flickered fully into life. Green lines ran across it.

'What's it doing?' he said.

I stared at the back of my own hands. How were they different from the front? Well, for a start I could see the veins standing out slightly under the skin.

'It's a *vascular* scanner,' I said. 'It's reading your blood. Which is the same as Elijah's blood.'

As I spoke, the green lines flashed and the screen shone with a steady glow. A second later, the concrete door slid open.

Theo glanced at me. He looked exhausted. There were dark rings under his eyes and grime mixed with smears of blood on his face. And then he grinned and my heart lurched with how gorgeous he was. Even in the middle of all this danger.

'After you,' he said.

88

Theo

I followed Rachel into the – what had she called it? – the bunker.

Our footsteps sounded loud on the concrete floor. The low ceiling meant I had to stoop slightly. Dim light from the open door revealed a set of stone steps leading down to a dark corridor.

There was no sign that anyone else was down here.

Ahead of me, Rachel was limping.

'What happened to your leg?' I asked.

'Hurt myself getting away from the house,' she said.

I remembered the voices I'd heard earlier. 'Who were you talking to?'

'Milo.' Rachel reached the stone steps and peered into the darkness below. Along the short corridor another door was visible.

Behind us, the bunker entrance started slowly closing. I glanced round, checking that there was a screen matching the one outside that we could use to get out. There was.

'Milo's in the woods?' I whispered. 'But he might have seen us . . . he's probably calling Elijah right now to tell him we're down here.'

'I don't think so,' Rachel whispered back. 'He's too scared . . . too scared of upsetting me to call Elijah.' She paused. 'Though he's also too scared of Elijah to help me. He was probably watching us outside the bunker, though.'

A shiver ran down my spine. *Great.*

'You do know that I made that up about liking him, don't you?' Rachel said softly.

'I know,' I said. 'I've got you figured out. You're like that door back there. Confusing until you understand how it works.'

'And you know how I work?' she said with a smile.

'Yeah. You're stubborn, full of stupid ideas and you'd rather stick pins in your eyes than ask anyone for help,' I said.

'So just like you then, don't you think?'

I stared at her. 'What I think is that we need to hurry up and get on through that door.' I pointed down the stairs.

Rachel nodded, and we crept down the concrete steps. The door here was similar in style and width to the sliding door at the bunker entrance.

'Careful,' Rachel whispered. 'If Elijah is working with other people then they might be through here.'

We stood either side of the door. Holding my breath, I tensed, ready to defend myself once the door opened, then held my hand against the screen attached to the wall.

Nothing happened.

I examined it more carefully. The screen on this door was much smaller than on the door above and positioned above it was a key pad. My heart sank.

'*Now* we need a pin number,' I said. '*Man*, and we're really running out of time, too. Why couldn't this door be like the one upstairs? Weirdo blood scan machines are my new speciality.'

'Well, cracking four-digit codes is mine.' Rachel grinned. 'Watch.'

89

Rachel

2509. The code Amanda Lennox had given me worked. We stood on either side of the door as it slid open.

'*Elijah uses three different kinds of security in that place,*' Milo had said.

I tensed, ready to attack if anyone – or anything – flew out at us.

But no one appeared. And there was no sound from inside the room, either.

After a few seconds I peered round the door. The room beyond was empty and still. It was some sort of lab.

A long table stretched through the middle of the room. Shelves to the side were ranged with microscopes and packets and jars of all sizes. A small box stood in the middle of the table. It was filled with rows of microscope slides. Each one contained a red smudge.

I limped over and took a closer look. The slides were all neatly labelled with a time and a date and the letters *Art*.

Theo came up behind me. 'What does *Art* mean?'

I thought for a second. '*Artemis*,' I said. 'My code name.' I stared at the times and dates again. 'These are my blood samples. This is where Elijah's been testing my blood for Eos.'

'For *what*?' Theo asked, examining another box on the ground.

'The Eos protein. Elijah's been trying to copy it.'

'Right.' Theo gave up on the box. He followed my gaze round the room and sighed. 'This doesn't make sense. All that security, just to shove a few slides under a microscope? He could have done that in the house.'

I nodded. 'There isn't even a computer in here.'

Theo walked past a huge bookshelf, laden with what looked like scientific and medical text books, to a tall cupboard in the corner.

'So why does Elijah want to copy this Eos protein?' Theo said. 'What's he going to use it for?'

'I don't know, but Amanda Lennox said it was for something terrible.'

As I spoke I remembered how she'd urged me to 'kill it', and shivered. What on earth had she been referring to? There was clearly nothing else here.

Theo was examining the contents of the cupboard.

'Anything?' I said.

'Oh *yes*.' Eyes shining, Theo turned to me, a laptop computer held proudly in his hand.

'This has to be it,' I said, clearing a space on the table for him to set the laptop down. 'This has got to explain everything.'

Nodding, Theo put the computer on the table, opened the lid and switched it on.

It took a few seconds to warm up, then the main desktop screen appeared.

It was empty, apart from the HD icon in the corner. Theo clicked this open, but all it revealed was the usual list of folders: Application, Library, System, User Guide. Theo clicked each one in turn, but they all just contained basic computer info, though the list of apps and software programmes was enormous.

'It's like it's just come from the shop, all loaded up and ready to go,' he said, looking bemused. 'Why would Elijah keep a brand new computer in his cupboard?'

I slumped into the single chair at the table. My ankle throbbed with pain. There must be something here we were missing. But *what*?

90

Theo

It didn't make sense. I paced round the lab, trying to work out why Elijah had built himself such an elaborately secure unit just to run basic blood tests.

'There aren't even any interesting-looking chemicals here,' I said, taking in the bottles on the shelves. A few were labelled with names that looked like they came off the periodic table, but they were all empty and, anyway, I had no idea what the names meant. The woman in the shop had said Elijah bought a special chemical – some kind of acid. Where was that?

'I don't get it.' Rachel limped over to the sink in the corner of the room. She turned on the tap but it just vibrated, making a low chugging noise. No water appeared.

'The pipes can't be connected up,' I said.

That was weird, too, wasn't it? I'd never been in a science lab that didn't have running water before.

I examined a big tank set into the wall between the bookcase and the sink. It was labelled *Hydratoroxide*. What was that for?

Rachel went back to the table and sagged into her chair. She rested her head in one hand and checked her watch. 'He'll be back in ten minutes, and we haven't found out anything.' She sounded completely defeated.

I bit my lip. Most of me just wanted to insist that we left while we had a chance, but the words Rachel had said outside, about Elijah, were still echoing in my ears.

It's up to us to stop him. For good. Right here. Right now.

Despite my anxiety for her safety – and my own – I knew she was right. We'd been living in fear since we escaped from the Washington complex last year. That had to end. And this was our best chance to end it.

I picked up the laptop again. It was a Vaio – a state-of-the-art model. Why would Elijah keep an ace computer in here with no data on it? Unless . . .

'Maybe he downloads the data onto something when he leaves the bunker,' I said. 'That's why the computer's empty, but loaded with apps and software.'

Rachel shook her head. 'Then where's the download?'

'I don't know. Man, it could be anywhere.' I groaned. 'It's probably *on* him.'

'Okay, but he must keep a backup here.' Rachel looked round. 'This is his safe place . . . it *has* to be here. It wouldn't make sense for him to take *all* the data out of this bunker.'

I followed her gaze round the messy room. I was standing close to the large bookshelf that occupied the end section of the wall. I pulled out several rows of text books, but no storage device emerged, so I turned my attention to the cupboard next to the sink. This was crammed with all sorts of scientific bits and pieces: from syringes and Bunsen burners, to a selection of rubber gloves in varying stages of disrepair.

No sign of a CD or a USB flash drive.

My guts twisted into knots. The data Elijah had downloaded could be hidden anywhere. Across the room, Rachel picked up a sheaf of papers from the table and shook them. Nothing fell out. She turned away, heading for the cupboard next to the table. I let my eyes travel round the room. If I were Elijah, which I genetically was, where would I hide something? Where was the last place you'd expect to find a fragile container of top-secret scientific data?

My eyes rested on the water tap above the sink. A water tap with no water.

Of course.

I strode over to the sink and turned the tap on again, hard. Again the pipes juddered and gurgled, but no water came out.

'Something's blocking this,' I said. I bent down, under the sink. The switch behind the U-bend pipe immediately below the bowl was switched to the 'off' position.

'Why are you looking there?' Rachel sounded incredulous.

'Elijah's turned off the water supply for some reason,' I said, examining the pipe. I grabbed a pair of rubber gloves off the table and twisted the nut positioned just above the U-bend. I knew there would be water in the bend itself but what about just above that?

With a grunt, I wrenched the nut off. It released more

371

easily than I expected, as if someone had loosened it recently. I shoved my fingers up the tube above. *There.* A small package was taped to the inside of the pipe.

I yanked it out and held it up. It was a memory stick in a plastic bag.

'*Whoa!*' Rachel's eyes widened.

Quickly, I ripped the bag open and pulled the top of the stick. I found the usb port on the side of the laptop and slid the memory stick in.

A long list of files opened up. Rachel and I scanned these together. Very few of the file names made much sense to me – most of them had long, complicated chemical-sounding names.

'There.' Rachel jabbed at the screen. She was reading a little further on than I'd got to, pointing to a file labelled Eos.

I clicked it open. It was a log, written like a blog with each entry dated. I scanned the top few reports – an incomprehensible mix of apparently random letters and numbers.

'Oh my God, look at that entry.' Rachel gasped. I followed her gaze to the bottom of the screen. It was dated the day after Rachel went missing – the day she arrived on Calla.

Today I have proof that the Eos protein is real. It heralds a revolution in biotechnology. If I can extract the protein and prevent its cells mutating, then I am just a few short steps away from creating a bioartifical implant that should prove flexible, biocompatible, and, ultimately, relatively

inexpensive to synthesise. This brave new dawn is the
elixir the world has been waiting for. Its implications are
as great, if not greater, than my original work with
somatic cell nuclear transfer. Eos – literally – is life. It is
youth. It is wellness. And it is within my grasp.

'What on earth does that mean?' I said.

'I'm not sure exactly,' Rachel said. 'But I think it's something to do with helping people stay young and healthy. Milo said something about Eos "saving lives".' She frowned. 'I still don't understand what Amanda Lennox was talking about when she said he was doing terrible things in here . . . I mean, what's so terrible about copying a protein that can help people be healthier?'

I looked round the room. 'This can't be all there is,' I said. 'There *must* be another room where he's carrying on other experiments.'

'Where?' Rachel was gazing round too. 'There aren't any other doors.'

I glanced back at Elijah's log. 'When did you arrive here?'

'Three days ago.'

I looked at the corresponding date. That was where the strange initials and numbers began. The first line of the first entry read: *I am the word.*

'Why does he have to be so bloody mysterious?' I read the sentence out loud. '*I am the word.* I mean, does that make any sense to you?'

'I think it's from the Bible,' Rachel said. 'Maybe it's a

password. We've had a scanner and a key pad . . . Milo said there were three sorts of security in here.'

I looked round. 'But like you said, there isn't another door, or anything that you could type a word into.' I sighed. 'And even if there was, we wouldn't know which word to use.'

Rachel stared at the log again. '*I am the word* . . . It's got to be a word Elijah uses about himself.'

'There are quite a few I'd use about him,' I said. 'Murderer . . . egomaniac . . . arsehole . . .'

'No, something personal,' Rachel said.

'What like a name?' I said, feeling doubtful. 'His surname is Lazio, but I don't think . . .'

'Maybe it's a name from the Bible.' Rachel checked her watch. Her face paled.

I gritted my teeth, we didn't have time for this.

I shook my head. 'But Elijah could have any number of names. We don't even know his *real* name. He told me once that he changed it when he was young—'

'That's it!' Rachel's eyes brightened. 'You've got it. It's a name he took for himself.'

'What d'you mean?' I said, bewildered. 'What name?'

'It's got to be his Greek God code name,' she said.

I stared at her. 'You mean *Zeus*?'

As I said the name, a creaking noise filled the room.

'What's hap—?' Rachel's hand flew to her mouth. She pointed behind me.

I turned. The bookcase was shifting . . . groaning as the shelves rumbled apart, sliding away from each other.

'It *was* a password,' I breathed. 'A voice-activated password to . . .'

'Oh my God.'

We stared as the bookcase slid along its tracks, opening wide to reveal another room.

91

Rachel

It was dark in the secret room beyond the lab. Impossible to see properly what was inside, though there was no sign of movement. I crept towards the door, the pain in my ankle barely registering. Theo hesitated. He looked round, his eyes falling on the chair on the other side of the table.

'I'm going to shove this chair in the doorway,' Theo said, 'in case the door tries to close on us.'

I nodded. 'Good idea.' Whatever was in the room, I didn't fancy being shut in there with it.

As he picked up the chair, I crossed the threshold, then stopped. I stood still, trying to identify the shadowy shapes all around me. There were tables of varying sizes. The nearer ones were cluttered with jars and bottles . . . Further away I could just make out the outline of another table with high sides. Whatever was on the table was concealed from view. My heart beat wildly.

This was it . . . what the Eos protein was really all about. Elijah had secured his work behind three doors and an electric fence. And now I was going to find out why. Another step forward and the motion sensor registered me. Lights flickered on.

I gazed round the room, trying to work out what I was looking at.

The jars and bottles appeared to contain human body parts. I walked over to the nearest table. *Yes*, there was an ear . . . and there was a hand . . . I gagged. It was disgusting.

Feeling sick, I checked the label on a small jar that contained a slice of something flat and greyish.

Ap 9 – liver section

Okay, so this was part of a liver. *Ugh.*

I glanced at the jar that contained the hand. The label said: *Ap 5.* I looked along a row of bottles, nausea swelling inside me. Each one contained a roll of something that looked like dried-out pork meat.

Ap 2 – skin tissue

Ap 4 – skin tissue

Ap 8 – skin tissue

I limped to the next table. A similar assortment of jars and bottles. I tried not to look at the contents too closely while I checked each container. Everything on this table was labelled as before, though several of the cases were far bigger . . . I couldn't help but notice what was in them.

Ap 13 contained a whole arm, *Ap 19* what looked like the side of a face and a shoulder and *Ap 22* held a faceless torso . . .

Horrific.

What *was* all this? And why was Elijah keeping it here?

I glanced round. Theo was still busy trying to wedge the chair in the doorway. I really wanted to wait for him to look at what was behind the screen on the next table, but our time was running out fast. Elijah would be back in less than ten minutes now.

I limped over. The screen that rose up from the edge of the table was labelled *Ap 24*. Holding my breath, I peered over it.

No.

My brain took a few seconds to register what I was seeing. I retched.

Lying on the table was the top half of a male human, down to the stomach. The body was normal size but hideous . . . deformed and twisted, the skin tapering off at the guts. It was impossible to say how old he was. The pallid, greying face was grotesque, with the nose missing and the closed eyes all slipped sideways down the face. There were no arms . . . just little skin buds where arms should be. The only part of the body that looked remotely normal was the mouth.

I stared at that mouth. It was familiar somehow . . . something about the shape of the lips . . .

And then I realised.

92

Theo

I raced over to Rachel. She was trembling . . . staring at whatever was behind the screen.

I followed her gaze. At first I couldn't work out exactly what I was looking at. I blinked, trying to make sense of it. A body . . . part of a body . . . distorted . . . deformed . . . I stared at the face . . . at the mouth . . .

It was my face . . . my mouth.

My head spun. What on earth was I looking at?

The truth hit me like a punch.

This was a clone of me. My legs threatened to give way. I grabbed the side of the screen. At the sound of my touch, the clone moved, turning towards us.

Rachel gripped my arm.

I was open-mouthed, unable to breath, choking with the horror of what I was seeing.

And then the clone's eyes opened.

For a long and terrible second we stared at each other.

There was no recognition of who I was in the clone's eyes. Just terror . . . and pain.

'Oh, God,' Rachel moaned beside me. Her voice carried with it everything I felt. The disgust, the pity, the horror.

I couldn't speak. Couldn't move.

I reached for Rachel's hand and held it tight.

We stood there, numbly, staring at the clone.

How could he even be alive? What was Elijah *doing* torturing someone like this?

'Who . . .?' I said. 'How . . .?'

The clone's mouth twitched, his face contorting. It looked like he was trying to speak. I leaned closer. His lips formed a word . . . he mouthed it again.

Help. I was sure that was what he was saying. *Hurts.*

'I'm sorry, I don't know what to do.' My voice was a tiny whisper. I'd never felt so helpless in my life.

The clone closed his eyes. Sick to my stomach, I turned to Rachel.

'I don't understand,' I said.

White-faced, Rachel pointed at the label on the screen concealing the clone. *Ap 24.*

'If *Art* stands for Artemis, then *Ap* must stand for Apollo,' she whispered.

I frowned. Apollo was the code name Elijah gave me, his first completely healthy, fully-functioning clone. I looked round at the jars and bottles on the other tables. They were all labelled with the same letters: *Ap*, but different, earlier numbers.

'All this . . . these are left over from Elijah's attempts to

380

reproduce himself.' I gazed back at *Ap 24*. 'And this one . . . this is the twenty-fourth version.'

I swallowed down the nausea that swelled inside me. It had never occurred to me that when Elijah had worked to clone himself it would have taken so many attempts . . . caused such terrible deformities. All of a sudden I thought of Milo . . . he was another link in the chain – another of Elijah's attempts to clone himself before succeeding in creating a totally healthy being with me.

I looked at *Ap 24* again. The clone's eyelids flickered. He moaned softly, then appeared to sink slightly against the table.

Was he asleep or unconscious?

My thoughts were running on so hard and so fast, that for a few moments I didn't notice that Rachel hadn't responded to what I'd said a moment earlier. I turned round.

'Rach?'

'I can't look any more,' she said.

93

Rachel

I limped across the room to a large, empty case that stood against the opposite wall. My breath was coming in short, shuddering gasps. I felt like crying, except I was beyond even that. Tears were too small a reaction to the horror in this room.

Theo followed me and put his hand on my arm.

'I . . . I can't believe even Elijah would do this . . . keep that poor creature down here . . .' I stammered. 'I mean he's *torturing* him . . .'

'I know.' Theo stared at the empty case in front of us. 'We have to help him,'

'The woman from RAGE . . . earlier, she said we should "*kill it*". I didn't know what she meant then but I think she must have been referring to . . . to that clone. And . . . and . . . maybe she was right . . . about killing it. I mean, like . . . killing as in putting him out of his misery . . .'

'But how?' Theo said. 'How would we kill him? How

would we *know* that we'd killed him without hurting him?
That can't be right either.'

'And what would you two know about what is *right*?'
Elijah said from the doorway.

94

Theo

We spun round. My guts spasmed in fear. He had caught us. We had spent too long . . . become distracted . . . and now Elijah had us both.

His eyes flickered across our faces. Hard and mean. 'Your tenacity and resourcefulness impress me, but you are *way* out of your depth here. The Eos protein is a miracle. Whatever it takes to develop it successfully is the right thing to do.'

I stared at him. Hate coursed through me. This man had brought me nothing but misery all my life: from his decision to let me grow up without having – or knowing – a father; to his attempt to keep Rachel and me apart; to this.

'What do you mean?' I said. 'We can *see* that the clone is suffering. How can that be *right*?'

'Yes, he . . . he asked us for *help*—' Rachel started.

'You don't understand.' Elijah's forehead creased in a frown. 'I am taking Experiment Apollo 24 *away* from suffering. In the end, it will be worth it.'

'How?' I said.

'Why is he even here?' Rachel added.

Elijah crossed his arms and leaned against the doorway. 'Very well,' he said. 'Experiment Apollo 24 was my last attempt to clone myself before Milo was born. I created Experiment 24 in a clinic near here . . . where I lived and worked a long time ago. He was born disabled and disfigured but he had healthy internal organs. I kept him hidden away in the clinic during my years working in London, and when I was in hiding in Germany and America and on Calla. When I arrived here a few days ago, I had the Experiment brought to the bunker in order to—'

'He's *not* an experiment,' I snapped, unable to bear the cold scientific way Elijah was speaking. I glanced over at the clone. His eyes were closed, though I couldn't tell if he was asleep or if he'd passed out from the pain he was feeling.

'Experiment Apollo 24 is not a proper human being,' Elijah hissed. 'Plus he is my creation . . . *mine*. To do with as I please.'

I moved sideways so I could see through to the outer room, beyond Elijah, who was still standing in the doorway. The guard who had held me captive earlier had set a wheelchair on the floor and was helping Milo into it. He finished, then turned without looking in our direction and disappeared up the stairs.

My heart sank. If Elijah and Milo were both armed our chances of getting past them were slim. Still, it had to be worth a shot.

Beside me, Rachel took a deep breath. 'When you said

385

you wanted to continue your experiments, did you mean you were . . . are . . . giving the Apollo clone the Eos protein?'

'Yes.' Elijah looked at her. 'I've been testing Eos on the Experiment for the past few days. I'd already noted some changes . . . increased haemoglobin levels, improvements in heart and liver function, even better muscular tone . . .'

'And *pain*,' I said.

Elijah shrugged. 'It's true that the introduction of the protein into the bloodstream does seemed to have caused some physical suffering but I'm sure eventually I will work that through.'

Unbelievable.

Rachel's mouth fell open. 'You mean the stuff that's inside me is what's making that . . . that poor clone . . . *suffer*?' Her face paled. 'He wasn't in pain before?'

'No.' Elijah took his gun from his pocket and held it by his side.

I exchanged horrified looks with Rachel. I couldn't work out which was worse – the casual way Elijah referred to the clone's suffering or the arrogance of his belief that his clones existed for his own benefit only.

'So the Eos protein works?' Rachel said slowly. 'But it is also agonisingly painful?'

'Exactly.' Elijah nodded. 'It's quite possibly my most impressive discovery to date. Can you imagine how much the world will pay for such a compound – once I've worked out how to prevent it from causing pain to the user, of course? The only problem is that it's fundamentally unstable. As you both know, Rachel carries the protein in her blood – but it loses its potency very fast and I can't find a way of synthesising it. Which means I need Rachel herself.'

'What does that mean?' I snapped.

Milo appeared next to Elijah in the doorway.

'You knew he was experimenting on this clone?' Rachel glared at him.

Milo looked away.

'What did you mean about needing Rachel?' I persisted.

Elijah gazed at me with an expression of amused disdain. 'Haven't you worked it out yet, Theo?' He glanced at the empty case by the wall.

Beside him, Milo stiffened in his wheelchair.

'No,' Rachel gasped, her eyes widening.

'What?' I said.

'I can't *copy* the Eos protein inside Rachel so I need access to fresh supplies of blood to stop it mutating,' Elijah said, briskly. 'Obviously, in order to do that I need to "preserve" her body in good working order and have easy access to it.'

'No,' Rachel breathed. 'You can't do that.'

'Can't do *what*?' I said. 'What's he talking about?'

Elijah smoothed back his hair. 'Tell him, Rachel.'

I turned to her. She was pointing at the empty tank.

'That's my coffin,' she said. 'My cage.'

With her final word it all fell into place. The world spun as I realised what Elijah was planning.

'You're going to put Rachel in that tank to preserve her

387

body so you can keep taking the Eos protein from her blood?'

'Yes,' Elijah said with a sneer. 'Caught up at last, Theo. Well done.'

95

Rachel

I felt numb. This couldn't really be happening. I couldn't get my head round what Elijah was suggesting.

'You can't kill her,' Theo protested. But his voice sounded hoarse. We both knew Elijah was capable of doing just that.

'She will, technically, still be alive,' Elijah said. 'Though all brain stem function will of course cease as soon as I inject her.'

Oh my God.

I glanced at Milo, shrunk into his wheelchair. He was gazing at me in total shock. I was sure that, although he'd known about the Apollo clone, he hadn't known until now what Elijah was planning to do with *me*.

Our eyes met. *Help me.*

Milo stared back, terrified.

I turned back to Elijah, my brain working at a hundred miles an hour. I had to reason with him . . . find an argument that would convince him that all this was unthinkable . . . impossible . . . Thoughts shot like rockets through my head.

'Please,' I said. 'Just listen to me, Elijah.'

He raised his eyebrows.

'The Eos protein that I carry is amazing . . . a brilliant discovery . . . but you have to make it work without causing pain – or taking life. It's just *wrong* otherwise. Why can't you see that?'

'The clones I have created are mine to control,' Elijah said stubbornly.

'But—'

'Enough.' Elijah sighed. For the first time since he'd arrived, he looked weary. 'How can I do this any other way?' he said. 'I can't risk you getting hurt, Rachel – I need access to your live blood. And I can't work like other scientists do.'

'Why not?' Theo snapped. 'What makes you so special?'

Elijah looked at him with wide, surprised eyes. 'I *am* special, Theodore. I have special talents that can't – *mustn't* – be regulated or limited by ridiculous legal restrictions. *That* is wrong.' He paused. 'Anyway, there's a more practical problem. I have no formal government support. If the full extent of my work was publically exposed and connected to me, then I'm certain much of my backing would melt away.'

'Elijah, just listen,' I pleaded. 'Can't you wait until—'

'No, Rachel. No more waiting. RAGE knows where we are. I just killed the head of their organisation. They are probably already on their way and this is the safest place for me to keep you.' Elijah picked up a syringe from the table by the wall. 'I am going to give you an injection to sedate you. It won't last long, just enough time to get you set up in the tank.'

390

'But you said you were going to keep Rachel's body alive,' Theo said. 'That tank is just an empty case. Where's the life support machine?'

'I don't need a machine,' Elijah said. He pointed to a tube that ran from the underside of the tank into the wall that separated the lab we were in from the outer room. 'Did you not notice the carton of hydratoroxide beside the sink out there?'

Theo nodded. He looked totally dazed.

'What's hydratoroxide?' I said.

'A kind of liquid oxygen. It was developed by the US government as part of a secret project many years ago. I was given access to it while I was based in Washington D.C. You saw it in use in my lab in Calla . . . inside the artificial wombs.'

'So I'm going to be breathing *liquid*?' I said.

'That's a little simplistic but yes.' Elijah paused. 'It's not such a strange idea. If you think about it, we all did exactly the same thing when we were in the womb. The technology really is amazing – hydratoroxide contains a blend of nutrients which are absorbed by the skin, plus oxygen to preserve the respiratory and cardiovascular functions, and tiny amounts of a special kind of acid. It even provides a resistance pulse that works the muscles, preventing atrophy.'

'So you're going to put me in that case and fill it up with hydrat . . . whatever it's called?'

'Yes. When you come round you will be "breathing" the liquid. Once I am certain the hydratoroxide is fully operational, I'll attach a series of wire nodes to your skin. These

391

will monitor all core functions, showing up on the machine over there.' He pointed to a large computer in the corner. 'Finally, I will give you another, simple, injection – and there will be nothing more to fear.'

'Because I'll be dead . . .' My heart pounded.

'Brain dead,' Elijah corrected, walking towards me. 'Your heart will still pump blood round your body, but you will have no brain stem activity . . . no thoughts or feelings.'

I shrank against Theo, who put his arm in front of me.

'You can't do this, Elijah,' he said. 'I won't let you.'

Elijah laughed and moved even nearer. He held up his gun. 'Big talk, Theo. Where's your weapon?'

I glanced at Milo. He was still in the doorway, his face consumed with terror. He caught my eye.

Why didn't he move? He had a gun, I'd *seen* it. Why didn't he shoot Elijah?

I pleaded silently with him to act, but Milo just looked away.

Elijah had almost reached us. Theo and I were backed against the wall. There was nowhere to run. Even if we could somehow get past Elijah without getting shot, Paul was upstairs, guarding the bunker exit.

Elijah raised his arm. The hand holding the syringe came nearer.

Theo pushed me behind him. He lunged at Elijah.

Elijah struck back. His gun cracked against the side of Theo's head.

Theo fell to the ground.

I stared down at him, shaking. It had happened so fast.

Keeping his gun pointed at me, Elijah shoved Theo out of the way with his foot, then turned back towards me, syringe raised.

'No,' I yelled. 'NO!' I hit out with my fists . . . my feet . . . lashing out. The calmness I'd felt just minutes ago had vanished. Now all I felt was fear, exploding in my head. 'NO!' I shouted. Elijah couldn't do this. He *couldn't*.

His hands gripped my arm. So tightly that I screamed in pain. And then I felt a sharp prick just below my shoulder. The room around me spun. I felt myself being lowered to the floor. The last thing I saw before I slipped into unconsciousness was Theo's body on the ground, eyes shut, hair falling over his face.

96

Theo

My head hurt badly – the back of my skull throbbed where Elijah had hit me. At least I hadn't passed out, though it had been a close thing. The blow had knocked me over and, for a few moments, pain consumed me. When I'd opened my eyes at last, Rachel was on the ground beside me and Elijah had already bound my hands.

He dragged me back out to the main room and tied me to the leg of the table.

I sat on the cold stone floor as Elijah went back to his lab. From where I was sitting, I could see some of the tables with their obscene load, but not Rachel or Elijah himself. They must still be round the corner – by the empty, waiting case.

I shuddered.

Milo wheeled himself over and looked down at me. He was wearing a black beanie hat pulled low over his forehead, almost covering his eyes.

It was more like looking in a mirror than ever, except I

knew my own eyes were flashing with anger and fear, while Milo's gaze was wary . . . and ashamed.

'What are they doing in there?' My head pulsed with pain as I spoke.

'Elijah's getting Rachel ready for immersion,' Milo said in a flat voice.

'You knew all about this, didn't you?' I couldn't keep the contempt out of my voice.

'No.' Milo shook his head for emphasis. 'I didn't know about the Eos protein causing pain and I didn't know he was planning to do this to Rachel, I swear.' He paused and looked down at his lap. 'Elijah doesn't exactly confide in me.'

At that moment, Elijah himself appeared in the doorway. 'I'm going to need your help in about five minutes, Milo.'

'Okay.'

Without a glance in my direction, Elijah walked back into his lab, out of sight again.

'You have to untie me,' I whispered. 'I have to get in there and help Rachel.'

'What?' Milo glanced over his shoulders to make sure Elijah hadn't heard us talking. 'But he's got a gun.'

'Come *on*! Elijah's distracted with what he's doing to Rachel. If you untie me I can run in and jump him – take him by surprise.'

'Elijah will see you coming,' Milo whispered. 'He'll kill you.'

'He's going to kill me anyway,' I said. 'Or else deep-freeze me for body parts. What other chance does Rachel have? Don't you *care* about her?'

'Of course I do,' Milo's face flooded with colour. 'It's just rushing in there like that—'

'Why are you so loyal to him?' I hissed. 'He doesn't care about you. Look at all those attempts to clone himself labelled *Apollo* in there . . . they were all created before you, but although you were born alive, Elijah didn't call *you* Apollo, did he? He gave that name to *me*, because I was perfectly healthy. What did he call you?'

'Hephaestus,' Milo said. 'The lame god. But that isn't—'

'You see?' I argued. 'Elijah's a bigot. A cruel, egotistical monster who looks down on you because parts of your body don't work.'

'You're not listening to me,' Milo said. 'You're behaving just like him. I'm trying to tell you that you don't have to do it on your own.'

I stared at him.

'We *can* be stronger, if we work together,' Milo said quietly. 'We don't have to be like him, just because we're genetically the same.'

There was a short pause. Milo looked over his shoulder again.

A series of bumps and thumps were emanating from the lab. No sign that Elijah had heard us speaking.

I hesitated for a second.

Could I really trust Milo? After all, he'd tricked Rachel into going to Elijah in the first place.

I looked into his eyes – the same shape and colour as my own – and I made the only decision I could.

'Okay,' I said. 'What do you think we should do?'

97

Rachel

I was drowning. *Help!*

My first instinct was to call out. Then I clawed at the thick, gloopy liquid. *Bang. Thump.* I hit something solid. The walls of the tank. I was *inside* the tank.

My eyes snapped open. There was water in my lungs. I couldn't breathe.

HELP!

'Listen to me, Rachel. You're okay.'

I registered Elijah's muffled voice. I turned my head towards the sound.

He was outside the tank, a dark shape looking in at me. And I was in here. Trapped. No air. My eyes stung from the liquid. It was lukewarm – body temperature – and had a slightly sour taste, like lemon, but very faint.

Panicking again, I beat against the sides of the tank with my legs and arms. Elijah had taken off my long top and socks but my leggings and vest clung to me, all wet.

'You can breathe,' Elijah said. 'The liquid is breathable.

Forget your nose and mouth. Focus on your heartbeat. It's like you're breathing through that.'

I stopped thrashing around in the dense, treacly liquid. Much as I hated to obey Elijah, what he said made sense. After all, I'd seen the embryos back on Calla surviving in the same fluid. And Grace.

Instead of trying desperately to breathe the ordinary way, I took my attention to my heart. It was pumping like it would explode. After a second or two the beats slowed a little and I felt it . . . the strange sensation of being okay with my lungs full of fluid. I still had to fight the instinct to breathe through my nose, but I could tell I was all right. It was like I was breathing through my skin . . . through my body as a whole.

Definitely the weirdest sensation of my life.

'There – you see, you are fine,' Elijah said triumphantly.

I turned towards his voice again. It was still muffled through the tank casing and the hydratoroxide surrounding me, but now that I'd stopped moving I realised that my eyes didn't sting any more and I could see fairly clearly – like I was looking through a pair of slightly smudged swimming goggles. There was Elijah himself, looming over the tank. Beyond him was the rest of his lab. I couldn't see the outer room at all. Was Theo there? Or had Elijah already killed him? My heart pounded. As far as I could tell, it was just me and Elijah. And I was trapped in this case. Totally at his mercy.

'Milo, get in here!' Elijah called. He turned to me. 'I need help placing all the wire nodes. It's a delicate operation, but it won't take long.'

I stared at him, taking in what he'd said. So this was it. Elijah was going to fix the wire nodes over my body, then give me a lethal dose of poison. I had just a few minutes to live.

I felt the panic rising again, my desire to breathe through my nose asserting itself. I shook my head violently from side to side.

'Calm down,' Elijah said. He held up a syringe. 'I can always sedate you again before I put the wires in. I don't need you conscious for that part.'

I stopped moving immediately. I turned my head towards the door, looking out for Milo. He was my last hope. Would he stand up to Elijah?

'Milo!' Elijah swore. 'Get in here!'

The wheelchair trundled towards us. Milo was sitting slightly hunched over, his head bowed. He was deliberately not meeting my eye. I fixed my gaze on the place where his beanie hat was pulled low over his forehead.

Look at me, I urged him. *See what he's doing. Stop him. Do something.*

Elijah glanced round. 'Get over here,' he snapped. Now Milo was in the room with him, Elijah had lowered his voice and it was harder for me to make out exactly what he was saying, but I got the gist of it. Elijah wanted Milo to help hold all the delicate wires while he fed them through the tiny hole in the top of the case and attached the ends to my skin.

As Elijah spoke, he laid his gun on the table beside him. The wires were on the table too. He picked one up, waiting.

Milo was wheeling towards him – a little faster now, his head bowed and his attention clearly on the gun on the table.

Something was different about him.

I strained to see more clearly through the hydratoroxide. *Yes.* There was definitely something different in the curve of his cheek . . . the hunch of his shoulders . . .

A second later he looked up and met my gaze. And suddenly I realised what was happening.

Hope surged through my whole body.

It wasn't Milo in the wheelchair. It was Theo.

98

Theo

I spun the wheels of Milo's wheelchair and moved forward again. It was hard enough controlling the thing, let alone looking as if I used it all the time.

Luckily Elijah was distracted by the wires he was separating out on the table. I knew Rachel, floating in that hideous tank, had clocked me. I could only hope Elijah hadn't noticed the flash of recognition in her eyes. I kept my focus on the gun on the table beside Elijah. It was just centimetres away from his hand. If he realised I was pretending to be Milo before I reached him he would shoot me. No question.

I turned the chair's wheels again and thought fast. Milo was outside, unable to move. Rachel was stuck in that terrible tank. Defeating Elijah, once and for all, was up to me alone..

You have to kill him.

The thought flashed through my mind as I drew close enough to touch Elijah.

I still didn't know how I was going to overpower him, just that I had to get that gun away from him.

Elijah threw a swift glance at me.

'Will you hurry—' His eyes widened with recognition. '*Theo?*'

Damn.

There was no time to think. As Elijah reached for the gun, I hurled myself out of the wheelchair. Everything that followed was a blur.

I knocked Elijah off balance. He stumbled sideways and fell to the floor, sending the table beside him crashing to the ground.

I threw myself on top of him, my hands reaching for his neck, my knees pinning his arms to his sides. He pushed me off with a roar.

I struggled back. He wasn't going to win again.

He wasn't going to kill Rachel.

I wouldn't let him.

'NO!' I forced him down again, my hands like steel against his windpipe. He was choking, kicking. A massive shove. Elijah released his right arm. Punched me in the gut. I loosened my hold on his neck, winded.

In a single movement he was pushing me back. One hand reached for the gun. Grabbed it. He stood over me, panting, the gun pointing in my face.

We stared at each other for a second. I glanced over at Rachel. She was staring, frantic, through the glass case that imprisoned her.

'Enough,' Elijah said. He wiped the sweat from his forehead and steadied the gun. The barrel was a thin black circle in front of my eyes.

'Stop.' The voice came from the floor by the doorway. It was Milo. His own gun was pointing up at Elijah.

I stared at him. I hadn't even realised Milo *had* a weapon. I could see from the terrified expression on his face that he didn't want to use it.

'Put your gun down, Elijah,' Milo said. His hand shook. 'I didn't want it to come to this, but I can't let you hurt Rachel and Theo.

'Don't be ridiculous,' Elijah sneered. 'You're too weak to shoot me and you know it.'

I gazed at Milo. His whole body was trembling, but there was real fury in his eyes.

'This is your last chance,' Milo said, his voice dark and intense. 'I've called the police and they're on their way and—'

'You're bluffing. Anyway, the police can't stop me.' Elijah laughed. 'Christ, Milo, I'd have thought even you weren't stupid enough to believe that.'

'I know they can't stop you,' Milo said. 'In the end, you always win, don't you?'

'*You'll* win with the Eos protein,' Elijah said. 'Think how it could help you . . .'

Milo glanced at the Apollo clone, then at Rachel. 'Not like this,' he said.

Elijah muttered something under his breath in Spanish.

403

And then, ignoring Milo, he turned back to me, took a step closer and cocked the pistol in his hand.

I shut my eyes.

Crack. With a deafening bang the gun went off.

For a split second I was too numb to realise I hadn't been hit. Then I heard a thud. My eyes opened.

Elijah was lying on the ground in front of me, a look of slight surprise on his face.

I crawled over, my whole body trembling. He was shot. I put my hand over his mouth. No breath.

I sat back. He was dead. This monster . . . murderer.

My creator.

Dead.

99

Rachel

Everything happened very fast after that. The local police arrived en masse, forcing their way past Paul and the electric fence.

Theo must have let them into the bunker. Shocked at what they found, they brought in a doctor to help release me from the tank. It was hours before I was free, coughing up hydratoroxide and breathing fresh, burning air into my lungs.

My first words were about Theo. Where was he? Was he okay?

I hadn't seen either him or Milo for hours, though there were people all over the lab . . . some examining the Apollo clone, expressions of utter horror on their faces; others standing over Elijah's body.

I couldn't quite believe he was dead.

Strangely, I didn't feel anything – except relief.

I was wrapped in a blanket and taken straight to a small hospital in the nearest town, Tromstorm. I was examined by about six different doctors and interviewed by two police officers. To be honest, it was all a bit of a blur. The only person I really remember from the whole afternoon was a petite female police officer with kind eyes who held my hand while I explained everything that had happened. I asked her where Theo and Milo were and, to her credit, she went away and found out for me.

Milo, she said, was still being questioned by police, but the statements from both Theo and myself had backed up everything he'd told them about shooting Elijah to protect me. The police officer was sure that, whatever happened, it was unlikely he'd serve a jail sentence.

Theo, it turned out, was in the same hospital as me. He was receiving treatment for the cuts he'd sustained during his fight with Elijah. I asked to see him, but the police office said the UK and US agents they'd contacted through our parents both said we should be kept apart for the time being.

In the end, a doctor took some blood from me and I was left on my own, in a small, white-washed room, just waiting. Now I knew Theo was okay, my thoughts turned to Lewis – hoping he was recovering in hospital back in Scotland – and to Grace. Had social services found a home for her yet? Was she all right? I couldn't believe it was just a few days since I'd seen them both.

At about eight p.m., the door of my hospital room opened. I looked up eagerly, hoping it might be Theo.

Mum and Dad walked in.

I got up off the bed, expecting them to cry or shout or hug

me. Instead they both just stood there, their faces lined and sad and exhausted.

For a moment, no one spoke. Then Dad cleared his throat.

'How could you just leave like that, Ro?' he said.

'It was for Theo,' I said, the words tumbling out of me in my eagerness to explain. 'I had to save him from Elijah.'

'Without telling us?'

'You'd never have let me go,' I said.

Across the room, Mum rolled her eyes.

Dad walked over and put his hands on my shoulders. 'Your life . . .' he said slowly, 'I don't think you understand how precious your life is to us . . . When you risk it like that . . . it's like you're risking our lives too . . . our happiness . . .'

I looked down at the white tiled floor. 'I'm sorry you were scared,' I mumbled. 'But I had to try and help Theo.'

'And why does Theo matter so much?' Mum snapped. 'We're your *parents*. Don't our feelings count?'

I stared at her. Why couldn't she understand how much Theo meant to me?

'I don't know who you are any more, Rachel,' Mum said.

There was a long pause as I felt the resentment build up inside me.

'No,' I said. 'You don't. And that's your own fault. You've tried to make me look and behave like the daughter you always wanted . . . like you imagined Rebecca would have been . . . and I can't be like that. I'm not her.'

Mum opened her mouth to say something else, but Dad cut in.

407

'We want to know who you are. Don't you see? That's the point – we want you to tell us who you are, what you want . . .'

He shook me gently by the shoulders then let his arms fall to his sides.

A million thoughts whirled in my head. What *did* I want? Where I lived didn't really matter. Having loads of nice things wasn't important to me at all. No, in the end it all came down to people.

'I want three things,' I said.

Mum raised her eyebrows. 'What?' she said. 'The right to disobey us? The right to upset us? The right to—?'

'Sssh.' Dad hushed her. 'Let Rachel speak.'

I took a deep breath. *Start with what's easiest.*

'I'd like to know if Lewis is all right . . .'

'He is,' Dad said, 'he's doing fine, well on the road to a full recovery.'

'. . . and I'd like to be able to keep in touch with him.'

Dad nodded. 'Of course. Nobody's stopping that.'

Mum said nothing.

'Then there's Grace,' I said. 'She's my sister . . . genetically my twin. It *hurts* to be without her and—'

'We've already been through this,' Mum snapped. 'We can't possibly take on another child at our age. It's not fair of you to ask, Rach—'

'I'm not expecting you to adopt her,' I said. 'You were right about that, she should be brought up by younger parents that really want her . . . but I have a right to still see her . . .

408

she's my family. She's *your* family. I know you can do that. There are a couple of girls at school who live with foster families but still keep in touch with their mums. Why can't I see Grace like that?'

Mum and Dad exchanged glances.

'What about Grace's safety?' Dad said.

'Elijah's dead,' I said. 'And RAGE aren't targeting clones any more. Amanda Lennox said so and I believe her. They might wish we hadn't been born, but they don't want to kill us. Grace isn't at risk from anyone. And I don't see why I can't be like a proper sister to her.'

Another long pause.

Mum and Dad looked at each other again.

'We've actually been discussing this, Ro,' Dad said.

'And?' I said eagerly.

'We've been talking to Liza Mitchell,' Mum said. 'D'you remember her?'

I nodded. Liza Mitchell was linked to the UK team who'd found Mum, Dad and me our new home in Roslinnon. I'd only met her a couple of times but I'd liked her.

'Well, Liza's here right now,' Mum went on. 'She's agreed to call the social worker we spoke to about Grace before and give her some part of the truth about the relationship between the two of you. Not the cloning side of things, but . . . anyway, they're going to make sure the two of you can see each other regularly.'

'They actually said that it would be a good thing for both you and Grace,' Dad added.

I blinked, my heart bumping with excitement. 'But that's brilliant,' I said. 'I mean . . . totally brilliant.' I flung myself at Dad, nearly knocking him over with the fierceness of my hug.

Dad smiled. 'It was your mum's idea.'

I turned to Mum, surprised.

'You've already lost one sister,' Mum said. 'I don't want to keep you from another.' She looked quickly away, but for a tiny fraction of a second I saw the vulnerability in her eyes.

I swallowed. Mum and I would probably never be close, but she did care about me. I could see that now. Under all her stupid rules and criticisms and advice about how I should behave, she cared.

'You said there were three things, Ro?' Dad said gently.

But at that moment the nice policewoman knocked on the door and called us into a meeting in a private room next door.

Theo and his mum, who'd flown to Scotland after he'd called her last week, were already in there. So was Liza Mitchell and the US agent who'd organised Theo's relocation last year, Drew Scott.

Scott was a portly middle-aged man with an ill-fitting jacket and slightly droopy eyes. Next to him, Liza Mitchell seemed energetic and trim in her smart grey suit. She smiled at me as I walked in. Theo didn't look up.

Scott spoke first.

'We've already taken all the statements we need concerning Lazio's death. We'll want you again, later on, to

410

testify . . .' he glanced from me to Theo, '. . . but for now you're free to go home.'

'Don't we need new homes?' Theo's mum sat upright in her chair. Her lips were drawn into a thin line. She looked furious, though I wasn't sure who with.

Theo carried on staring at the floor.

'No, there's no need to move you to a new location,' Scott went on. 'With Elijah Lazio dead, the main threat against you is removed. The agent who sold details of Rachel's whereabouts has confessed and been charged – so he's no longer a danger. And all our intel confirms what Amanda Lennox told Rachel, that RAGE's current agenda is to fight ongoing scientific work, not the results of that work.'

'So we're all safe now?' Dad said.

Liza Mitchell smiled. 'The risk assessment suggests you no longer qualify for our protection, though we still strongly advise caution about your genetic heritage.'

'You mean the fact that Rachel and I are clones?' Theo said, looking up at last.

He kept his gaze on Liza Mitchell as he spoke. He sounded as tight-lipped and surly as his mum.

My heart sank. Why was he so angry? This was all *good* news, wasn't it? If there was no security reason to keep us apart and we could all go back to living in London, then Theo and I would be able to see each other whenever we wanted.

Why didn't he look pleased?

411

'We will still need you to be available to our research teams,' Liza Mitchell went on. 'But the check-ups will only take place every six months. That doesn't need to affect where you live.'

Mum sat back in her chair, a smile curling round her lips. Dad reached out and squeezed her hand.

'So we can go back to London?' Dad said.

'Absolutely,' Mitchell said. 'To be honest that suits us very well. We've been in touch with government scientists from both the UK and the US . . . we've emailed them some of Lazio's notes on this Eos protein Rachel carries.'

I looked up in alarm.

'There's absolutely no risk to you, Rachel,' Mitchell said reassuringly. 'In fact it looks as if the Eos protein was a blind alley. As you saw, it offers some health improvements but only at the cost of terrible pain.' She sighed. 'Elijah Lazio *was*, undoubtedly, a genius. But there are other experts in this field and our preliminary findings suggest Lazio was wildly exaggerating the Eos protein's value, not to mention under-estimating its cost.'

I nodded, glancing round at the others. Mum and Dad looked relieved. Theo had gone back to staring at the floor so I couldn't see his expression. Beside him, however, his mum still seemed furious about something.

Drew Scott cleared his throat. 'The one thing we must insist on is that any discussion of what you saw and heard in Lazio's lab remains confined to those sessions. For your own safety.'

412

'What about the Apollo clone?' I said. 'What's going to happen to him?'

There was an uncomfortable silence.

'A doctor examined him. His body was in terminal shock from the pain he had endured. I understand he passed away an hour ago,' Mitchell said gently. 'A proper burial will follow after the post-mortem is complete . . .'

That was something, I supposed. At least he was no longer suffering. In my head I could still see the pain in that clone's eyes.

I suspected the sight would prey on my mind forever.

'So when can I take Theo home?' his mum asked.

As she sat forward, her long, dangly earrings jangled like wind chimes. Theo sat, rigid, in his chair. He was still staring at the floor.

Surely this was where he was going to jump in and say that he wanted to see me? Which was the third – and most important – thing I wanted for myself.

But Theo said nothing.

What was going on? We'd had that whole conversation just a few days ago about wanting to see each other . . . about not letting our parents keep us apart.

Why didn't he say something now?

I racked my brain and could only come up with one possible reason for the change: was the fact that I'd lied to him about liking Milo sinking in, making him question us being together?

If we'd been on our own I'd have tried to speak to him but

here, in front of the two agents and all our parents, it was impossible, so I kept my gaze on his face, willing him to look at me . . . to give me some clue as to what he was feeling.

But Theo just stared straight ahead.

100

Theo

'Another coupla days and you'll be flying home.' Drew Scott grinned that big stupid grin of his that I remembered from when he was setting us up in Philadelphia last year.

Man, he was annoying.

'Good.' Mum sat back with a satisfied smile.

I could feel Rachel's eyes boring into me. I knew she was wondering why I hadn't asked about us seeing each other.

The truth was, that after the conversation I'd just had with Mum, I wanted to hit something so badly that I didn't trust myself to speak.

'There won't be any problem with us . . . er, me and Theo . . . travelling now, will there?' Rachel said.

'Well, we'll want to know where you go and keep a track on your movements, but no . . . most destinations will be fine.'

'So we can see each other?' Rachel persisted. 'I mean, visit on holiday?'

The atmosphere in the room grew tense.

'I'm not sure that's such a good idea,' her mother began.

'I agree,' Mum added.

I gritted my teeth.

Rachel was looking at me again.

I took a deep breath.

'I'm not going back to America,' I said. 'I'll be sixteen in a month. I don't want to be at High School. I want to be in a sixth form at home.'

'But we have a life in Philadelphia,' Mum said.

'No,' I said. '*You* have a life. I want to be in London.'

The UK agent, Mitchell, and Scott exchanged glances. Everyone else was looking at me, including Rachel, but I kept my eyes on Mum.

'The money the government paid us when we went to the States last year will be enough to send me to college in London, won't it?' I went on. 'Maybe even accommodation? And I can work, get a job . . .' I turned to Rachel's dad. 'I know I took your money to find Rachel with and I promise I'll pay you back.'

'That doesn't matter now, Theo,' Mr Smith said.

His wife pursed her lips.

'None of this is the point . . .' Mum drew herself up.

I could see she was getting ready for a full continuation of the row we'd had earlier.

'It's not about the money or even the legal position,' Mum went on. 'I'm your mother and I want you with me. You're being very selfish.'

That was rich.

'*I'm* being selfish?' My voice rose.

'Perhaps everyone could just calm down?' Mitchell suggested.

'I *am* calm,' I said. 'I'm just telling you what I want. I'm entitled to do that, aren't I?'

'Of course,' Mitchell said, soothingly. 'And there's really no reason why we can't fix you up with a school in London but—'

'What about *me*, Theo?' Mum said.

'I'll visit in the holidays,' I said, looking down at the floor. 'Or *you* can visit me. And I can do all the genetic check-up things then, as well. But I'm not going back to Philadelphia to live. I'm almost sixteen, Mum. You can't make me.'

A tense hush descended on the room.

Mum's lips tightened into an even thinner line.

'Why, though, Theo?' Drew Scott was frowning . . . concerned. 'Is it school? Friends? Tell us why you don't like Philadelphia.'

'It's not that I don't like it,' I said.

I could feel everyone looking at me. I kept my eyes on the floor.

'Well, what then?' Scott sounded bemused.

I took a deep breath.

This was it. My chest tightened. Suppose I'd misjudged her? Suppose she wasn't interested any more?

'I want to live in London so I can be closer to Rachel.'

As I spoke, I looked up and met her eyes at last.

And in that moment I knew that if I had to live the whole

of the last year again with all its threats and terrors – from nearly being murdered to give Elijah a new heart, to saving Rachel from a living death – I would go there like a shot.

Because the look in her eyes was unmistakable.

'Rachel, what do you think?' her dad said faintly.

'That's what I want too.' She beamed at me. 'More than anything.'

'For goodness' sake,' Mum muttered.

Across the room, Rachel's mother whispered something that sounded suspiciously like, 'He's not exactly a good influence.'

I didn't care.

Whatever happened, we weren't going to let anyone keep us apart.

Not ever again.